WAYWARD GIRL

Sandy Greening loses her virginity at fourteen to a drunken neighbor. Her mother doesn't care. She's drunk herself all the time on cheap wine. So Sandy starts running with a gang, The Blue Devils, and that's where she first turns on to marijuana, and not long after, heroin. That's when she starts to sell herself to anyone with the bucks to pay for her highs. But the night Tommy asks her to hold his knife before they rumble with The Black Cats is the night that changes Sandy's life forever. A kid gets killed, and the cops put the finger on Sandy for information. And when she won't give it up the easy way, they set her up and go after it the hard way, all the way to reform school. And that's where Sandy starts to learn the real lessons of life.

THE WIDOW

When Jerry Rebner starts working for Mrs. Sprague as her cook at the Dells, he figures he knows what he wants—Linda. Lush and ripe, Linda has everything Jerry likes in a woman, and more. Linda is married to Frank, Mrs. Sprague's shiftless hot rodding son, who widows her when he plows into a tree one drunken evening. Then Jerry meets Norma, sweet, virginal Norma, who used to pose as a nude model! Torn between the two women, and by the memory of his first wife, Jerry begins to drink. Then Linda comes to him with a plan—Mrs. Sprague's property is worth $50,000 to a development company, but she won't sell. Linda is all she has left, her sole heir. And those steps leading down to the cellar are awfully steep...

WAYWARD GIRL
THE WIDOW

TWO NOVELS BY
Orrie Hitt

Introduction by Brian Greene

Stark House Press • Eureka California

WAYWARD GIRL / THE WIDOW

Published by Stark House Press
1315 H Street
Eureka, CA 95501, USA
griffinskye3@sbcglobal.net
www.starkhousepress.com

ISBN: 978-1-944520-62-5

Book design by Mark Shepard, SHEPGRAPHICS.COM
Original cover art from Beacon Books edition of *Wayward Girl*
Proofreading by Bill Kelly

First Stark House Press Edition: June 2018

FIRST EDITION

Contents

Victims of Desire
By Brian Greene

When working on a career overview article on Orrie Hitt (1916-75) in 2013, I interviewed the pulp author's two living children, daughters Joyce Gordon and Nancy Gooding. They both made it clear that their dad—who so often wrote fictional accounts of lust-driven characters who couldn't have been more different from the wholesome, family-oriented likes of Ward and June Cleaver—was a devoted father to them and their siblings, and forever and faithfully in love with their mother. They talked about what it was like to be raised by the man who churned out steamy paperback original novels for a variety of small publishers—their dad banging away at his typewriter incessantly while slurping glasses of iced coffee, often taking breaks from writing to get on the phone and hit up an agent or publisher for overdue royalties he had coming and that they were always too slow to turn over, etc. My conversations with Hitt's daughters were interesting and enlightening. And they were comfortable, easygoing chats … until we began discussing the contents of their father's books.

The constant and unbridled sexual scenes in Hitt's innumerable novels were not something Gordon or Gooding necessarily wanted to discuss at length, and not things they wanted brought up when socializing with the people they grew up around in the small town of Port Jervis, New York. But what I pointed out to them, and what I wrote into my article, was that there were often concurrent, socially and morally conscious themes that ran parallel to all the hanky panky in their pop's books. I read roughly thirty of Hitt's titles one after the other while working on the piece, and I noted as I blitzed through them that "the Shakespeare of Shabby Street" often went to bat for society's underdogs in the stories, working in bits of compelling human drama that showed these people's uphill battles, even while including a sex-related scene about every fifth page. This is not to make the case that Hitt was some kind of literary saint, or that his books can be viewed as crusades for social justice. Ha! In fact, there's a scene in one of these two novels that will challenge the moral sensibilities even of people who seek out risqué content in their pulp fiction. Still, he did at times take up causes in his stories.

One such cause Hitt took up in his fiction was the impact of the lives of youthful characters who are being raised by parents who are no damned good. These hardened-too-soon teens live in dismal, squalid, rough and tough environments, and they have to fend for themselves amid such circumstances, because their moms and dads are no help to them. 1960's *Wayward Girl* contains this theme.

The title character of *Wayward Girl*, Sandy Greening, is 16 at the time of the story. And she's already more street smart and world weary than most people ever become. She slings hash at a greasy diner down by the docks, but she makes her real money by selling the use of her voluptuous body to the eatery's sex crazy male customers, at five bucks per party. She's a high school dropout, a heroin addict, and a member of a street gang. So who and where are Sandy's parents, you might wonder, and why have they allowed their child to fall into this kind of lifestyle? Well, Sandy's dad, who actually seems to be a decent enough guy, is serving a long-term jail sentence as the result of a botched gas station holdup attempt. So he's out of the picture. And Sandy's mom is a wino and a floozy who doesn't have much of a conscience and who just can't be bothered to care much about her daughter. As is made clear in the novel, to Sandy her mother is just some drunk lady who happens to live under the same roof as her. So, like the main character of *Call Me Bad* and other Hitt tales, Sandy is a teenager who is on her own and has to take care of herself any way she can in this cruel world, without parental protection or guidance.

Sandy's mom is hardly the only adult who does the teenager wrong in the pages of *Wayward Girl*. Sandy's first sexual experience came when, at age 14, she was raped by a grown man. Her mom's slob of a boyfriend, who sells street drugs to Sandy and other underage users, makes it known he'd like to get into his ladyfriend's teenage daughter's pants. The pig who owns the diner where Sandy works can't keep his greedy paws off her private parts. And there are other disturbing experiences Sandy has with grownups—who are all too happy to use and manipulate her in whatever ways suit their interests and desires—after she gets busted for hooking and remanded to an experimental reform school.

Sandy Greening isn't exactly a sympathetic character, because by the time we meet her she has already become so stony hearted by all the hard knocks she's sustained, that she's just another irresponsible street teen who's out to get what she needs, without much care for other members of society. Yet in telling Sandy's story, Hitt showed clear empathy for the difficulties of a young person who has to make her way in life without the aid of good parents and while becoming victimized by various other villainous adults.

Something else I wrote into that article on Hitt is that in many ways his novels can be seen as the literary equivalents of the movies made by softcore porn master Russ Meyer (1922-2004). *The Widow* (1959), the other title included here, would have been ideal as the basis of a Meyer film. The main characters are pure Russ. There's Jerry, a drifter who works as a highway repair laborer and a dishwasher/cook at a diner over the course of the story. The two women with whom the always horny Jerry becomes involved are also Meyer-esque characters. Linda, the wife of the restaurant owner's son, is sex on wheels and likes to hang around the eatery wearing the kind of skimpy clothing that shows off her salivation-inducing body. And Norma, the daughter of the foreman who runs the highway road crew, is a beautiful and well-built young girl whose face and figure have appeared in the nudie magazines through which the diner's workingman clientele like to greedily pore.

The Widow's setting is also similar to the kinds of out-of-the-way, lightly populated, backwoods towns in which Meyer tended to set his films. The never-ending quests for carnal pleasures is a constant, à la Meyer, but there are plenty of basic human dramatic conflicts here to offset all the sex and demonstrate that the characters occasionally have some other kinds of motivations besides what they act on in the sack, same way Meyer always worked those sorts of things into his cinematic tales. Yeah, Russ could have taken Jerry, Linda, Norma, and the side characters, setting, and various subplots of *The Widow*, exaggerated everybody and everything to make it all a little more cartoonish, and produced a classic Meyer movie.

Note that one of the women in Jerry's life in *The Widow* is the wife of his employer's son. They all live together on the property in which the restaurant is located—Jerry, Linda, Linda's grease monkey hubby, and that guy's miserly mother, who owns the joint. That kind of highly risky romantic foul play is something that occurs routinely in Hitt's novels. And it makes me think of something one of the author's daughters told me: she said, in a mischievous way, that she'd often wondered if some of the characters and situations in her dad's books were based on people and events from his own social circles. If this is the case, the citizens around Port Jervis during Hitt's days there, as well as those who knew him in his non-writing working life (at various times he was employed as a radio announcer, insurance salesman, manager of a hunting and fishing club, etc.), could have experienced his novels on a whole different level from how we casual observers do. In *The Widow*, as in other Hitt works, the characters' lustful pursuits often drive them into romantic and sexual partnerships in which they really shouldn't be engaging, unless they want to put their marriages, jobs, familial relations, neighborhood reputations—and sometimes their lives—at risk. Hitt used the potent combination of sexual desire and existential danger to concoct explosive literary cocktails in *The Widow* and in countless other novels. And the idea that he did all that while writing stories that were based on the exploits of people he actually knew? Wow.

If you're new to the novels of Orrie Hitt and have been looking for an entry point, this package will make an excellent introduction. Both *The Widow* and *Wayward Girl* are among Hitt's better titles and together they give a clear impression of the kinds of characters and situations he included in his numerous books. If you're already a Hitt enthusiast and haven't read one or either, what the hell are you waiting for?

Brian Greene writes short stories, personal essays, and features and reviews of books, music, and film. His writings on noir fiction and film have been published online and in print by Criminal Element, Literary Hub, Crime Time, Crimeculture, Mulholland Books, Paperback Parade, and PM Press. Brian lives in Durham, North Carolina.

Wayward Girl

By Orrie Hitt

1

The sixteen-year-old girl, Sandy Greening, meant to be around when the Blue Devils hit the Black Cats gang. The Black Cats, who controlled the Cannon Street area, were going to pay for what they had done to Ruth Sloan. They were going to pay big.

True, it was four o'clock by the battered clock on the dresser, time for Sandy to leave for work at the diner. She worked from four till eight daily, helping out during the dinner hours, but today the diner would have to get along without her services.

The girl figured the Blue Devils had better use for them.

Sandy crossed the room she shared with her mother and halted at the window to look down into the back yard, but she had no idea why she bothered. There was nothing down there but old cans and high weeds and a woman's girdle some smart guy had stuck up on the end of a stick. The girdle had been flopping there for a week now and nobody had claimed it. Sandy had examined it carefully when she had hung out the wash the day before and had thought the girdle too expensive to have come out of the Central Avenue area. Probably some girl uptown had ventured into Devil's Corner and had run into more than she had bargained for. Sandy wondered, vaguely, who of the Blue Devils had taken care of the girl. But there were twenty-three boys in the gang, counting their leader Tommy Forbes, and they all had the same idea of what a girl was for.

She shrugged and turned from the window. The view inside had not much more to offer. She saw two beds with sagging springs, and the clothes her mother always left scattered around. It did no good to pick things up because her mother would just throw more stuff down and the room would look the same. When they had first moved to Central Avenue, Sandy had tried to keep the living quarters neat and clean but it had been a waste of time. All her mother cared about was the wine she drank at Chuck's Tavern with Marty White, and the pleasure of Marty in bed.

"He ain't so bad," her mother often said, usually in the morning when she and Sandy were by themselves and her eyes were still red from the drinking. "He's better than your old man. If your old man had had any sense, he wouldn't be sitting it out in prison."

The Greenings had been living on Central Avenue for only three years. Sandy could still remember the nice house they had occupied on Sherman Place at the other end of Mayville, where most of the people were honest and hard working. Her father had been a furnace salesman earning a fairly good income, but her mother, Flora, was an extravagant sort and had plunged him deeply into debt. He had been on the verge of losing his car when he had made a desperate attempt to stick up a gasoline station with a borrowed gun. But he had been nervous and inexperienced and the owner of the gasoline station had slugged him with a wrench, grabbing the gun and holding him until the police had arrived. That had been the end of Leo Greening. He had been charged with armed robbery and had been given from ten to fifteen years.

There were times, like now, when Sandy thought about her father. He had been a pretty right guy and she supposed she ought to go and see him more often. But the prison was nearly two hundred miles away and there never seemed to be enough money for bus fare. At first Leo Greening had written once a week, assuring Sandy and Flora that everything would turn out for the best, but their replies had dropped to nothing, so that he had finally stopped writing altogether. The last time Sandy had seen her father had been on Christmas, nearly a year ago.

"You shouldn't be living on Central Avenue," he had said then. "It's no place for a fifteen-year-old girl."

"I'm almost sixteen. Sixteen next month."

"How's school?"

School she had hated but had not said so. She had said exactly the opposite. The following month, however, as soon as she had turned sixteen, she had quit. She had been relieved to get away from the girls who had looked down on her because of her convict father. In Devil's Corner nobody snubbed her for that. On the contrary, in that section of the city bounded by Central Avenue, Bolton Park and the river, she was a big shot, especially with the gang. Her old man was doing time and she was in a class by herself.

"He should've pumped the bastard full of lead," Tommy Forbes had told her. "He should've blown the guy's brains out."

Tommy, nineteen, the oldest of the gang, worked the day shift on the docks. He was also Ruth Sloan's steady. Ruth was Sandy's age, sixteen, going on seventeen, and Tommy had made her pregnant the year before. But Phil Landers, who supplied the marijuana and heroin to most of Devil's Corner, had managed to dig up some pills for Tommy, and Ruth had lost the baby.

"Wonderful things," Ruth had told Sandy at the time. "One day you've got a gut filled with misery and the next day it's gone. I got six pills left and I'm keeping them. You ever need some you just ask me."

Sandy was sure she would never need them. Her mother had told her how to avoid having a baby, so when Sandy took a man to the back room of the Blue Devils for a five-dollar trick she refused to let him take chances with her. Sometimes she got ten dollars—if she were really obliging to the customer. It depended. The men who drifted into the diner where she made most of her contacts could seldom afford more than five. The ten-dollar deals were with guys who happened to come from uptown. Some men were married and some single. To Sandy it meant absolutely nothing as to who or what they were. It only mattered that they give her the money in advance; she made it a point of honor, however, to give them what they paid for.

"You're gonna get yourself an extra load," her mother kept telling her. "I was only fifteen when I married your old man. Why do you think we bothered?"

"And what about you and Marty?" she would counter. "Nights you think I'm asleep I hear you in the next bed. I know what you're doing."

Marty usually met her mother after she finished work at the brassiere factory. The only nights Sandy shared the room with them was when it stormed, or she had no date, or she had no idea of what else to do. Frankly, she was afraid of Marty. She was sure her mother did not know that she smoked marijuana and sometimes mainlined for kicks, but she was equally sure Marty could detect her addiction. Marty White was a pusher, although apparently he never used the stuff himself. Marty supplied Phil Landers who in turn sold the grass and horse to the teeners. Almost all the Blue Devils hit one or the other and they would do anything inside or outside the law to pay the fare.

Saturday nights were hot nights at the Blue Devils' basement club because by the end of the week most of the kids had accumulated some money. Everybody drank and many sucked the weed; and a few, if they had a girl, made love. When they did, they did not necessarily use the back room.

Saturday night, however, was about the only night during the week Sandy could not use the club to entertain her men friends, so she would have them take rooms in one of the cheap hotels along Central Avenue. She and the customer would register as man and wife and nobody ever said a word. The hotels collected at the time of registration and it made no difference to them what the room was used for. Once in a while she picked up a man who still had most of his pay-check cash and she was able to charge double. The week before she had had somebody like that and after she had left him she had gone down to the club. She had tried the weed without satisfactory results and so she had mainlined.

The next day Ruth Sloan had told her one of the fellows had taken Sandy into the back room while she had been under the influence. Sandy could not remember doing that, so it was possible Ruth might have been lying. Ruth did not have her build, at least not so far as her breasts were concerned, and frequently Sandy thought Ruth was jealous. But, jealous or not, Ruth was a good friend and she had had a racking experience the night before. She had been crossing the park about ten o'-clock and half a dozen Black Cats had jumped her. It was rumored that Slim Jefferies, leader of the Black Cats, had raped her, along with some of the others. It was, Sandy decided, a hell of a thing.

She moved to the dresser and took stock of her bare body in the mirror. Her white-blonde and naturally curly hair fell in long waves down to her shoulders, framing her face and making her lips appear wet and red and pouting. Her nose was slightly tilted, her chin firm, her neck lines good. But the best part of her, she knew, was her bosom.

She swung away from the mirror and began putting on her clothes. She felt no self-pity. In a city of a quarter of a million, a lot of girls did the things she did, the only difference being that some made as high as a hundred dollars a call. She wished that she could. If she could only connect uptown, she would lie about her age and cut a piece of cake for herself. This five-and-ten-dollar business was no good, not when you needed money desperately for dope.

She twisted into a black sweater, low in the front, and then into a pair of tight black jeans; high in the rear. Most of the girls who followed the gang wore the same kind of an outfit and the boys wore clothes which matched. What did not match was the gang's name—the Blue Devils, but somebody had started the black costume bit and the others had fallen into line.

As she continued to dress she thought about the first time she had known a man. She had been fourteen at the time and it had been shortly after she and her mother had moved into the room on Central Avenue. There had been a man in his thirties living across the hall and he had come in on her one afternoon after she had returned from school. He had had a bottle and he had offered her a drink but she had been frightened and she had refused him.

"You must be close to eighteen," he had said.

"No, I'm only fourteen."

"Don't hand me that. You've got a body that says you're eighteen."

He had put the bottle on the dresser and then he had chased her into a corner. She had fought him, screaming a couple of times, but it had been no use. He had been too strong for her and screams meant nothing on Central Avenue.

"I'm gonna take what I want," he had promised.

And he had. He had ripped the clothes from her body and thrown her upon the bed. She had crawled over to the wall, terrified.

She had pleaded with him, warned him that this would be rape.

"I don't care about that," he had said. "I'm getting out of this rotten town anyway. The only reason I hung around today was because I've seen you coming home before.

"Ain't no girl on Central Avenue as big as you are who don't know what it's like to have a man."

She had bitten him and had scratched his face but he had laughed at her, had pinned her arms to the bed. Then she had felt the pain....

The fellow had been gone by nightfall. She had not even bothered to complain to the cops about him.

All that had followed since, she now assured herself, had come naturally. If you ran with the Blue Devils you were expected to put out and all of the girls did—either for a physical lift or because some boy had bought them a couple of sticks of grass. But she had been over fifteen before she had drifted into prostitution and that had been because of Phil Landers.

At first Phil had given her the smokes for nothing but as soon as she had acquired the habit he had asked for money. There had been only one thing to do. She had started picking up men on the street and bringing them up to the room. At the beginning she had charged two dollars for her favors but she'd grown wiser with the passing of time and had boosted her price to five—and ten if she could get it. Soon she had had too many men to continue using the room and Tommy had given her a key to the club. A few of the other girls also had keys and they used the back room for the same purpose. There were two cots and more than one night she had made her money on one cot while another girl had been making hers on the other. She had felt no shame, simply a regret she could not promote more money for her wares.

Sandy left the room, locking the door behind her, and walked down the foul-smelling hall. There was an empty whiskey bottle on the stairs and she kicked it. It bounced from step to step, making a lot of noise. She left the building and wandered out to the street. A stiff breeze blew from the river. In spite of the sweater she felt chilly.

There was a butcher shop next door and the owner was outside. She gave him a smile as he stared at her jouncing breasts. Then she crossed the street, feeling the wind grow sharper as she left the protection of the buildings and walked toward a brick apartment house. Ruth Sloan and her parents lived on the first floor and because both mother and father worked they were always buying new furniture or a new television. They had jobs in one of the all-night factories and they worked from four until midnight. That gave Ruth the opportunity to be with the gang, and the chance for Tommy Forties to come and visit her if he were not tied up at the club

Sandy walked up the steps, pulled the big door open and entered. The hallway in here smelled fresh and clean. She did not bother knocking on the apartment door. She just shoved it open and walked in, closing it behind her. Ruth was watching television. She looked very small sitting in a big chair, her dark hair pulled back away from her face, a faded blue robe covering her youthful curves. Her face, while not exceptionally pretty, had a quality of grave appeal, something older than her years. Ruth smiled.

"Turn the damned thing off, will you?" she asked Sandy. "These programs they have about all the goodness in life drive me nuts,"

Sandy shut off the set. It became quiet in the room. She noticed Ruth had been reading a confession magazine. Ruth read a lot of confession magazines and she thought they were the most.

"You had a bad deal," Sandy said, sitting down on the davenport. She had not realized until then how tight her jeans were and she had to shift around to get comfortable. "They must have given you a rough time."

Ruth's eyes clouded. The smile left her face.

"Six of them," she said. "Or seven. I don't know which. But that Slim got his three times. He said he was paying me back for not dating him."

"I didn't know he tried to date you."

"Oh, sure. He knows I'm Tommy's girl and he thought it would be a big mark for him with the Black Cats if he got me away from Tommy. He tried it lots of times but I told him where he could go."

"What were you doing in the park?"

"Mailing a letter for my mother. I took it over to the other side of the park because they pick up the mail there early in the morning. On the way back I had to pass where the Black Cats meet. You know where it is—near that wall and that little pond. I didn't think anything of it. I was minding my own business. But they must have seen me cross the park and waited for me to come back. That's about all there is to it. They caught me and then they forced me. I didn't have a chance."

"What did you tell your folks?"

"Nothing. Tommy was in the diner and I told him. What good would it do me to tell my old man and old lady? They'd just say I was out asking for it and that I got what I deserved."

Sandy leaned forward, her elbows on her knees.

"We'll get them," she promised. "We'll get them tonight. And we'll cut their bellies out. You know how it is when somebody cuts in on the Blue Devils and especially when you're Tommy's girl. They've got their territory and we've got ours. We don't bother them none so why should they bother us?"

Ruth lit a cigarette and made a face.

"I wish I had some grass," she said.

"Sorry. No got." This was a lie because she had three sticks in her purse but she was keeping them for later. "I haven't seen Phil in a couple of nights."

"I'd like to go with you," Ruth said, her tone hard. "I'd like to see those bastards pay. They always meet in the park and it's a cinch you can jump them easy."

"You stay here and rest up."

"I've got a choice maybe?" Ruth's mouth twisted. "I've got trouble standing on my feet, let alone walking to the park. I told the old lady I'm coming down with a cold or something and she's gonna call me every hour."

Sandy longed for the feeling a stick of grass would give her but she could not light one in front of Ruth. The thing for Sandy to do was to return to the room and sit out on the fire escape. That way the room would have no odor when her mother came home with Marty. A few hours remained before darkness and if she smoked the three she had she could get a little high. If she had known Phil Landers' whereabouts she had earned the money the night before—she could have mainlined it. But Phil did not come around until late, so that was out. The weeds would have to do.

"We'll slash them," Sandy said, getting up from the davenport. "We'll slash the Black Cats until their blood flows down Central Avenue. They may have done this once but they won't do it again."

"I know where you can slash them where it counts."

"We might even do that."

Once Sandy reached the street again she found the bite had gone out of the cold. The wind had died down, and what was left of the sun crept in between the buildings and splashed across the street. A boy whistled at the way she was built and she told him to go to hell. There were a lot of punks along the street but what they wanted they wanted for nothing. Sure, once in a while you gave it away, at the club for instance, but that was different. You got high and no longer cared what you did. The next day, if you were able to remember it at all, it meant very little.

Thinking she might read a paper while on the fire escape she stopped and bought the local tabloid. It headlined the same old jazz. Too many call girls in Mayville. Too many kid gangs. Something, the paper said, had to be done to turn back the wave of crime breaking over the city. Just the night before a secretary had been raped in her room by a prowler, the fifth rape in that section of the city. Where, the paper demanded, were the police? Where would it all end? Most of the crimes, the paper contended, were born in Devil's Corner. From there sex-mad men fanned out to seek their victims in every part of the city, prowling through the night and striking with all of the fury of the insane.

Sandy dropped the paper into a garbage can before she reached the rooming house. Where was the truth in the paper? A reporter could have been sent down to Devil's Corner to see the rats running across the street, to see the kids who had nothing but the hard pavement to play on. A story could have been printed about the factories that refused to pay enough for a family to die on, let alone live on. There could have been interviews with landlords who didn't care whether their poor tenants were petrified by cold or burned out by heat. But catch a newspaper really giving a reaming-out about the things that were important. Catch the City Fathers talking about what really mattered. Devil's Corner was the goat for everything that went wrong in the city and probably always would be.

She began to hurry as she neared the rooming house. She had three sticks and they ought to give her a charge, a good charge. Later that night she would see Phil Landers and she would get something that would really make her world spin, a world in which everything would be possible and nothing impossible.

Once Sandy was inside she went up the steps two at a time.

She could not wait.

She honestly could not.

2

It was dark when she crawled through the open window from the fire escape into the room. The grass had done her no good. For several minutes she had had a lift and then it had left her. But it had been that way lately. She had to have some H before she really rode the broom. The trouble was that Phil Landers or somebody else had been cutting the horse and she had found that she had had to take more and more to get a boost.

She closed the window and walked across the room to turn on the overhead light. She had bought a cheap shade in a five and dime, one of those things you pushed up over the bulb, and it gave a pink effect to the room. But as she rolled up the left sleeve of her sweater she could see her arm clearly enough. The marks of the needle did not show as yet. She had only been on the heroin since summer, using it when nothing else would work. More than once she had tried to cut it out, not wanting to go down the ladder any further than she had already gone, but she had usually ended up looking for Phil and a fix. Each time she had taken one she had told herself it would be the last but she had known she was deceiving herself. The first jab demanded a second—the second, a dozen more.

There were kids on the avenue who spent as much as forty dollars a day for the junk. The girls who were hooked earned the money to pay for it by selling their bodies, and the boys stole anything they could lay their hands on, sometimes going so far as to mug men and women along the streets. The muggings, however, did not take place on Central Avenue because nobody there had anything worth stealing. The boys worked uptown around the theatre district where they were almost sure to get enough take for their trouble. Occasionally one of the boys would hit it good and then they would all have a hell of a time at the Blue Devils' club. Nearly everybody would go for the needle and they would live for awhile in a dream world.

Sandy pulled the sleeve of her sweater down and glanced at the clock on the dresser. It was a few minutes past eight, nearly time to meet Tommy and the others at the corner of Central and Fourth. The corner of Central and Fourth was directly opposite the entrance to Bolton Park. The overhead light across the street enabled them to gather in the shadows and make plans without anybody noticing them. Then they would filter into the park, one or two at a time, and the hunt for Slim Jefferies and the Black Cats would be on. Everybody knew where the Black Cats held their meetings, over near that wall. They thought the park belonged to them but it did not and they did not have enough money to pay for club rooms. During the winter, when the weather was bad and they could not meet outside, the Black Cats came close to breaking up but when the weather was favorable they went into action again and fanned out from their Cannon Street area.

Sandy's back was to the door when it opened and she thought it was her mother and Marty coming in. Turning around, however, she saw it was Marty, alone.

"You got no hands?" she asked him. "You could've knocked."

"I never knock."

He closed the door and leaned against it. He was big, with dark hair, and his suit looked expensive. He wore a large diamond on one hand and never missed a chance to show it off. He claimed the ring had cost him more than a thousand but she had seen some in the store windows that had looked as good for a lot less than a thousand.

"I don't like you walking in here," she said. "When you're with my mother that's different but when you're alone that's something else again."

He took out a package of cigarettes and flipped one into his mouth. He was very good at that. She had seen him do the same thing a hundred times and she could not remember him missing once.

"The traffic held me up and I was late getting to the factory. I checked and she had already gone. Then I stopped in at Chuck's, thinking that she would show, but she didn't. I figured she had come up here and that's why I came."

Her mother had probably met some other man and gone off with him. Flora Greening did that once in a while and a couple of times she had been away from the room overnight. Marty was just another man to her and, to her way of thinking, one man was just as good as another.

"You might better wait for her in Chuck's," Sandy said. "She won't come here without getting her wine."

Marty grinned and moved away from the door.

"Ain't often I'm alone with you," he said. "And don't think I haven't noticed you. I have." His grin grew wider and she noted that his teeth were well-kept and white. "I've noticed you plenty."

She backed away from him.

"Who's touching you?"

"I'm just telling you, that's all. I've got no time for you."

He stopped, still grinning, and rubbed the side of his face. He left the cigarette in the comer of his mouth as he spoke.

"I know everything that goes on along Central Avenue, baby. And I mean everything. You've been putting it out for money and most of your take goes to Phil Landers. Your old lady, bad as she is, would blow her roof if she knew the whole thing."

She was unhappy Marty knew about her but she was not surprised. Marty had many connections extending all through the Devil's Corner. Since her mother would learn about her sooner or later, Sandy was not too concerned. What could her mother say? Her mother was stupid; she gave her body away when she could have capitalized on her favors.

"I'm in a hurry," Sandy said, walking past him. "And you've got nothing to say that interests me."

He grabbed her arm and twisted it.

"I'll pay you the same as the others do."

She swung around and kicked him in the shin, hard.

"Pay my mother," she said as he let go of her. "You get in your licks and you give her nothing. Why don't you pay her?"

"She has her fun."

"Well, go ahead and find her and let her have some more."

She jerked the door open and stepped into the hall, considering she was lucky to get away from him. She slammed the door and hurried out into the street. Let him go to her mother. Let him shoot his mouth off. She could always get a room and make a go of it. She had nothing in common with her mother. In fact Flora Greening was simply another person with whom Sandy shared the same room.

The wind had stopped blowing. There was a full moon overhead which would help in the park, giving at least some light by which the Blue Devils could see the rival gang, seek them out and destroy them.

Sandy's blood pounded as she continued along the street. There was almost as much excitement to this as there was to a needle in the arm. All the Blue Devils were big strong boys and they would give the Black Cats something to remember.

She arrived at the comer of Central and Fourth and saw nearly everybody was there—about two dozen boys and half again as many girls.

"Thought you weren't coming," Tommy said to her.

Tommy was tall with blond hair cut short, and he had the shoulders of a football player.

"You couldn't keep me away," she assured him. "Not after what they did to Ruth."

She saw the flash of chains in the dim light. One boy had a zip gun. For some reason she was afraid of that thing. The chains were bad enough but the zip gun was worse.

"You carry this for me until we get into the park," Tommy said.

He handed her something and she knew it was a knife, long and sharp. The other fellows took this as a signal and began loading up the girls with their weapons. A cop occasionally patrolled the park but while he could search the boys if he thought something was up he could not search the girls.

"All set?" Tommy wanted to know.

Everybody nodded.

Tommy issued orders. The first of the boys moved across the street and disappeared into the darkness of the park. They were followed by other boys and then the girls. Pretty soon only Tommy and Sandy were left.

"I'm gonna rip that Slim Jefferies," Tommy said as they stepped off the sidewalk. "I'm gonna rip him until there ain't nothin' more left to rip."

No cop was in sight and nobody stopped them. In a matter of seconds they were inside the park with only the light from the moon overhead. They assembled near a deserted bench and moved in a group toward the distant wall. As they came nearer to the wall the boys claimed their weapons from the girls.

"Keep your hand outa the front of my sweater," one girl complained. "You want your chain or a hunk of flesh?"

"Both," the boy replied.

They moved on and Tommy cautioned them to be quiet. Now that Sandy had become accustomed to the moonlight she could see fairly well.

She heard the Cats before she saw them. They were laughing it up, possibly passing a bottle around and more than likely planning how they could catch some other girl who might venture into the park, bending her to their will as they had bent Ruth Sloan.

Tommy pulled the boys aside and told them in a low voice what they should do.

"Well cut them off on all three sides," he said. "They won't know where to go or what to do. But Slim is for me. You guys got that? He's mine."

The boys understood and they moved off through the shadows, Tommy in the lead. One of the girls said she wished she had not come and another girl told her to shut up. A dead silence seemed to settle over the park, and the sound of the cars moving along the avenue was at that moment far away, a part of life in the city which to Sandy was very unreal.

It came suddenly when it came—the shouts and the screams and the curses—and Sandy rushed forward with the other girls to see what was going on.

Boys were everywhere, clubbing each other with chains and clubs and calling each other four-letter words. The Black Cats met in a clearing, away from the trees, and the light was fairly good. Sandy saw Tommy, the knife flashing above his head, and she heard Slim Jefferies pleading. But the pleas did no good and the knife came down, not once but many, many times. Presently Tommy stepped back and Slim Jefferies sank to the ground, his hands over his stomach, his body lying there without movement.

The fight was short. A cop's whistle shrilled through the night and they all got out fast. Tommy had Sandy by the arm, dragging her along with him, and as they neared the street he threw the knife into some weeds. Once they reached the sidewalk they started walking casually, as though nothing had happened. The cop was coming from the other direction, from over Cannon Street way, and they had plenty of time.

"How about stopping at the diner for coffee?" Tommy inquired. "I could do with something."

"I hadn't better. I didn't show up for work this afternoon. The old man'll blow a gasket but if he doesn't see me I can tell him tomorrow that I was sick."

They crossed the street and continued down the avenue. Now that Sandy fully realized what had happened back in the park she was somewhat frightened.

"You killed him," she said, her mouth dry.

Tommy ran his fingers up and down her arm.

"I cut his guts out," he said. "I ripped him from side to side and up and down. He won't bother no other girl ever again. And if the others have any sense they'll learn a lesson from it."

Her arm trembled beneath his touch. "What if they catch you, Tommy?"

"Nobody's gonna catch me."

"Some of the Black Cats might talk."

"Let 'em talk. I was with you all night." His fingers dug down into her arm. "You got that? Me and you, we had a little ball at the club. They can't prove no different. All I gotta do is say we had a shack-up and I can thumb my nose at 'em."

There was one thing he had not considered—Sandy was only a little over sixteen and he could get himself into additional trouble if he said he had fooled around with her. But she said nothing about that just then. Maybe the police would be stymied and Tommy's act would just go as another unsolved stabbing. If it did it would not be the first in Mayville. The cops would chase after the gangs for a while and break them up on the street corners. The newspapers would kick up a big stink but, as in the past, only the parents and relatives of the dead would remember, and often they too had short memories.

The moon now was clouded over and the wind had risen again, blowing in once more from the river. Sandy felt a few drops of rain against her forehead and her whole body shook, not from the wind or the cold but from what she had seen back there in the park. Somehow, she thought, killing was not right. One boy could beat another boy up and teach him a lesson but he did not have to kill him.

"He had it coming," she said without conviction.

"He sure did. If you knew how many girls those guys have knocked off in the park, girls who didn't say anything, you wouldn't be able to keep count." He let go of her arm long enough to light a cigarette. "They should've had some debs along. Then they would really have got what was coming to them."

She knew that a lot of girls had been taken care of by the Black Cats in the park but she knew that a lot of them had asked for it, too.

"I have to go in," she said when they were opposite her rooming house.

He took a firmer grip on her arm and kept her from stepping off the sidewalk.

"Nuts to that," he said. "The cops may take a look in at the club and I want you to be there with me if they do." He pulled her in closer to him. "And we can have that ball I spoke about." He leaned down and kissed her on the cheek "You know what I mean, baby."

She knew what he meant and she longed for a jolt that would send her up high into the clouds.

"You're Ruth's fellow," she reminded him, trying to pull away.

"Yeah, and what good is she to me now?" He kissed her again, on the mouth. "I've been sorta watchin' you all the time." His hand moved up. "You've got a pair," he told her, his fingers driving pain into her. "You've got a real pair."

The club rooms were at the end of the block, down in the basement, and as he let her in she wished desperately she had a fix. If she had one she would be able to endure anything at all.

"You got something to make me bounce?" she asked him.

"I never use the stuff."

"What about liquor?"

"Liquor I've got."

He switched on the lights and they moved toward the back room, past the chairs scattered around and the table where some of the fellows played cards. There was a dart board on one wall and a huge picture of a nude girl.

Tommy had hidden a bottle, nearly full, beneath one of the cots and they drank the liquor straight. Sandy sat on one cot and Tommy sat opposite.

"You make a lot of dough down here," Tommy said, pouring her another drink.

"Some," she admitted.

"If you worked uptown you could get out of the five and ten dollar class and hit it big."

"Well, I've thought of that."

"What's the use of thinking? You oughta do something about it."

They drank and smoked and she felt the liquor taking hold. The feeling did not resemble the one she got from mainlining but it was better than nothing. That Phil, she decided, must be selling her low-quality grass or those three sticks she had had would have hit her hard. Most of the time she needed only one or two to get herself jacked up off the ground. The suspicion that he had cheated her made her angry. She had paid him a buck a stick and he should have supplied her with the real thing.

"The cops aren't coming," Tommy said. "The crazy bastards are running around like they had their heads chopped off and they don't know up from down."

The liquor and the absence of a visit by the police caused her to relax. She noticed with a twinge of regret that the liquor was low in the bottle. Tommy ought to go out and get another jug, she thought. It was too late for her to work the streets and it was too early for her to return to the room. For all she knew, Marty was still there waiting for her. And that, on second thought, might not be so bad. Marty could get her a fix and by tomorrow she would need a fix as much as she had ever needed one.

"Couple of dummies lookin' at each other," Tommy said, getting up from the cot. "You sit there and I sit here. What kinda romance is that?" He sat down beside her, putting one arm around her middle. "You got somethin' for me, baby?" he wanted to know. "You got somethin' you and me can have a little fun with?"

She did not resist when he kissed her and slowly forced her head and body back. It hardly mattered. He was just one more and by tomorrow she would have forgotten him the same as the others. The only trouble was this was not for money.

He had trouble with her jeans and she lifted her hips so that he could get them free.

"You know what you have to do," she said.

"Sure."

"Be sure you do it. I don't want to hold any screaming brat in my arms."

He laughed at her.

"I'd make a great father, baby."

It was her turn to laugh.

"You'd make one hell of a father. A girl has a kid by you and she might as well hang herself."

She was certain that he would be careful with her but at the last moment she knew he was not.

"Louse!" she screamed at him. "Dirty louse. Dirty—"

She had been determined that she would not respond to him but she did. There was something inside her, a powerful urge to be pleased, that would not be denied. Before she realized it her arms were around his neck, pulling him closer, her mouth wide-open and demanding. Each time was like the first time. But unlike the previous times she was unprotected. The knowledge of this screamed through her mind but it died in a wave of emotion. Many girls did the same thing and nothing happened to them.

"Tommy!" she gasped. "Tommy!"

"You're something all right," he said later, trying to force a drink from the nearly empty bottle. "I should've tied up with you and not Ruth. Since what happened last year Ruth is scared all the time and she gives me the jitters."

Sandy got up from the cot and began to dress.

"I don't want a steady," she said. "A girl has a steady and the first thing she knows she's got a big belly." She stepped into her jeans. "Those who want it can have it but it's not for me. I'll take my lumps for what the guys can pay."

Tommy threw the bottle on top of one of the cots.

"You didn't make much tonight," he reminded her.

"That was charity and payment for the key to the club." She walked to the door and paused. "Consider our debts square."

"Until the next time."

She left him alone and made her way out. The rain was coming down harder now, a cold rain driven by a sharp wind, and the street was deserted. She might just as well go to the room. She could run naked up and down the avenue but with this storm she would not be able to turn up a dime.

A smile pulled at her lips as she crossed to the other side.

Tommy Forbes had been quite a man.

She tilted her head and smiled up into the rain.

Man?

Hell, he had been all man.

3

Her mother stayed away from work the next day and the two slept until noon. When her mother did get up she paced the room like a caged animal.

"Four o'clock," she said. "What a time to get in. And now I've got a head like a barrel."

Sandy yawned at her mother. Flora Greening at thirty-two had lost none of her shape. Her stomach was still flat, her hips rounded and her breasts full. If she would only choose the right shade of lipstick to use with her red hair she would be more than attractive.

"Marty was looking for you," Sandy said, sitting up. "I guess he figured you were with somebody else."

Her mother leaned forward to examine her face in the mirror.

"He figured right. What the hell does he think I am, anyway? Some nut who's going to stand on a corner waiting for him a half an hour? If he hasn't got ambition enough to show up there's always somebody else. If I dated all of the guys who are fishing for me at the factory he wouldn't even get up to home plate."

Sandy lay back and closed her eyes. What a life, she thought. Now that she was sober the memory of the night before returned to her, making her skin first cold and then hot. Tommy had gone the limit with her and that had been poor sense on her part. She should have made him do what she made the others do. What if he had started a kid? But, she assured herself, it was nothing to worry about. Ruth Sloan had those aborting pills. But there were times when they did not work. All Sandy could do was hope she would not have to try them at all.

It was around one by the time they dressed and her mother asked her to go out for a paper.

"You want a hot dog from the Texas Lunch?" Sandy inquired.

Flora Greening made a face.

"I couldn't eat a thing. Not a damned thing. That wine has got my guts tied up into knots."

The newspaper stand was only a few doors from the rooming house and Sandy picked up a copy of the *Record*.

"Can't get enough papers today," the man said. "Everybody wants to read about the stabbing in the park."

She lingered on her way back by the side of a deserted brick building to read about the killing. Slim Jefferies had been well known on Cannon Street and his parents were grief-stricken. He had been a good boy, they said, and he had gone to church every Sunday. The minister of the church called for swift and decisive action by the police and an official of the police department said that the men in blue were doing everything they could to uncover the killer. The newspaper said that every youthful gang in the city should be crushed and that the young offenders, no matter who they were, should be given full punishment for their crimes.

The same slop, Sandy thought, as she returned to the room.

Her mother read the paper, starting with the comics first, and then threw it aside.

"That boy got his," she said.

"Yes, he did."

"Well, he probably deserved it. He probably cut in on somebody and got cut up instead."

Flora Greening walked to the window and stood there silent for a long time.

"You run with the Blue Devils," she said finally.

"Once in a while."

"I want you to give it up. These gangs are bad. The same thing could happen to you as happened to that boy." Her mother sighed. "I wish I had enough money to move off of Central Avenue. I wish your old man hadn't been so stupid as to pull a gun in that gasoline station. He ruined everything, he did. Everything we had went for the trial and they stuck him away anyhow."

Her mother talked on and on, raving about the police and the laws, and Sandy was glad when it came time for her to get ready for the diner. She was nervous and on edge and her need for a fix was worse than ever. That night she would have to grab a needle and give herself a ride.

"I could use a ten," her mother said,

Sandy thought about it before replying. Phil Landers would be in the diner just before closing and since he had trusted her before there was no reason why he would not trust her again. It was pay-day on the docks and she would be able to line up four or five men for the night. And there were some regulars she had whom she could depend on.

"It's in my pocketbook."

"Thanks. I'll pay you back."

Her mother never paid her back. If she got overtime at the factory it only went for wine. She would haul a couple of bottles up to the room and when Marty White appeared they would really sex it up.

Sandy waited until her mother had left the room before she changed into the white uniform she wore at the diner. The uniform was a good fit, low enough in front to excite the men, but she objected to the short sleeves. If she continued with the needle the marks were bound to show, the veins getting big and lumpy as she had seen them on some girls.

Sandy stepped into the hall and locked the door behind her. Someday she ought to kick the habit and maybe she should start doing it now. She had seen enough of it to know it was an endless chain. You started out with a little, just as an experiment, and before you even knew it you were hooked, hooked hard.

She experienced a sharp pain in her stomach as she emerged on the street, a pain that crawled all the way down into her legs. That was part of it, part of the need, part of the hunger that screamed for the needle to bring release and satisfaction.

The rain had long since stopped and the sun was out bright and warm. She did not feel cold without a coat or a sweater but after it got dark the dampness would drift up from the river. If she saw Phil, though, she could make a deal with him so she would not mind the night in the least. She would not mind anything. All she had to do was to arrange for three or four tricks and she would have it made.

The diner was three blocks distant, near the waterfront, and its outside needed painting. It had needed painting ever since she had lived on Central Avenue but Old Dick would never go to the expense.

"I should make it a palace?" he often demanded. "I should maybe plate the counter with gold for guys with strong backs and weak minds?"

Old Dick was about fifty and he shaved about once a week. He never bothered the steady girl, Hester Carlton, a woman his own age, but whenever Sandy had to go into the kitchen for a dinner he liked to pinch her.

"Am I an orphan?" he would say. "I give you a chance to make your contacts and you oughta show some appreciation by making an old man happy."

But Sandy had steadily refused to have anything to with him. A guy played and he paid. She brought business into the diner he would not have otherwise got, guys who ordered steaks and big meals and who hung around to look down the front of her uniform when she bent over the sink behind the counter to rinse out glasses.

She found the diner empty except for Old Dick sitting at the counter. This was unusual for four o'clock. Most of the shifts finished at that hour and the men crowded in to eat.

"Everybody die?" she asked.

Old Dick grunted and his fat stomach moved up and down. He was about due for his weekly shave and his face was covered with a heavy, gray beard. He was a short man, not much taller than Sandy, and when he walked he also grunted.

"Might as well have," he said. "You hear about the docks?"

"No."

He took a drink of black coffee from the mug sitting in front of him.

"Strike," he said. "They walked out this morning and it don't look like the strike will be over with right away. They got paid, same's always, but they've only got one more pay—the week that's held back—and they won't be spending their money like they usually do."

This was bad news to Sandy. The last strike, just the year before, had lasted more than a month and a half. She had made peanuts during that time but she had only been using grass and she had been able to get by. But now she was on the H and that cost a lot more money.

Old Dick got up from the stool and wandered off toward the kitchen, mumbling to himself. A couple of men came in for coffee. They tipped Sandy a nickel and she sneered at their backs as they went through the door. How far did they think a girl could go on a nickel?

None of the regulars came in and this burned her. Why did they have to have strikes? The people on strike generally lost more than they gained and prices went higher and higher. Somebody, Sandy decided, had a bolt loose.

Phil Landers came in around five-thirty and ordered bacon and eggs. Phil was small, with narrow shoulders, and he looked like a well-dressed rat who had just crawled up from the sewer. She guessed him to be in his late twenties or early thirties, although with his schoolboy complexion it was difficult to tell.

When she went back to the kitchen to get the bacon and eggs, Old Dick slapped her on the fanny.

"Some ham," he said.

"Keep your hands to yourself."

She reached for the plate of bacon and eggs but he delayed giving them to her.

"You won't be doin' nothin' tonight," he said. "We could go some place and iron the sheets."

Usually she had a couple of dates by this time but the strike had really thrown a wedge into things.

"You put your money on the line," she said.

"Pay? Me pay? Why should I pay? I get all I want without comin' across with a buck."

"Then get it and don't bother me."

She carried the bacon and eggs out front and buttered the toast for Phil.

"I need a fix," she said, putting the toast before him. "I need one so bad my guts are rubbing against my spine."

Phil nodded and dug into the eggs. "You got the money?"

"No, but I'll get it."

He glanced at her and she could see the question in his dark eyes.

"Where?" he demanded. "You got a printing press?"

"No, but—"

"You heard about the strike?"

"I heard."

"Those guys will be hanging onto their money until it's over with. Most of them are married and those who aren't married have got steady girls. Why should they fork over a five or ten to you? What they've been paying you is just money to throw away and now they don't have it to throw away. You follow me, huh?"

Sandy nodded, so terribly in need of a fix she was almost sick.

"You trusted me before," she reminded him. "I never cheated you any. If I owe you dough I pay you dough. You know that, Phil."

Phil finished the bacon and eggs in silence.

"You gonna help me?" she asked him.

"Yeah, when I see the money. The other times I gave it to you on the cuff I knew you had some dates and you'd come across. Now you ain't got no dates. So where do you figure on digging up the money? Not in this dump."

"Damn strike," she said bitterly.

Phil put a dollar on the counter.

"Maybe you should try uptown," he told her. "You've got a better shape and face than most of the girls who coin cash. You could get twenty-five bucks a trick without any trouble at all. Once you learn the ropes you can hit it even better."

"But that ain't now," Sandy pointed out. "And now is what counts." She leaned across the counter toward him. "Those sticks you sold me stunk," she said. "If you could get a lift out of them you'd have to be in an elevator."

He shrugged and stood up.

"I don't make 'em," he said. "I buy 'em and I sell 'em. I don't know what's inside and I don't ask nobody. If you're not satisfied with what I give you, go find somebody else."

A few minutes after this Phil left but he said he would be back again before Old Dick closed.

"You may score," he said. "You may pick up a live one and then you can live."

After he was gone she took the dishes out to the kitchen and Old Dick made another pass. Sandy jumped away from him and told him again what he could do with his hands. Then she returned to the front of the diner and sat down on one of the stools at the counter. She remembered what the girl had told her how you felt when you had to go without a lift and it frightened her. If only she had not given her mother the ten dollars she could have done something with that. But she had not known about the strike and she had been sure that it would be a good night. Payday night she often made as much as fifty dollars.

Tears filled her eyes and she listened to the cars moving along the avenue. What was she going to do? What could she do?

The door opened and somebody came in. Sandy hoped it was somebody she knew and she got up, smiling, turning as she did so.

"Hello," the man said.

He was a stranger. He was tall, probably around six feet, and he appeared to be fairly young, with brown hair and a slightly red face that told of the sting of the wind outside.

"Coffee," he said, taking a stool.

"Black or regular?"

"Black."

Sandy drew the coffee.

"Going to storm," the stranger said as she put the coffee in front of him.

"You think so?"

"Yes. You can tell by the moon. There's a ring around it and it's all clouded over."

She washed some glasses to give the stranger a chance to look down inside the front of her uniform. He might be a trick and she would do anything for a trick. Not only that but he looked like he could afford more than ten bucks.

"Nothing doing down here," he said.

She straightened and dried her hands on a towel.

"Did you think there would be?"

"Well, you hear things."

"Such as?"

"How you can have fun down here."

Sandy gave him her best smile.

"It depends on where you look," she said. "And how much money you're willing to play around with," she added. "The money has a lot to do with it."

"Naturally."

He had another cup of coffee and he said he was new in the city and he traveled for a firm which sold road equipment. This information pleased her. If he were a salesman he had an expense account and a salesman was not tight with his money.

"You work late?" the stranger asked her.

"Until eight."

"What do you do then?"

"Oh, hang around."

He worked up to it slowly, talking about himself some more, things which she did not even listen to, and while she did not come right out and tell him what she was she left no doubt in his mind she was available.

"How much?" he asked her finally, stirring his third cup of coffee.

"Twenty-five." Sandy had decided he could afford that much. "Twenty-five, whether we go to the club or take a hotel room."

"Club?" he inquired.

"That's a place a few blocks away."

"I'd rather go to a hotel room."

"Suit yourself. But you pay for it."

"I'd expect to do that."

He made arrangements to meet her promptly at eight and left a dollar on the counter. She watched him go, satisfied that the night would turn out all right after all. Sandy would not be with him more than an hour, and she would be able to meet Phil Landers and pay him for what she had to have.

She laughed to herself as she cleaned off the top of the counter. She had nothing to worry about. Something always turned up. All you had to do was sit and wait and fate hit you right between the eyes. One minute you were down and the next minute you were riding it sure and fast.

Sandy laughed again and threw the cleaning rag under the counter.

Hell, it was a great life.

4

The stranger returned for Sandy shortly before eight and sat at the counter waiting for her. He had, he said, got a room for them in the Bell Hotel on Fourth Street and he had picked up a bottle of gin. Sandy did not care much for gin but she did not tell him that. He was a twenty-five dollar sucker and she was lucky he had come along.

When it got to be eight she went back to the kitchen to tell Old Dick that she was going. He merely grunted at the announcement. He was reading one of his filthy books and he was more interested in that than he was in her or business or anything else.

"I may have to lay you off if the strike keeps up," he said as she started for the door.

"All right."

"But you come in tomorrow, same as usual. I'll let you know then."

"Okay."

The stranger was waiting at the door for her and they went outside together.

"I don't know your name," Sandy said to the man beside her.

"Just call me Harry."

She giggled and took his arm.

"Bet it ain't your right name. Bet you got a wife and kids at home and you don't want nobody to know who you are."

"You aren't far wrong."

She squeezed his arm tight.

"What the hell do I care?" she said to herself more than to him. "You got a room, nice and warm, and you got the money." She giggled again. "And I got what it takes to make a man happy." She paused. "I got lots of it, honey."

He did just what she had expected he would do. He freed his arm, put it around her and she felt his long, heavy fingers pressing at her breast. They all did that. Some wanted to put their hands down inside of her dress but she would not permit that on the street.

"You're nice," the man said.

"I'm glad you like me."

"You'd better be nice to me in the hotel."

She stopped, turned toward him, pulled his head down and kissed him on the mouth.

"Oh, I will," she promised. "You won't be sorry none."

The hotel was on the opposite side of the street and they crossed to it.

The lobby was small and there was just an old man at the desk. He paid no attention to them.

There was no elevator so they had to walk up to the room on the third floor.

"Rat's nest," the man said.

"Like the whole area," Sandy agreed. She forced a laugh. "A rat would give up in disgust and drown himself in the river."

The room was the same as the other rooms she had been in. The woodwork around the door and windows needed washing and the paper was faded. The rug on the floor had a big hole in it and both chairs looked as if they were ready to fall apart. Shoved up against the wall was a double bed with a pink spread on it, the pink nearly white in some spots from age and repeated washings.

"Well, here we are," Harry said and closed the door. He did not bother locking the door. "Here we are and now we play."

She looked him over. He was not as bad as some she had been with and a lot better than others.

"You could pay me now," she said.

His eyebrows lifted and a faint smile tugged at his lips.

"You don't waste any time, do you?"

"Why should I? We aren't up here to talk. I know what you want and you know what I've got."

He reached into his pocket and brought out his wallet, fingered through it and then handed her two tens and a five.

"What are you waiting for?" he asked.

"Nothing."

She knew what he wanted. They all wanted the same thing. They all wanted her to strip first, to see her naked body. She had never understood the reason for this but she guessed it was just one of the idiosyncrasies of the male.

She folded the bills tightly in her left hand and began to undress. Harry sat on the bed watching her, something sad and unhappy in his eyes as he looked at her.

"Now I'll show you what little girls are made of," she said.

While she was getting out of her uniform he left the bed and walked to the window, standing there with his back to her for a moment. When he turned around she was already unhooking her bra.

"You like?" she asked him as she removed the bra.

"You're all girl," he admitted. Beads of sweat stood out on his forehead. "You're a very pretty girl."

She got out of her other things and then stood in front of him. She still had the twenty-five dollars in her hand and that was where she intended to keep it. If she put it on the dresser he might pick it up and then she would have difficulty getting it back again. One night she had done that and the man had scooped up the money and kicked her out without a cent.

"Well, what are you waiting for?" she asked as she walked to the bed. "I haven't got all night, honey." She lay down on the bed. "You've seen all there is to see. Now it's up to you to make me earn my dough."

She closed her eyes and waited. What was the matter with him? Most guys would have been after her already. Sometimes she did not even get a chance to undress. But this fellow certainly was taking his time. Maybe he was bashful.

Her eyes were still closed when the door was flung open and she was aware of somebody else in the room. Quickly her eyes leaped open. She let out a frightened squeal. The man standing there, just inside the door, wore the uniform of a policeman.

"I hurried as fast as I could," he said to the man named Harry. "But the old man on the desk tried to give me an argument."

Her glance moved to Harry, or the man who said he was Harry, and she took a deep breath as he reached for a cigarette.

"She's got the marked bills," he said. "It's open and shut and there's no mistake about that."

"And her only a little over sixteen," the cop said. "Yeah. A little over sixteen."

"Too bad."

Sandy barely remembered leaving the hotel or the ride in the police car uptown. Inside she was dead, dead as a fish lying along the river bank in the sun. She had been so sure of making enough so that she could get a fix from Phil Landers and now she was in trouble, big trouble. She began to cry. There was nobody to help her, nobody at all. She was a prostitute and the cops had caught up with her. What would happen to her now?

Sandy soon found out when she reached the police station. They booked her as a wayward minor and then she was led into a little room where an elderly man sat at a long table.

"Sit down," he told her.

She sat, the tears still wet in her eyes, trembling all over. If she only had a fix all this would not be so bad. If she had a fix it would kill the pain in her stomach and it would make everything fine.

"How old are you?" the man asked.

"Almost seventeen."

He shook his head sadly.

"Too young for the business that you're in."

She said nothing. There was nothing to say. He could keep talking and she would listen.

The man called Harry came in and joined them. He was a cop and she hated him. Hated and feared him. A cop could do a job on you if he put his mind to it. The cops had slammed it to her father and now he was spending his time in a cell.

"I'll brief you in on her," Harry said to the older man. "She lives with her mother in a room on Central Avenue but most of the time her mother is hitting up the wine. She runs with a guy named Marty White and you know what we think of Marty. He isn't a pusher but he's a supplier and one is as bad as the other. I don't know if the girl has been on the dope but from what I've heard she's been willing to sell herself to the men who work on the docks. I passed out five dollars to one of the strikers and he gave me her name as being a right dish. The rest of it was easy. She's a pro."

She longed, for a cigarette but would not ask either of the cops for one. They would talk to her for a while and then they would let her go.

"Where were you last night?" the older man asked her.

"I don't think I have to answer that."

His face became stern.

"Answer the questions I ask you and don't be so smart," he said sternly.

Sandy had heard that a person had a right to have a lawyer but she did not know much about such things. And she had no money to hire a lawyer. It seemed to her that her best bet was to go along with them and get out of this as easily as she could.

"I was down at the club," she replied, thinking of what Tommy had told her.

"The Blue Devils?"

"That's right."

"Were you alone?"

"No. I was with Tommy Forbes."

"From when until when?"

"From around seven until midnight."

The older man looked unhappy.

"That tallies with what Forbes told us," he said to Harry. "He didn't give us any time but he said they were down there half of the night. That kind of lets him out on the Jefferies killing. He couldn't have been two places at once."

"Unless she's lying."

"Lying? Who can prove it? It's the same with the rest of the Blue Devils. Their parents cover up for them. They were home watching television. They were reading. We've talked to all of them during the course of the day and it's been the same story. Nobody was any place and nobody did anything." He slammed his fist down on the top of the table. "That's the trouble today. The kids roam the streets, raising hell, and their parents stand behind them. If I had my way I'd make a law to put them all in jail."

She saw then that the police had not been inactive. They were on the prowl for the killer of Slim Jefferies and they had struck at her because she was Tommy's alibi. As long as she maintained that she had been with him they could not touch Tommy. It gave her a sense of victory, of being bigger than the cops were.

"What were you and Tommy doing?" Harry asked her.

"What do you think we were doing?" she sneered. "Holding hands?"

"You're not of age. He can be held for impairing the morals of a minor."

"You mean because he kissed me a couple of times?"

"You probably did more than that."

"Go ahead and prove it."

The two men looked at each other and they both shrugged.

"What are you going to do?" the older officer asked. "It's like trying to knock down a brick wall with a car that's only going fifteen miles an hour."

Sandy listened to them talk but hardly anything that they said made much sense to her. She gathered that the cops were putting on a blast against kid gangs, that they were going to drive them from the streets. The death of Slim Jefferies had lit a fuse and the effort would be all out.

"What's going to happen to me?" she asked finally.

The one she had known as Harry looked at her a long moment before saying anything.

"It depends," he said. "You're young and with the right kind of care and help you can make something of yourself. It'll be up to the judge. My guess is you'll go to reform school, probably Edgewood."

Her heart almost stopped.

"Oh, my God," she whispered.

A matron was called and the matron took her away. She was searched in an adjoining room but she had no weapons and she was taken to a cell.

It was a long time before Sandy closed her eyes and even longer before she went to sleep.

If only she had not been such a little fool.

If only she had a fix.

So many things, she thought, had gone wrong.

It was hell.

5

The courtroom was not a big place and Sandy saw her mother was there, sitting to one side and simply staring at Sandy as she entered. Her mother's eyes looked red, as though she had been on the wine all night long, and it was obvious she had been crying. A tiny sneer pulled at Sandy's mouth. What was her mother crying for? You took your chances and sometimes the turn of the wheel came against you. What did her old lady expect when you lived on Central Avenue? You gave it away or you sold it. Was there much of a difference?

There were several others in the court, including the man she had known as Harry and the elderly cop who had questioned her the night before in that tiny office. She glanced at them and then away. They were cops and she hated them, hated everything they stood for. They would probably get a pat on the back for giving her the business, for picking up a kid who had not been hurting anybody except herself.

Presently Sandy was before the judge and she looked up at him. He had a bald head and a face that seemed to be kind. The blood raced through her veins and the pain in her stomach from being without dope was not so bad. Perhaps he would listen to her and let her off easily.

"I'm Judge Ferris, Sandy."

"Yes, sir." Her voice was tight and strained and did not sound like her own voice.

"What is your last name?"

"Greening."

"How old are you?"

"Sixteen, going on seventeen."

"Ever been in trouble before?"

"No, sir."

"And you don't go to school?"

"No, I quit. I wasn't doing good and I quit. I work in a diner down by the docks."

The judge studied some papers on his desk, then rubbed one hand across his forehead and leaned forward.

"You were an average student," he said. "We checked with the school authorities and while you weren't at the top of your class you weren't at the bottom either. You could have made out if you had stuck to it."

"Well, I didn't."

"And your job at the diner isn't much. Four hours a day. It's hardly enough to support yourself."

"I manage to get along."

His eyes, very dark and piercing, searched her face.

"The way you were getting along last night, Sandy?"

What could she say? She had had the marked bills in her hand and she had been offering herself on a pay for fun basis.

"I think I ought to have a lawyer," Sandy said, not sure if this were right or not.

"A lawyer?"

"Other people have one, don't they?"

He nodded and straightened in his seat.

"Do you have money with which to hire a lawyer?" he inquired.

"No."

He looked at her thoughtfully for a moment.

"You're entitled to a lawyer," he said finally. "If you don't have the money the court can appoint one." He surveyed those who were sitting in the court. "Would you accept the task, Mr. Summer?"

A young man, hardly more than in his early thirties, stood up.

"Yes, Your Honor."

"If you wish, you may have a conference with your client in an adjoining room."

"Thank you, Your Honor."

A court attendant led Sandy away and she began to feel better. A lawyer would get her out of this. Lawyers got lots of people out of lots of things.

The room into which she was led was small. It had but one window. There were bars on the outside.

"You can wait here," the man said. "I'll stay outside by the door."

"All right."

She heard the door close behind her and she walked to the window. The sky was overcast and a few flakes of snow were falling, big flakes that melted as soon as they touched the window or the building next door.

It was several minutes before the lawyer came into the room and she swung around to face him, her hopes rising again.

"Why don't we sit down?" he said.

There was a long table in the room—at least, it was long for the size of the room—and she sat on one side and he sat on the other.

"This could go to trial," he said, offering her a cigarette.

She accepted the cigarette.

"Trial?"

"By a jury." He held a light for her. "But I don't suggest it."

Some of her hopes began to die slowly.

"Why?" she demanded, her hand shaking as she fingered the cigarette.

"Because it would be a waste of your time and a waste of mine." He smiled faintly. "You were caught and you were caught properly. All the evidence is against you. You were selling your body and you took marked money. There isn't a thing you could tell a jury that would make them think you were innocent."

"But I've never been in trouble before," she wailed.

"That's not the point. You're in trouble now and that's what counts. You're in it up to your ears," he added. "And, I might say, above your ears."

She sat there stunned, unable to move. She had counted on him and now he was letting her down. It just went to prove that the police and the lawyers worked together.

"What should I do?" she asked after a while.

He spread his hands wide.

"What can you do? Plead guilty, that's all you can do, and hope for the best."

"And what is the best?"

He shrugged.

"A reform school, perhaps." He held up his hand. "Oh, don't get alarmed. It isn't as bad as you may think. A reform school isn't a prison. They'll help you and put you on the right track. When you come out you'll be a different girl. They'll teach you that the clean life is the good life and someday you'll be grateful for it."

She stubbed out her cigarette in an ash tray.

"Oh, brother!" she breathed.

"You haven't had much of a home life," he went on. "Your father is in prison and from what I gather your mother hasn't been much of a mother." His tone softened. "You aren't too young to make a mistake but you aren't too old to be helped. Be happy about that and look to the future rather than the past."

She pushed her chair back and stood up.

"Thanks for the speech," she said.

"I'm only trying to guide you."

"Yeah, but which way?"

She walked to the door and opened it.

"You might as well take me back," she said to the man standing outside. "I've had all of that lawyer that I can stand."

In the courtroom the judge motioned Sandy forward. She walked toward him, her legs numb, the pain in her stomach a sheet of fire.

"Did you talk to Mr. Summer, Sandy?"

"Yeah, I talked with him."

"And what did you decide?"

"What could I decide?" she countered bitterly. "He's in it with you and you're in it with him."

"You're aware of the evidence which we have against you?"

"I know about it." Her voice rose. "Sneaking cops, running around and picking on kids. Ain't they got nothing better to do?"

"A sixteen or seventeen-year-old prostitute violates the law as much as she would if she were twenty-five."

The policeman who had trapped her was called before the court and he told the story as it had happened. He was backed up by the one who had been in uniform.

"How come he waited for me to undress?" she wanted to know. "He after a free peek or something?"

But the officer had an answer for that. He had gone to the window to signal his partner and she had undressed quickly.

"I didn't intend for her to strip, Your Honor. All I wanted to do was get her with the money in her hand."

"I believe you," the judge said.

When the officers had completed their testimony she was asked how she wished to plead.

"I've got no choice," Sandy replied. "I guess I'm guilty."

The judge nodded his approval.

"You are making a wise choice," he said. "From what we have learned about you you haven't had a chance to live in our society as you should. A few months in Edgewood Reform School will do you a world of good. You may learn a trade, if you wish, or, to the extent of the capabilities of the school, you may resume some of your studies."

Sandy was just interested in the facts.

"How long am I getting?"

"Six months to a year but you can get out in less time if you show progress and the desire to be a decent citizen. When you are released the school will help you to find a suitable job, either here in Mayville or somewhere where you're not known." He paused. "You should be pleased that I am sending you to Edgewood."

"Oh, I'm jumping up and down."

He refused to be annoyed by her remark.

"Edgewood is something new, an experiment by the Department of Correction. My personal opinion as to whether it will work out or not is hardly important. For what it's worth, I think that a juvenile can be just as big a criminal as an adult and deserves the same sort of treatment. But because this is your first trip into court, though I think you should have been here before, I am giving you the benefit of the doubt. It's all up to you, Sandy. If you look upon this as an opportunity, rather than punishment, you will profit by your experience."

"Okay." But she was not convinced. What a hell of a way to gain experience. "Okay, sir."

As she was taken from court she was led past her mother—her mother had changed her seat—and their eyes met briefly.

"Whore," her mother said. "Cheap little whore."

"Stop calling yourself names," Sandy flared.

The man led her into the same little room which she had been in before with the lawyer.

"A couple of policemen want to talk to you," he explained.

"That's just dandy. I suppose they gotta know how many times I did it."

The man made no reply, stepped out into the hall and closed the door after him. Alone, very much alone, Sandy felt the hot sting of tears in her eyes. The bastards, the dirty bastards, they had really given her the works. Six months to a year in some damned reform school. How would she ever be able to stand it? Living on Central Avenue was no prize but she would rather do that than have to go through with this. But, she reasoned, six months or a year went fast and when she got out she would be a big shot with the gang. Anybody who had done time was a big shot on the avenue.

She walked to the window and looked out again. It was snowing harder and now the flakes were not so big and the building opposite was beginning to gather a coat of white.

Sandy walked away from the window and sat down at the long table. Jesus, she needed a fix, needed one in the worst way. Those pains in her stomach were getting sharper, almost driving the air from her lungs, pains that did not stop at her middle but spread out all over her body, causing her to tremble and sweat and then get cold. She thought about the needle, of plunging it into her arm, of the glorious relief that would soon follow. Silently she cursed Phil Landers. Those sticks he had been selling her must not have been up to par. The weed had been cut down, purposely, making it necessary for her to go for the H. She had heard of that being done but it had never happened to her before. Until the night before one or two sticks had been plenty, enough to get a little high on, but even with three she had not felt a thing. They had cost her a buck a stick and again she cursed Phil Landers, out loud and viciously this time, using a four letter word common along the avenue. He had sought to get her in deeper, to get her to depend on the needle. Well, she would show him. She would show them all. She did not have to depend on that and she would kick the habit before she became a slave to it. This caused her to smile. Kick it? How—in this situation?

The door opened. The man she knew only as Harry, and the older man who had questioned her the night before, came in.

"You did the right thing," Harry said, sitting down at the table. The other man sat down too. "A plea of guilty was, under the circumstances, the only plea you could give."

"I've got no truck with you," she said, feeling as though she might retch because of that pain in her stomach. "You're a big man, aren't you? Stickin' me away in some reform school. So you got what you wanted. So what the hell do you want with me now?"

"It won't do you any good to act tough," the older man told her.

Sandy laughed at him.

"Maybe I should give you a medal, huh? Maybe I should send you a bunch of flowers for what you did? Is that it? You want me to thank you for stickin' me with this rap?"

The older man offered her a cigarette but she shook her head. She wanted nothing that belonged to cops. She had had enough of them. First they had slammed it to her father and now they were slamming it to her.

"We want to ask you some questions," Harry said.

"Well, I can't stop you. But that don't mean you're gonna get any answers."

Harry nodded as though he understood and then reached into his coat pocket. He brought out a knife and laid it on the table before her.

"Ever see that before?" he asked.

"Not that I know of."

He tested the blade with the tip of one finger and she could see it was sharp.

"We found it in the park," Harry said. "We found it not far from where the Jefferies boy was killed."

"Why tell me about it?"

"Because we thought you might know how it got there."

"Ask the man who had it. You think I run around keepin' track of everybody who has a knife?"

"Not exactly and we don't have to ask you who it belongs to. We found it before the snow and there were fingerprints all over it. The fingerprints belong to Tommy Forbes."

This was bad, very bad. Tommy should not have been so foolish as to throw the knife away in the park. Anybody with any sense at all was bound to know that the cops would look for it. The cops had a murder on their hands and the pressure was on them. They would drive into it from every direction.

"He must have lost it," she said. "But don't ask me. How would I know?"

"There wasn't any blood on it," the cop said.

She smiled faintly. Tommy must have wiped the blood off on his pants and that had been a smart thing to do. If he had, she hoped he had got rid of the pants. But why had he forgotten about the fingerprints? He must have been in a hurry and overlooked them. She had read once that anybody who did a murder always made one mistake. But, she reasoned, it was not serious. The cops might find one knife or a dozen in the park—which proved nothing.

"He was with me," she told the policemen. "He couldn't have done nothin' wrong. We were down at the club, just like I said. You ask my old lady if I was home."

"We did and she said she didn't think you were, but she was half gassed when we talked to her and I don't think she knew what she was saying."

"Sounds like her."

"What did you and Tommy do at the club?" the older man asked.

"Sat around and talked. What else was there to do?"

"Did you have sexual intercourse with him?"

"That's for me to know and for you to find out."

"Did he give you any dope? Anything, say, like marijuana?"

"No."

"Or a few drinks?"

"No."

Harry regarded her with interest and, she thought, a touch of defeat.

"So you just sat and talked, is that it?"

"That's what I told you and you can take it from there. Tommy and me have been friends for a long time and we had a lot of things to talk about."

"Such as?"

"Things. They don't have nothin' to do with what you want to know. I got a right to talk to somebody, haven't I? There a law against that or something? You got laws that say you can talk to this guy and not that guy?"

Harry frowned and returned the knife to his pocket.

"You could help yourself," he said. "You could tell us the truth."

"So I did tell you the truth," she retorted hotly. "I tell you the truth and you have to go and crap it up. I was with Tommy at the club, like I said, and we were there for a long time. He didn't score with me and he didn't even try. We talked about the weather and how the docks were on strike and things like that. If somebody got gutted I don't know nothin' about it. And neither does Tommy. Instead of askin' me all these damn fool questions why don't you go out and get the guy who did it?"

"You know Phil Landers?" the man called Harry asked.

"Should I?"

"He sells dope in the Devil's Corner."

"Then I wouldn't know him." Jesus, those pains in her stomach were bad. "I've never been on the stuff. But if he's what you say he is why don't you go out and put your hooks into him?"

"Because we have to have proof."

"Well, you won't get it from me. I don't know any guy by that name. I never even seen the guy."

"Some of the Blue Devils use marijuana, don't they?"

"You'll have to ask them. I've got my own grief."

"What about Marty White?" the older policeman asked. "Are you acquainted with him?"

Sandy thought of lying and then decided that she should not. If they had checked out Marty White they must know that her mother went with him.

"Not good," she replied. "He takes my mother out once in a while."

"Did you know he was in the dope business?"

"I never asked him what he did. He came to see my mother, not me. Why should I care what he worked at?"

"Did you ever have any relationship with him?"

"Why don't you come off it? You think I went to bed with every man I met?"

"I only asked you."

"And I'm tellin' you."

"I think they should have sent you to a tougher reform school," Harry said as he got to his feet. "You're hard, Sandy, hard as they come, and my guess is that being nice to you isn't going to pay off. Some girls deserve to be treated fairly but you aren't one of them. A lie rolls off of you just like water off a roof."

"The judge told me where I'm gonna go," she reminded him. "You got any objections you go out and tell the judge."

The two men paused at the door.

"It wouldn't do me any good," Harry said slowly. "Judge Ferris is a man of rather firm convictions."

"So I guess you're kinda outa luck, huh?"

"No," Harry said, opening the door. "You are. You're the one who ran out of luck."

As the door closed behind them Sandy began to cry, crying hard for the shot she could not have and crying for the life being taken away from her, crying as much as she had ever cried.

Damn them, she thought.

Oh, damn them.

Damn them, damn them, damn them ...

6

It was eighty miles to the reform school and Sandy rode with three other girls, a matron and a deputy sheriff. Sandy rode in back, in the middle, and the other girl and the matron rode up front with the deputy.

"I wouldn't mind so much if it wasn't for the baby," the girl on Sandy's right said. "Now I'm three months gone and the poor little thing will be born in a reform school. Ain't that a nice start to give to a kid?"

The matron turned her head and removed the cigarette from her mouth. She was a woman of about fifty and she tried her best to be pleasant.

"You don't have to worry about that," she assured the girl. "It's against the policy in New York State to have a baby born in a reform school or a prison. You'll get prenatal check-ups and as soon as you go into labor you'll be moved to the local hospital, along with a nurse from the school. When you're released from the hospital you'll be assigned to the nursery at the school where you can be with your baby and care for it."

Later during the drive the matron told them more about the reform school.

"The ages of the girls range from sixteen to thirty," she said. "They're in for prostitution, drug addiction, petty larceny, bigamy, assault, neglect of children and for being wayward minors. For the most part they are first offenders, none of them violent, and the school offers them a rehabilitation program, a program designed to make them useful citizens when they get out. Those who are young enough, or who have not finished high school, go to classes for half a day and the other half a day is devoted to learning a trade. Every effort is made to help you, to assist you to see that you have done wrong in the past but that you can do better in the future."

"It don't sound so bad," the girl in front said.

"It isn't. You learn to work with other people, to help them, to be a person in your own right."

"Jesus, a speech," the other girl next to Sandy said.

The matron merely smiled.

"No, it isn't," she said. "I simply think you should know what you're going into and to realize how lucky you are. Other reform schools have almost the same projects but in Edgewood you are visited by people from town and you may, if your behavior is good, accept an invitation to their homes for a weekend, starting on Friday night and ending late Sunday afternoon. In this way Edgewood is entirely different from any other reform school. You have something to work for, something to accomplish, other than merely time off for good conduct. If you are lucky and a local family takes an interest in you, you can spend two days out of seven away from the school. It gives a girl a sense of security, of being wanted."

"When does this start?" Sandy asked.

"You're on probation for six weeks, to see how you fit in with the school, and then you're on your own. After that you can make or break yourself. Not all girls, of course, get away for weekends. There are just so many people who can take them in—people who are interested—and there aren't enough to go around. But the program is gaining favor in the community and most girls get at least a couple of weekends away from the school. It is remarkable what this does for them and how it brightens their outlook."

The snow was coming down heavily and the deputy was not driving very fast. At one point they skidded and almost went into the ditch. The girl in front screamed and covered her face with her hands.

"Tricky," the deputy said as he straightened the car. "They must've had an ice storm up here before the snow." He glanced at the matron. "Back in the city they'll think we got lost or something. They figure two hours coming up and two hours going back but they never figure on driving conditions."

A truck loomed ahead of them and the deputy slowed the car, leaning forward in an effort to see better through the whirling snow that came back from beneath the truck's tires. There was a heater in back of the car as well as in front but Sandy felt cold. Before leaving somebody had tried to find a coat for her but there had been none available and there had not been time for a cop to go down to her room and pick up the only one she had. For this reason, hoping that she would keep warm, she had sat between the two girls, but it was not much good. The one girl had on a cheap, thick perfume, and the other girl had a cold that made her cough every once in a while. Once the matron had suggested that the deputy stop and get some cough drops but he never did.

The truck ahead turned off into another road and the deputy drove a little faster. The fall of the snow had increased and the windshield wipers were having all they could do to keep the glass clean.

"That defroster isn't worth a hoot in hell," he said once. "I could almost see better if I was locked up in the trunk."

They entered a small town, paused for a stop light and then continued on. People walked the streets of the town, their heads bent into the snow, and as Sandy saw them she thought of them as being free people. They could stop in at a bar for a drink. They could go home. There was hardly anything that they could not do. There would be no confinement for them, no rules they had to live by—just the rules that were ordinary rules—and they were not shut away from the rest of the world.

Suddenly, watching the people, Sandy felt sorry for herself, sorry for her father, even sorry for her mother, sorry for everybody who had made a mistake. How had she? But she knew the answer to that one. It had been easy, easier than going to school and enduring the remarks of the kids and making something of herself. In that instant she hated her past life, hated Phil Landers, hated Tommy, hated the cops—hated everything and everybody that reminded her of what she had been. But mostly she was unhappy with herself because she had been so stupid. She should have stayed away from the grass and the H and she should have made her connections uptown, getting from twenty-five dollars up for a throw instead of from ten dollars down. A guy did the same thing to you for fifty bucks as he did for five. Why sell yourself short? The prostitutes who knew the ropes seldom got caught while dumb girls like herself fell into a trap.

"There it is," the deputy said after a while.

The snow had let up and Sandy could see the brick buildings crowding the crest of a hill. A couple of the buildings were fairly large but most of them were inclined to be small, like pleasant looking homes in the country. Or, she thought, they looked like homes in the country. She had never been out of the city before.

"Home," one of the girls said bitterly. "Three cheers for nothing."

They drove along a high wire fence for a considerable distance before the deputy turned off the highway and brought the car to a halt in front of the gates.

It did not take them long to be cleared by the guard. The gates opened and they rolled forward, climbing the hill, the rear wheels of the car spinning in the snow.

"The first place you go is the administration building," the matron said. "The clerk in charge will check you in and any valuables you have can be left in the school's safe."

"Who's got any valuables?" the girl who was pregnant wanted to know.

"You have," the girl on the other side of Sandy said. "You're carrying a kid, aren't you?"

"That's not very funny."

"Maybe not but you could get real dough for it on the outside. Some people go as high as five grand to adopt a kid."

"I'm keeping my baby."

"Go ahead and be a sucker. Who the hell cares?"

The building in front of which they stopped was impressive but forbidding, like a school nobody wanted to attend. It reminded Sandy of the first day she had gone to high school, of her fear that somebody would ask her where her father was, of her shame because she had no bra to wear under her sweater.

They were herded out of the car and up the high cement steps coated with ice and snow.

"It might be better if I fell down," the pregnant girl said. "It might be better if I lost the baby and didn't bring it into the world."

The wind was cold and the uniform little protection. Sandy felt her teeth chatter, stop, and then chatter again.

"That's no way to talk," Sandy said. "You had a bad break and you have to make the best of it. Others have had worse happen to them. What if you were dead? That would be worse. As long as you're alive you can solve things and do the best you can."

The office into which they were led was a fairly large place with a bench along one wall. The matron told them to sit on the bench and wait their turn.

"Hurry up and wait," the girl who had been riding in front said. "Jesus Christ."

The bench was hard but it was warm in the office and the girl at the reception desk tried to be pleasant enough. She had a smile for all of them, not just the matron and the deputy, and then she checked over the papers which the matron had brought along. Finally she nodded, indicating that everything was in order, and the matron and the deputy departed, the deputy grumbling about the weather and the drive back to the city.

The first one called before the girl at the desk was the girl who was pregnant. It was too far away for Sandy to hear what they were saying but she did not care. That pain in her stomach was like a mass of fire and once she bent over, pressing in with her hand, in the hope that it would go away. But it did not. The pain seemed to be all through her, long tongues of it reaching out and gripping each nerve and muscle.

Sandy was the last one called and her legs were weak as she moved up to the desk. That pain was in her stomach again, grinding out in sharp flashes that shot up into her chest, nearly pulling the air out of her lungs. She had not had a headache before but she had one now, an ache that seemed to start at the base of her skull and move all the way forward across her head to above her eyes.

"You must be Sandy," the girl at the desk said. "Sandy Greening."

"That's right."

"I'm Miss Nolan." She studied a paper in front of her and then looked up.

"You're in for prostitution, aren't you?"

"So they say."

"Aren't you rather young to be mixed-up in such a mess?"

"Young enough, I guess."

Miss Nolan smiled, a smile reserved for those considerably beneath her.

"It's none of my business," she said. "We have three psychiatrists who come in to work with the girls and you will be assigned to one of them. I'm sure you will be helped and that by the time you leave here you'll feel like a different girl."

"Oh, sure."

Standing up and walking to the desk had helped Sandy's headache but the pains in her stomach were very violent. Maybe, she decided, she was just hungry but the mere thought of food sickened her so much that she had to swallow hard to keep from retching.

"You aren't wearing any rings," Miss Nolan observed.

"I don't have any."

"And no locket or beads?"

"Nothing."

"You're entitled to wear a religious emblem but that's all or if you're married you can wear your wedding ring."

All this seemed pretty stupid to Sandy.

"I'm not married and I don't have any ring," she said. "And I never went to no church so that other stuff is out. All I got is what's on my back and nothing more."

"You must have been cold on the way up."

"Well, I wasn't warm."

"Is that why you're trembling?"

Sandy had not realized that she had been trembling but when she looked down at her hands she saw them shake.

"Maybe," she replied. "But it's warm in here and I'll get away from it soon."

The girl swung to the left and inserted a yellow form in a typewriter.

"Your first name Sandy?"

"That's right."

"Any middle name?"

"No.

"Address?"

She gave the number of the house on Central Avenue.

"Live with your family?"

"My mother."

"And what is her name?"

"Do you have to have that?"

"Yes. In case something should happen to you we have to notify somebody."

"Forget it," Sandy said, remembering her mother's red eyes after her mother had been on the wine. "She don't count with me and I don't count with her. I could drop dead tomorrow and you'd have to pay her to come to my funeral."

Sympathy filled Miss Nolan's eyes.

"Don't think you're alone," she said. "It's that way with a lot of girls. If parents only took more interest in their children there wouldn't be so many reform schools. About eighty percent of wayward minors are the products of poor home lives. It's the job of the reform school to teach them to live on their own, to become a part of society through their own desires."

They were fancy words, too fancy for Sandy, and she merely nodded. What they would teach her at the school would not be worth the powder to blow it to hell. As soon as she hit the city again she would cut loose in a storm that would make her past seem dull.

"It's my job to brief you about the school," Miss Nolan was saying. "You'll be in quarantine for two weeks."

"How come?"

"For medical examinations and observation. All the new girls have to go through the same thing. About four or five girls out of a hundred have some social disease which requires treatment."

Sandy tilted her chin stubbornly.

"I don't have no disease."

"Perhaps not but we have to be sure. Few girls would admit it if they were sick. You'll have a Wassermann test for syphilis and a smear test for gonorrhea. If you're found to have either one of these things you'll be taken care of. If you don't, and you're all right in every other respect, you'll be out of quarantine in two weeks and assigned to a room in one of the cottages. A house-mother will be in charge of you and she will be responsible for your welfare. Each cottage has a recreation room—so do the quarantine sections—where you may read, listen to records or the radio or television or just talk with the other girls. At nine o'clock you must be in your room and your lights must be out. While you are in quarantine the door to your room will be locked but after you move to a cottage your door will not be locked. However, you are not allowed to visit another girl's room and another girl isn't allowed to visit yours. Not under any circumstances. Is that clear?"

"I—guess so."

"The rules we have are for your protection and welfare. After you have been on probation for six weeks you will be assigned to a parole officer who will determine if you are suitable for weekends in the village." Miss Nolan smiled. "Most girls work very hard for this opportunity and we have found that the plan has been quite effective. Some of the girls have even found jobs in the village after their release and are now leading decent lives." Miss Nolan paused and tapped her white teeth with the end of a pencil. "Follow our rules, Sandy, and you will make out fine. We don't ask for the impossible. We know that what has happened to you isn't wiped out overnight and we're willing to work with you to overcome it. Do you have any questions?"

"Not right now."

"Then I'll turn you over to a correction matron. She will see that you have a shower and that you are issued a hospital uniform. When you are released from quarantine you will be given the regulation clothes of Edgewood. Your personal things you will wash out yourself but your dresses and things like that will be done in the school's laundry. Perhaps you will be put in the laundry for half of each day. It all depends on what our guidance counselor thinks you are best suited for."

Miss Nolan had little more to say after that. Sandy was led to the elevator by a heavy-set woman who must have been in her middle fifties. Sandy was amazed that the elevator always had to be unlocked before it could be used and she asked the woman about it.

"All doors are kept locked," the woman explained. "You'll get used to it."

The door closed behind them and they began moving slowly upward. Sandy doubted very much if she would ever get used to it.

"I'll try," she said.

It was the only thing that she could do.

7

The two weeks that followed were terrible ones for Sandy. She had to kick the habit and she had to kick it cold and when she was alone in her room she alternately paced the floor, doubled over with cramps, or lay upon her narrow iron bed and twisted in agony. When she was not with the doctor or other people who wanted to see her—these were ordeals because she had to keep up a good front—she made every effort to sleep. Sleep brought temporary relief but it also brought wild dreams—she was sticking the needle in her arm once again and riding high or she saw that knife in Tommy's hand flashing in the moonlight, bringing death to Slim and, with it, trouble to Central Avenue.

"You're improving," the doctor told her near the end of the two weeks. "You're making some good progress, Sandy."

The doctor had seen her several times, more than he had seen the other girls, and she had wondered about that. At first Sandy had thought she might have picked up something from one of the men she had been with but he had assured her that this was not so. Both the Wassermann and the smear test had indicated she was free of disease.

"I'm doing the best I can," she told him.

"Well, the worst is over."

"Huh?" She did not know what he meant.

"You were on the dope," he said. "You lied to me when I asked you about it but a doctor who works with as many girls as I do can tell. That's why I've been seeing you rather often and keeping an eye on you. The withdrawal is difficult but I doubt if you've been on it long enough for it to be serious."

Sandy was shocked that he had been aware of her condition but she was glad, too. She was glad the secret was out. Her dark hours of misery had cried out for somebody to talk to, for somebody who would listen and understand.

"It all started so easy," she said, the words rushing out.

"It always does."

She looked across the desk at the doctor. He was neither young nor old and most of the girls liked him. He never made a girl feel ashamed of herself. He always made a girl feel as though she were somebody important.

"The first was grass," Sandy went on.

"Marijuana," he corrected her.

"Yes. Marijuana. I was with some other kids and they were all trying it. There was a man who gave us the stuff. For nothing," she added. "He just passed the sticks around."

"To get you to want more." The doctor nodded. "And then he charged you?"

"Yes."

"It's an old racket. A pusher usually works that way. It's like giving away a free razor if the man who gets it will keep on buying blades from you. The investment is made with the intention of future profit."

Sandy felt ill at ease in her poorly-fitting hospital gown, a gown which hid all of the curves of her body. But she was no different than the other girls in this respect. The only one who showed her shape at all was a girl seven months pregnant. She was in for neglecting another child, a boy of two, and was unmarried.

"It's getting better now," Sandy told the doctor. "Last night I had the pains but they didn't last and today I've hardly got any at all."

"That's a good sign. In a few days the longing will be gone and you'll have gotten rid of the habit. You should feel proud about that. And it should be a lesson to you not to get into such a thing again."

"I won't," she promised.

"Dope only leads in one direction and that's down. Usually it starts with marijuana, just as it did with you, and while the marijuana isn't supposed to be habit forming—there are authorities who say that it isn't—the pusher cuts the quality of the merchandise he delivers to you and then when you don't get the response that you think you should he suggests that you go to something else. Heroin is usually the next step and that is habit-forming. Did you start sniffing it first?"

"No, the man showed me how to use a needle."

"Then he got you off to a fast start. The pattern is usually more progressive but some pushers can't wait. They can also cut the heroin—or H as you probably called it—and this makes you spend more and more money for relief. The need for money probably led you into the profession which finally brought you here to the reform school."

"More or less but there were men and boys before that."

"At least you're being honest."

"There's no use in lying about it."

He folded his arms across his chest and leaned back in his chair.

"Was it due to the fact that you were seeking sexual satisfaction?" he asked.

"Do I have to answer that?"

"No, certainly not. I was merely curious. The psychiatrist will go into that with you and it is really no concern of mine." The doctor smiled. "His job is to treat your mind and mine is to treat your body. Your body, so it happens, is in excellent condition. Once you get yourself squared away you'll be able to lead a normal life."

Something bothered Sandy, something that had bothered her ever since that night with Tommy. The topic among the girls in the recreation room dealt with sex but she had not found one to whom she could confide her fears. However, the doctor was impersonal and several times she had been on the verge of talking to him about this very important thing.

"I may be pregnant," she said.

He unfolded his arms.

"I found no evidence to show you are."

"It only happened the night before I was picked up."

"Then it's too early to tell. You'll just have to wait and see. If you are it will complicate your situation."

"Yes, it will."

"Do you love the boy?"

"I haven't thought about that."

"Well, don't until you're sure—sure one way or the other. If the boy is single that would help matters."

"He's single."

"Then I wouldn't worry too much about it. Most worries are for nothing. If it weren't for worry there would be very few sick people. You'd be surprised at the number of physical complaints which originate in the mind."

She left the doctor feeling somewhat better and received permission from the correction matron to join the other girls in the recreation room. She was kicking the habit, kicking it, and she smiled as she walked down the hall. And that doctor was smart. He was very smart. Nobody fooled him much and he was patient, giving his time where he thought it had to be given.

There were about a dozen girls in the recreation room and they were all in quarantine. Some of them were Sandy's age, some older. The older ones tried to put on the dog, as if they knew everything, and it became slightly boring. The oldest girl, in her late twenties, was in for forgery and she kept telling everybody that she would not make the same mistake again. Once she was out she would spread a little paper in one town and then move on to another before the checks bounced and the store owners ran to the cops. A couple of the girls were dope addicts, kicking the habit the way Sandy was kicking it, and they were not much fun to talk to. The younger of the two, just turned eighteen, had been on the junk for four years and she was living a life of hell, suffering only as an H user could suffer. Sometimes she banged her fists on the walls and screamed with the agony tormenting her. Then the correction matron would show up and drag the girl off to her room, staying with her until the attack let up and the girl drifted off to sleep.

There were two davenports in the room, plus several easy chairs, and Sandy sat down on one of the davenports, next to the girl who was seven months pregnant. The record player was playing, not rock and roll, but soft music, pleasant to the ears.

"You see the doctor again?" the girl asked.

"Yeah."

"You see him a lot, don't you?"

"Enough."

"More'n anybody else."

"Maybe."

The girl tried to adjust the hospital uniform, a smock-like affair, over her swollen stomach but the effort was wasted.

"You shuck out for him?"

"I don't get you," Sandy said.

"The hell you don't. He's got a private office and there's a couch in it and there's a lock on the door. I'd like to have five bucks for every girl he's given the business to."

"I don't think you would have very much," Sandy said curtly, cutting the topic short.

Sandy shifted her attention to watch the other girls and wondered what would happen to them. Everybody seemed to be waiting, waiting for they knew not what. Afternoons they spent in the recreation room but at five they had to go to their own rooms. Bars were on the windows of all the rooms and food was brought to them on a tray. There was no such thing as a community bathroom. There was a commode in the night-stand in each room and a girl had to tend to her needs with this. It was, to Sandy, as bad as being back on Central Avenue, and as cheap. However, she had been told that it was different in the cottages, that there were bathrooms and that life was closer to being normal. The term "normal" forced a smile to her lips. How could it be normal?

Sandy missed the dope, though much of the need was gone now, and she missed the men. Of the two she guessed she missed having a man the most. A girl had to have a man, especially if she were used to one. Even though she had sold her body for money there had usually been pleasure in the act for her. But Tommy, she decided, had been the best. Tommy had been like a bull that had been locked up for six months. If it were not for the fact that she didn't know whether she was pregnant, she could remember those moments with him and cherish them. But, to be truthful about it, he had not been the only man who had sent her. Even that first time when she had been forced it had ended up being good. She asked herself, staring through the smoke, if she were abnormal and she guessed she was not. A girl was meant to be with a man, to give her body to him, to enjoy the act of physical relationship as much as the man did. The last few nights when she had not been dreaming of a fix she had dreamed of Tommy, of his strong arms around her, of the offering of the male for the female. More than once she had come awake from the dream, clutching the pillow tightly to her body, the sounds of her heavy breathing filling the room, her desire and need so great that they threatened to consume her.

She had just finished her cigarette when Mrs. Graves, the correction matron for quarantine, came in and told her the doctor wanted to see her.

"I was just there," she protested mildly.

Mrs. Graves smiled and ran her hands, palms first, down over her ample hips.

"Not this doctor," Mrs. Graves said. "This is Doctor Francis."

"Who's he?"

"The nut-doctor," the girl beside Sandy said. "He takes a peek into your skull to see if you've got any sense. But he ain't so bad. All he does is ask a lot of screwy questions."

Sandy rose from the davenport and followed Mrs. Graves into the hall. She had already seen the medical doctor several times and now there was this one. How many were there anyway?

"Don't pay any attention to her," Mrs. Graves said. "She's pregnant and she's mad."

"Maybe I would be, too, if I was in her place."

"I suppose you would. Most girls who get themselves in trouble act that way. Their trouble is the result of their own foolishness but they take it out on the world. I don't mind, though. I've gotten used to it. Each girl is different, each girl is a challenge, and I only see them for ten days. I make out a report of my observations, which goes with them to their cottages, and I try to be as fair as I can. I try to think of how I would feel if I were in here."

"You couldn't possibly imagine," Sandy said.

"Perhaps not exactly. They say you can't know what pain is like unless you hurt yourself and I suppose it's that way with this. But I do my best. The girl you were talking to will never get along and eventually, either before or after the birth of her baby, she'll do something bad and she'll be sent to a prison. There is no fooling around in Edgewood. It's the best reform school in the state and only the best girls stay on here. Those who can't be helped by kindness have to be punished. It isn't a nice thing to think about but each girl has an equal chance when she enters and it's up to her to make the most of it. We're trying to show all of the doubtful people who say this experiment won't work that it will work, that the only way to make a girl decent is to treat her decently."

The doctor's office was at the end of the hall and the door was open. Mrs. Graves left her there and she entered the office, wondering what to expect.

"Please close the door," the doctor said.

He was about the same age as the other doctor, probably a few inches taller, and he had very dark hair and eyes to match. He sat behind a small desk and there was a chair in front of the desk. She sat down on the chair without being told.

"I'm Doctor Francis," he said.

"Yes, sir. I know. Mrs. Graves told me."

He smiled and toyed with a key, possibly the key to his car. Everybody who drove a car and who worked at the school was required to lock his car when he left it in the parking lot. A year before, just as the school had been getting started, a girl had hidden in the back of an unlocked car and had escaped. She had never been captured and it was a bad mark against the school, one which the officials did not want repeated.

"You're about ready to move to a cottage," the doctor said.

"Either tomorrow or the next day."

"The reports I have on you seem to bear out that you are willing to co-operate, that you keep your room neat and clean that you don't cause any trouble."

Sandy was not quite sure why she should but she felt relaxed in front of Doctor Francis. At least she was fairly sure he would not ask her to disrobe, though while she had done it for the other doctor and it had not bothered her much she would just as soon not do it again.

"I don't have much choice," she said. "You get put in here and you do as you're told or you're in a jam."

"A wise way to look at it."

"Is there another way?"

The doctor leaned forward, still fooling with the key. "You're in for prostitution, aren't you?"

"That's right."

"Tell me about it."

She crossed her legs under the hospital uniform and she wished that she had a cigarette. There would be another cigarette after supper and that would be all for the day.

"There isn't much to tell," she began. "It just—happened."

"Because of money?"

"Mostly."

"Or because the other girls were doing it?"

"That may have had something to do with it, too."

Sandy saw he had a file on her and Dr. Francis studied it carefully for several moments, putting a pencil check here and there and then pushing the file aside.

"You've used dope," he said. "Haven't you?"

"Some."

"How do you feel about that now?"

She uncrossed her legs and crossed them again. It was difficult to get comfortable on a wooden chair.

"It was bad at the start," she replied. "I was sick as a dog and I had pains and cramps all the time. But most of that is gone now."

"Would you go back to it again?"

"Not if I can help myself." Why tell him the truth? "It just costs you money and it doesn't do anything real for you. The more you take the more you need and after a while you can't get enough."

"And you go to something more dangerous, more effective?"

"Maybe. I don't know. I wasn't on it too long so I wouldn't know about that."

The doctor sat silent, staring at her. His eyes were so dark and so piercing that she found she could not look into them. She glanced down.

"I don't think we have to worry about the dope," he said finally. "You don't have to be very smart to know that it can destroy you, that it destroys thousands like you every day. From what I know about you I think prostitution is your problem. It isn't something that you kick in two weeks. Once you've done it you're apt to go back to it again. You've found a way of making easy money and you're used to selling your body. The experience leaves a scar on your mind that isn't easily erased. The important thing is for you to understand yourself and to realize what a return to your former way of life can mean to you. You don't want to be old at thirty, do you?"

Her shoulders lifted and fell.

"I guess not," she said.

"Well, you would be. At thirty you would be old and at forty you would be finished. The way you are now, you can command decent prices but as your beauty leaves you the price goes down and down, until you reach a point where you give yourself for a place to sleep or a drink of booze. Surely you don't want to end that way, do you?"

"Hardly."

"Besides all this you run the chance of becoming pregnant or contracting a disease. The first, under certain circumstances, is almost as bad as the second. Hadn't you ever considered these things?"

"Naturally."

"But you kept on?"

"Yes, I kept on." He seemed to be pleasant enough and Sandy was now looking at him again, looking straight into those dark eyes that regarded her with interest.

Dr. Francis had put the pencil down but he reached for it as she spoke and also picked up a yellow pad.

"I have to ask you some personal questions," he said. "Do you mind too much?"

"It wouldn't do me much good if I did, would it?"

For the first time he smiled.

"Well, you could lie to me but that wouldn't help either of us. I will see you from time to time while you're here in the school and if you aren't honest with me my efforts are wasted. If you are honest with me I can help guide you into a better way of living."

It seemed to her that everybody was trying to change her but there was not much she could do about it. Let them have their fun, let them earn their money, and when she got out she would do as she pleased. To fight against them was only to make matters worse for herself.

"All right," she said. "You ask the questions and I'll do what I can."

The doctor smiled and nodded while he wrote her name across the top sheet of the pad.

"How many men have you had sexual relations with?"

"I don't know. I don't have any idea."

"How did it happen the first time?"

"I was raped. He lived in the same house where we lived and he caught me one afternoon. That night he moved out and I never saw him again."

"How did you respond?"

"Huh?"

"I mean, did you fight him?"

"I tried to at first," Sandy admitted.

"And then?"

"It wasn't so bad. He hurt me at the start but after a while he didn't hurt."

"Could you say that you enjoyed it?"

"Maybe."

"Have you enjoyed intercourse with any other men you have been with?"

"Some of them." She felt as though she were being stripped naked. "It depended on the guy."

He turned the sheet over and started on a fresh one.

"What about girls?"

"What about them?"

"Did you ever have a relationship with a girl?"

"No."

"Ever think about it?"

"I don't think so."

"But you're not sure?"

"I'm not sure of anything right now." She wet her lips with her tongue. "I never talked to anybody like this before and that's the God's truth."

"It does you good to talk."

"Well, I guess it doesn't do any harm."

Dr. Francis reached into a drawer of the desk and brought out a package of cigarettes.

"Care for one?" he asked.

"I already had my three and I've got another one coming after supper. They only allow you four a day."

He pushed the cigarettes and a lighter toward her.

"You don't have to mind about that in here," he said. "I want you to be at ease and I can tell that you're nervous. It isn't anything unusual. Most of the girls are nervous."

She took one of the cigarettes, lit it and took a deep drag. This Doctor Francis seemed to be a regular guy, the kind of a man a girl could talk to.

"What about since you've been in here?" he inquired.

"It isn't as rough as I thought it'd be. The only thing, there isn't a mirror where you can fix your hair and you can't go to the bathroom. But they say that when you get in one of the cottages—"

"No, I'm talking about the other part of it."

"What other part?"

"The sexual part. Have you had any desire to be with a man?"

"A little," Sandy admitted, watching him through the smoke from her cigarette. Her voice had a ragged edge to it. "I should be ashamed, huh?"

"Not at all. It's perfectly normal," the doctor assured her. "A girl who is used to being with men doesn't overcome the desire so easily." He finished writing something and then put the pencil aside. "In many respects men and women are alike. The sex drive is powerful in both, and it isn't slowed down because you put iron bars across a window. Those of us who deal with the mind realize this but the problem is to get others to realize it, too. You can't lock a girl or a man up for a number of months and not have a certain amount of frustration stemming from the physical needs of the individual. There are some for whom this isn't true but they are few and far between. In Edgewood we try to appreciate that a girl's emotions don't die just because she is confined. Most reform school authorities, I am confident, accept this theory."

A few minutes later the doctor excused her and Sandy left his office and walked down the hall toward the recreation room. The pains, she was pleased to note, no longer tore at her stomach, no longer tortured her mind. She had kicked the habit, kicked it cold. All that remained was the other thing, the thing which the doctor had been talking to her about. Still walking, she closed her eyes and thought of a man taking her to his body, her nakedness alive and hungry to be pleased, more violently alive than it had ever been before. If she could only be with Tommy for just a few minutes, feel the crush of his arms, the search of his lips, the glory of him as he searched her out with love.

If only ...

She opened her eyes and wiped away the tears.

She had to get over it, simply had to.

There was no other way.

8

There were twenty girls in the cottage, each with her own room, and there was a recreation room on the first floor quite similar to the one in the quarantine section.

"It could be worse," one girl observed. She was in for running a con game that had backfired. "It could be a hell of a lot worse."

It could have been. The room which Sandy had in the cottage was nicer than the first room she had had at the school, and there were three bathrooms on the second floor. All the rooms were on the second floor and Miss Hunt, the matron, had her quarters on the first floor.

"She's young," one of the girls had pointed out. "You think of a matron as being somebody fat and fifty."

Miss Hunt was young. Sandy judged her about twenty-three or twenty-four. She was not very tall, probably around five-four, and in spite of the uniform she wore she showed off a nice shape. Not only that, but she was quite pretty, with long black hair and brown eyes and full red lips that had a ready smile whenever she spoke to the girls or met them in the recreation room. Nights when she came around, checking on the rooms, she still had the smile.

"I like my work," she told Sandy one time. "I always wanted to be helpful to other people and I guess this is about as close as I'll ever get to it."

"Are you from town?"

"No, I was born in Georgia. But I moved up to New York when I was ten and I soon lost my accent. My parents still live in the city. I took this job because it offered a challenge and because I could see that I might be in the same situation as some of these girls if I hadn't been lucky."

When Miss Hunt came around to check on the rooms she never entered any. It was against the rules of the school for a house-mother to go into a girl's room without another mother being present. At first, Sandy had not understood this ruling but it had not taken her long to find out its meaning. Some of the girls were homosexuals. They held hands in the recreation room and, if nobody seemed to be looking, they sometimes kissed. Sandy had not been in the cottage more than a week before she knew that a lot of girls visited each other after lights were out, sometimes sleeping together until morning. It was obvious that Miss Hunt knew of this practice but she did nothing to prevent it.

"The top brass knows that it goes on," one of the girls told Sandy. "They might not approve but when you shut up a group of girls who are used to being with men they have to find some outlet. A lot were that way before they came in here and although it isn't the real thing it's better than nothing at all."

"I'll take mine straight," Sandy had said.

"You won't in here."

"No, I guess not."

"When they first started the school they had guys working around the cottages, making repairs and like that, but some of the girls got pregnant and they gave up the idea. All the guys wanted was to get a girl into a corner. Now when a cottage has to be done over, all the girls are moved out and they don't see anything of the men. The only men you see are the doctors and you're lucky if they give you the right time of the day."

Sandy had been back to Doctor Francis a second time and after that he had turned her over to an elderly woman who was the guidance counselor. After two sessions with the guidance counselor it had been decided that Sandy would attend school in the morning, taking typing and other courses, and that she would work in the school library in the afternoon.

Sandy had dreaded going back to school again but it had proved to be interesting and the work in the library was not hard. Only a few of the more than five hundred girls in the school took out books, most of them showing a preference for the cheap magazines some of their parents sent from home. A confession magazine was passed around until it was worn out and whenever Sandy saw one she was reminded of Ruth Sloan. One night she had written a letter to Ruth but she had received no reply; and another one she had written to her mother in a wave of self-pity had brought nothing, too.

The only letter she had received had been from Tommy, a brief note which had said that everything was all right. She had taken this to mean that he was no longer bothered by the police and that the cops still did not know who had killed Slim Jefferies. A couple of times she had tried to fashion a reply but the efforts had seemed weak and she had destroyed them. But nights when the darkness of her room closed in around her and she lay on her cot she would think of him, want him terribly. In this respect Doctor Francis had been right. Bars could be over your window but bars did not shut out your emotions. Her longing for dope was entirely gone but not her longing for sex. Often she thought that she had not been a prostitute just for the sake of the money. She must, she decided, have a gland that worked overtime, a gland more female than she had previously suspected. She wanted a man to make her, to do with her as he pleased, to send the joy flooding through her in wave upon wave of ecstasy.

"Just wait'll I get out of here," a girl told her in the recreation room one night. "The first guy who can find me a bed can have it for nothing."

Most of the girls were very blunt in expressing their feelings. Those who were girl lovers, and there were about eight of them, even went so far as to ask the head office if they could wear boy's clothes if the clothes were sent to them. The request, quite naturally, was turned down. All the girls, they were told, were to dress the same.

Evenings Sandy spent in the recreation room, talking with other girls, listening to records, watching television—all the shows they were able to get seemed to be Westerns—or watching the homos. The homos disgusted her but in a strange sort of way she got a kick out of them. They stayed by themselves, fighting almost as much as they made love. One night a redheaded girl approached her but Sandy showed no interest and the girl soon forgot the matter. There were too many others who were willing, girls who sought love even if they had to travel the forbidden road.

"These damned homos," Fran Peters often said. "Why don't they stick them in a cottage where they can be alone?"

Fran was a small girl, nineteen and pretty, and Sandy liked her. Fran was in for passing bad checks and for prostitution, but it had been the checks that had tripped her up in the beginning. She had made the mistake of going back to the same store twice and the man had recognized her. He had stalled her, saying that he had had to get money from the back room, and he had called the cops. From that moment on she had been as dead as a duck shot by a gun.

"Believe me, I'm not going back to it," Fran would say. "No more wallpaper for me. And no more of the other, which I was crazy enough to admit when the cops questioned me. Nope, when I get out of here I'm living it straight. I'll get a decent job in a store or a factory, meet some guy, marry him and give him his brats. You'd be smart if you did the same."

Sandy did not honestly know what she would do when she was released. She kept thinking of Central Avenue and Tommy and the gang and she was all confused. Once she was outside of Edgewood she would be on her own and she would have to make a life for herself. In the school you were taught to respect the law but she did not know about that. She was afraid of the law and afraid of cops. The thing to do, she was fairly certain, was to make the right connections and make the money she knew was possible. And there was only one way she knew how to make it. She would never develop into a good typist—she was too slow and unsure of herself—and, anyway, most offices did not pay much of a salary. Fifty or sixty dollars would be high for a start; they paid less for a file clerk, and if she had to support herself that would be tight to get along on. Waiting on tables in some restaurant might be better. Tips were usually good and she would be able to meet men who could pay the freight on a bundle of curves. That would not amount to doing the same thing she had been doing before. No more five- and ten-dollar tricks. Twenty-five would be the lowest and if she played it right she could get more than that. One of the girls in the cottage said she had been getting a hundred, sometimes from four or five different men each night, and the girl was nothing to rave about. The girl had had a pimp, giving him part of her earnings, but she had done all right just the same. She spoke of a car that she had back in the city, one of those foreign expensive jobs, and a couple of closets of the best clothes. There was no doubt that the girl would return to the world's oldest profession as soon as she was free.

"But the next time I'm gonna be more careful," the girl said. "I won't take on anybody who hasn't been cleared by my contact and I won't pick up no guys in bars. You pick up a guy in a bar and he's apt to be a cop, the way it was for me this time. You figure you've made a hundred and all you've made is six months to a year."

There was an office near the main entrance to the cottage, where the records of the girls were kept, and Miss Hunt often called Sandy into the office to talk to her. They did not talk much about anything, just the school and how Sandy was doing and usually Miss Hunt got to talking about herself, how she was confined herself and could hardly go anywhere.

"But you're lucky," she would say. "You may be able to get away for a few weekends."

"I haven't heard anything about it."

"You will. It takes time. You're watched carefully and then a parole officer is assigned to you. He knows of the people in town who will take a girl in and if a girl is all right he suggests her to a family. Most of the girls who get out are the younger ones, girls about your age. The older they are the less chance they have of somebody getting interested in them."

Her talks with Miss Hunt were always friendly and Miss Hunt was very sweet about the whole thing. She did not ask a lot of stupid questions nor did she keep reminding Sandy of what she had been. She often remarked about how pretty Sandy was and that she thought Sandy had the best legs in the cottage.

"Not to mention your bust," she frequently added. "I never saw a girl with a better shape."

Nights when Sandy did not go down to the recreation room she stayed in her room and read one of the books she had brought along from the library. Until her confinement at Edgewood she had done very little reading, only newspapers, and much of the stuff she read made no sense to her. She would start a book, trying to read every word, but after a while she would jump from place to place and by the time she was done with it she was thoroughly confused. Then she would throw the book aside, suspecting that she would never make a student, and go down to one of the bathrooms for a shower.

As soon as she finished her shower she would wash out her bra and panties, sometimes singing as she did so. She was shut up, true, but her biggest fear was gone. She was not pregnant, something she had learned the day after she had been moved into the cottage. Tommy might have been careless with her but he had not scored in a way that would make her life more miserable. He had missed, just as the first man had missed.

Sandy generally showered early, before the other girls came up from the recreation room; then she would walk down the hall to her room, hang up her dress and drape the bra and panties over the radiator near the window.

One night she left the bathroom, carrying her things, and almost bumped into Miss Hunt.

"You shouldn't be out here that way," Miss Hunt said.

"What way?"

"Naked."

"Is it a rule?"

"It's a rule, a rule in every cottage. You aren't supposed to expose yourself to anybody."

"Then they should give us robes."

Miss Hunt smiled her customary smile.

"We've fought for robes but we haven't gotten them," she said. "There seems to be a budget and somebody forgot to include the robes in the budget. As long as there aren't any you have to make your dress do."

"I see."

Sandy stood there and she knew that Miss Hunt was looking at her, looking at all of her. Miss Hunt, at the moment, was not smiling. There was something different about her mouth, something Sandy had not seen before, and the expression was mirrored by Miss Hunt's wandering eyes.

"You have a wonderful body," Miss Hunt said at last.

"Thank you."

Miss Hunt moved on and Sandy continued toward her room. Sometimes she did not understand Miss Hunt. Miss Hunt had looked at her as—well, almost as a man would look at her.

Once inside the room Sandy closed the door and put the bra over the radiator. She turned out the light and crawled into bed, covering herself with a sheet and a blanket, feeling the top and bottom sheets against her body. She lay there staring up into the darkness, wondering if the dock strike were over with, wondering about what Tommy was doing, wondering about a dozen things. It was the same every night. She had not enough to do at the school to make her tired and these things kept running through her mind.

"I wish I could give you more," a five-dollar customer had told her one night. "You're worth top dollar, baby."

She smiled as she thought about it. She would be worth more now, worth a lot more. The ache of her need was in every part of her body, not for a jolt of the H but for the physical love of a man. It would be wonderful to have a young man, possibly Tommy, to hear his heavy breathing as she lost herself in the fury of his embrace. It was a disease worse than dope, worse than drinking, worse than any other a girl could suffer. It was a longing that could not be controlled, a requirement only one act could satisfy. Doctor Francis had touched on the subject briefly, the need for sex, but she had not thought much about it at the time. Now she did. Sex was like a lovely flower that would not die, a flower which should be picked and treasured beyond all else.

Sandy heard the girls coming up the stairs, some of them laughing, going into their rooms. All she could do was lay there and blink the tears from her eyes.

It was a long time later, possibly two or three hours, when she heard her door open and saw the light spill in from the hall.

"Are you all right?" It was Miss Hunt.

"Yes, I'm all right."

"Have you been asleep?"

"No."

She turned her head and saw Miss Hunt was wearing a filmy, revealing, nylon negligee that clung to her body.

"Can I come in?" Miss Hunt asked.

"You aren't supposed to, are you?"

"I didn't ask you that. I asked you if I could."

"Well—I don't care."

Miss Hunt closed the door behind her. She had put on some rich, thick perfume that reminded Sandy of the perfume Ruth Sloan sometimes used and which the boys had said was very sexy.

"I can't turn on the light," Miss Hunt said.

"No. I know that."

"But we can talk and nobody has to know the difference."

"I won't say anything."

"It wouldn't do you any good if you did. I would only deny it."

The perfume became stronger as Miss Hunt sat down on the bed beside her.

"I could use a cigarette," Sandy said.

"That's against the rules."

"We're already breaking one."

Miss Hunt laughed.

"So we are," she agreed. "One more shouldn't make too much difference. In fact, I was going to offer you one. I thought we could smoke and gas a bit." She paused a moment. "It's just as bad in here for me as it is for you. Don't think that it isn't. I get lonely, too."

Miss Hunt snapped her lighter on and Sandy accepted a filter-tip cigarette. In the glow from the lighter she could see the cleavage between Miss Hunt's breasts. She had seen it once before, when Miss Hunt had bent over the desk in her office, and it was warm and deep and dark.

"You can call me Betty," Miss Hunt said, closing the lighter.

"I'd feel funny doing that."

"Not in front of the other girls, of course. But when we're alone like this. When we're alone other ears don't hear and what other ears don't hear can never cause you any trouble."

"I guess not."

"You're doing very well here, Sandy."

"Well, I'm trying. I don't dig the school very much but the library is a lot of fun. I get a kick out of making sure that the books are in the right places. The only thing is we should have some books that are a little racy. I'll bet half of the stuff has never been read. I know I've tried a lot of them but I didn't get very far."

"That makes two of us. When I first came here I used to go to the library but it wasn't long before I stopped going. Hardly any of the stuff is popular and most of it is as old as the hills."

"That's what I thought, too."

They talked some more about the school and the library and after Sandy had smoked the cigarette all the way down to the filter-tip she reached for the ash tray, sitting up as she did so. The sheet and the blanket slid down from the upper part of her body and one breast touched one of Betty's arms.

"I'm putting in a good report on you," Betty said.

"Thanks."

"I was talking with your parole officer today and I told him I thought you should be permitted a weekend in town."

"In the crummy dresses we wear around here?"

"No. That's one thing the school does take care of. You'd get a nice dress—they have a supply of them on hand—and nobody on the street could tell that you were from the school. You'd be treated like a real person and when you got back from your trip you would feel like a new girl."

Sandy thought of getting out of the school for a short while—she had thought of it several times before—and it was almost too much to hope for. Why should she be picked when there were other girls just as deserving?

"It would be nice," she said.

"I can arrange it for you. Anybody in charge of a cottage carries a lot of weight with the parole officer. They don't want somebody getting a pass who will bring discredit to the school. There is enough pressure from high up for a get-tough policy and Edgewood is only an experiment."

"I understood that."

"Just because a girl made one mistake she is supposed to be treated like a criminal. In many reform schools she is and there is no real effort to help change the picture. They get six months and they serve six months. Here, if a girl shapes up in the right way, she can get out in a lot less time. Take you, for instance. You could get out in three months if you continue to show the progress that you've already made."

Sandy had not been aware of this. Hope swelled within her.

"It's something to work for," she said. "It really is."

"Some girls don't think so. Some girls have to stay here for their full terms. They won't cooperate and that makes it hard on them. Most of them get in trouble again as soon as they get home and then they get the rough treatment."

There was plenty of room beside Betty. Sandy pulled her legs out from under the covers, swung around and sat up. A slight chill had invaded the room but she did not mind. Just the possibility of being let out in three months made her feel warm all over.

"Could I have another cigarette?" she asked.

"No reason why not."

The cigarette tasted good, better than a cigarette had ever tasted before, and it was several moments before Sandy spoke.

"What does the parole officer ask you?"

"Not much. He has your record and he questions me about you, about my observations of you and how you conduct yourself. It isn't complicated. Once you're cleared a dress is issued to you and on Friday night the people come out to pick you up. The people who go in for this thing are nice people and they don't look down on you. You'll be treated as one of the family, perhaps taken skating or something like that—there's only one movie in town—and if they like you and you qualify you may have several of these outings."

Sandy thought about what it would be like to be free for several days, to have a pretty room she could call her own, to go and come as she pleased.

"It would be wonderful," she said, and Betty's perfume seemed stronger than ever. "But I don't know how I would act. I'd feel—funny. I don't want no charity from nobody."

"It isn't charity, Sandy. Get that out of your head. People want to help you—everybody wants to help you—but if you won't let them they can't very well do it, can they?"

"I guess not."

"Let yourself go a little bit. Relax and don't be so stiff. You're as good as anybody and don't ever forget that. What if you did make a mistake? We all do. Some get caught and some don't. You happened to be caught or you wouldn't be here. But it isn't the end of your life. It can be the start, a start that will wipe out everything that happened to you before."

Sandy thought it over and she knew that it was true. She was young, terribly unsure of herself, and if she worked it right the future could be promising. Once she was out she did not have to go back to the gang, or back to prostitution. What if she did take a low-paying job? Thousands of girls got along on jobs that did not pay fortunes and she could, too. Back home in Mayville, when she had gone uptown to the business section, she had seen many of these girls. They took a room in a private home or they took a room together and they got along, got along as good as anybody. Eventually they met nice boys and they married and raised families. There was no fear of the police in this kind of girl but there was, instead, love and respect for the community. They were the girls who gave their souls and bodies to their husbands. Until this moment she had not seen her life in such a light but she saw it that way now.

"I feel sorry for you," Betty said.

"Why?"

"Because you're so pretty. When you first came to the cottage I thought you were pretty but when I saw you in the hall without anything on I knew that you were. You have a delightful body."

"I guess I'm just lucky," Sandy murmured.

They had two more cigarettes. Sandy thought there was something funny about Betty, very funny. Men had talked to her this way but no girl ever had. Sitting there in the darkness beside Betty, Sandy felt the color rise up into her face and sting her skin.

"You must miss the men," Betty said after a while.

"In what way?"

"In a sex way. It's natural for a girl who used to love to miss men. That's why we don't have any boys working around the cottages while the girls are present. It isn't anything to be ashamed of. We all want love. We all need love. The only difference is that to some of us love means one thing and to others it means something else. Do you follow me?"

"Not all the way."

Sandy felt Betty put her arm around her, became aware of the soft fingers that lingered over the flatness of her stomach.

"I've stood this as long as I can," Betty said with sudden thickness in her voice. "I can't stand it any longer."

"Can't stand what?"

"You. Seeing you. Seeing you every day and knowing how pretty you are, and knowing that your hunger, though it may be different, is as great as mine."

Sandy found the ash tray and stubbed out the cigarette. She was too nervous to smoke.

"I want to touch them," Betty said, also putting out her cigarette with her free hand. "I've got to touch them. I've got to feel all of their goodness for myself."

"But—"

"You want a weekend away from here, don't you?"

"Yes, but—"

The hand that had been at Sandy's stomach moved up.

"Don't think you can avoid me," Betty whispered. "You can't. If you tell anybody I approached you I'll tell them that it was you who approached me. I could have you sent to another reform school, one where you would be miserable. They would believe me and not you. They always believe the house-mother. But it doesn't have to go that far. All you have to do is let me be nice to you, let me love you, and I'll see to it that you have all the freedom possible. Isn't that fair enough?"

Sandy felt herself being pushed back on the bed, became aware of the hungry lips that sought her mouth, lips that were parted and hot and whispering crazy things she did not understand.

"Baby," Betty moaned. "Baby, let me make you live."

"Please—"

Betty's kiss was the kiss of fire.

"Kiss me back, for Christ sakes!" Betty commanded.

Sandy closed her eyes, returning the kiss, trying to make believe that it was a man, trying to think that it was Tommy. It was not so bad when she did that. The darting tongue pushed her lips apart, opened them up wide, and then Sandy began to kiss blindly. Betty cried out, saying that she was wonderful, saying that she was sweet, and then Betty was kissing the twin mounds.

"You're the best," Betty exclaimed.

"Please—"

"You'll live, baby. You'll live!"

Sandy was both sickened and exhilarated.

Sickened because this beautiful creature was a lesbian, and exhilarated because Sandy had never dreamed of the completeness of this kind of love, had never believed it possible.

Later, long after Betty had left her, Sandy lay upon her bed and sobbed. It was wrong, so terribly wrong. When she finally went to sleep she did not dream of Betty.

She dreamed of men.

Not any particular man.

Just men.

9

The next week wore on.

In the morning Sandy went to school; in the afternoon she worked in the library; at night, after the others in the cottage were in bed, Betty came to make violent love.

"It's all wrong," she told Betty one night. "This whole thing is wrong."

"Wrong?" Betty laughed at her. "Nothing is wrong when it means something to you. You're here alone, shut away from the rest of the world, and you need somebody to love you. Your body is meant for love."

"But this kind—"

"This kind or any kind, but this kind is the best of all. Don't you feel the same way when I'm with you and I give you pleasure?"

Sandy did not know and her work in school suffered because she thought about it so much. She did not want this relationship but she was helpless to avoid it. If she wanted to get away for a weekend and obtain a parole as quickly as she could she had to remain a prisoner of the flesh.

"Love me," Betty told her one night. "You love me, honey."

"I—I couldn't."

"You will if you want me to say nice things to your parole officer about you."

It was one of those nights when the heat was up and it was hot in the room. They were on the bed, their bodies close, tight, and it seemed to Sandy as though Betty had been kissing her for a long, long time, each kiss more demanding than the one before.

"You keep saying that," Sandy said. "But when will I see him?"

"I could arrange for him to visit you tomorrow. I could tell them at the front office that you're ready."

"And then?"

"There'll be a weekend for you in town, a weekend when you'll be away from this place. Isn't all of that worth it? Isn't it?"

"Well—"

"Or I can fix it so that you won't see your parole officer for months, not until your time is almost up. There is a lot I can do for you—or against you."

Sandy was crying, looking up into the darkness of the room.

"Why did you pick on me?" she asked.

"Because you are so lovely. The moment I saw you I wanted to have you love me as much as I love you."

"And what will you do after I'm gone?"

"Other girls will come. Some girls leave the cottage and other girls come to take their place. There is always one who is willing and beautiful."

"But there are some who wouldn't care. There are some who—"

"I don't want a girl of that type. They can love each other. The girl I want has to be fresh and young, a girl who can satisfy me as much as I can satisfy her."

"Is that why you stay here? So that you can keep on finding new girls and make love to them?"

"Partly. I could find girls on the outside but here they are more desperate and here I can pick the girl I want."

There was a kiss and Sandy knew, knew as much as she knew anything, that she would have to bend to Betty's will.

"Make me live!" Betty breathed.

And she did, listening to Betty's instructions. Her tears came, tears of hate and disgust, and when it was over with, when she fell down upon the bed sobbing, wishing that she could die, she thought she would never be able to do such things ever again.

"You were delightful," Betty said before she left. "With a little more practice you should be a very satisfactory lover."

Sandy could not sleep that night. She thought of her former life on Central Avenue and while she admitted that she had done many rotten things she was sure she had never done anything as bad as this. On Central Avenue, in spite of all of its poverty and sin, a girl was meant for a boy or a man.

"A lesbian," Tommy had said, spitting, of one girl who had tried to join the gang. "Get her the hell out of here."

Nobody had any use for a lesbian, who was of a world apart, violating the basic law of human nature. Woman was meant for man and man was meant for woman. There were those women who strayed, who found pleasure with their own sex, but on Central Avenue there had been no place for them. Even those who had come from uptown, making love to each other on the park benches during the summer, had been driven from the park by the gang.

"You either take it straight or not at all," Tommy had decided. "We got no time for a bunch of queers. They should put 'em in cages with the rest of the animals."

All during the night Sandy lay there and wished that Tommy were with her, that his arms were around her, straining her to him, his truly male body finding her in a storm of passion. If only he could be with her, if only she could know him, she would not even make him take precautions. But she realized that it was not just Tommy she wanted. Betty had been right when she had said that sex was an important force, that you did not leave it outside the gate when you entered Edgewood.

Sandy thought of getting out of the reform school, of going back to the gang, of taking up where she had left off. By the time she returned the dock strike should be over with and she ought to be able to get ten dollars a trick for herself. Uptown, of course, would be better but she did not know anybody there and it would be difficult for her to get started. She would have to have connections, bartenders and cab drivers and people like that, but she did not know how to go about it. But all this, she assured herself, was in the future.

Sandy was still awake when the bell rang at seven—everybody got up at seven—and she began to dress. As soon as she was finished, she straightened up the room and made the bed, yawning as she did so. It had been a miserable night, a night she wanted to forget. But she knew Betty would be back again that night and any desire Sandy might have had for food immediately left her. How could she go on this way, living a lie she did not want to live? But, she reasoned, there was no way out of it. She was a toy in Betty's hands, a toy that had to respond with each pull of the string. Going to the main office and putting in a complaint would only lead her into real trouble. It would be Betty's word against hers and Betty could count on being believed.

Sandy went to the mess hall, walking with Fran Peters, and the wind was sharp and cold.

"Just twenty-nine days to go," Fran said.

"You count the days or something?"

"Who doesn't in here?"

"What will you do then?"

"What can I do? The same thing. What you learn in here you could stick in your ear. You work in the laundry, the way I do, and you don't learn up from down. So I learn that you weigh the clothes and that you put so many pounds in an automatic washer. You gotta be a genius to get that through your head?"

"How come you don't go to school the way I do?"

"Because I graduated from high school and you didn't. Not that I was any good at it. I wasn't. But all of my teachers were men and I was nice to them. They had cars and they took turns at taking me home and I let them make their time. You might say that I graduated on the flat of my back. They wanted something young and I gave them something young. I wanted my diploma and they gave me my diploma. It was a fair exchange."

Sandy and Fran ate at a long table. One of the girls was cracking jokes because she was going to get out in a day or so. She was in for cutting up a boy and she said she would do something else to him if she ever met him again.

"I'll shoot the bastard," she said. "Since when is it a crime to defend yourself?"

"But you had his watch," another girl pointed out.

"Yeah, I guess I did," the first girl admitted. "I thought he was out stone cold drunk and the watch looked like it was worth something. Then he come out of it, all of a sudden, and I hadda do something."

Sandy only drank her milk, did not touch any of the food, and she left in time for her first class, in English. She hated English. She did not know the first thing about it and the whole business was a waste of time for her. You read a lot of jazz that made no sense and then the teacher asked questions.

"Who wrote *The Red Badge of Courage*?" the teacher would ask.

That was one thing Sandy did know. Some fellow by the name of Crane had written it. It dealt with the Civil War and he had not been in the Civil War. What, she wondered, was the point to it?

Somehow, still thinking about her relationship with Betty, Sandy got through the morning. She missed a question in English, made a terrible mess of her typing—her fingers just could not find the proper keys—and sneered to herself when the teacher in citizenship said that the object of the school was to make every girl useful in the community.

"You will find people tolerant," the teacher went on. "You can forget your past and live in the future, creating homes and families which will, in turn, bring about a better America. Some of you will live with your mistakes for a while but in time they will soon fade away. We all learn by making mistakes and all of you have the golden opportunity to learn."

"Oh, brother," one of the girls said when they left for lunch. "Somebody wound up her spring so tight that it'll never get unwound."

The afternoon was better than the morning and there was not much doing in the library. Sandy swept the floor, straightened up some books and then sat down to read a magazine. The woman who had charge of the library, a Mrs. Something-or-Other, worked a crossword puzzle at her desk.

"I've got the easiest job at the school," the woman said, pausing for a moment. "Hardly any of the kids seem to be interested in the books we have. You'd think they'd want to improve their minds."

"What? With the books we've got?"

"We have some very good ones. Even the library in town doesn't have the selection of fine literature we have."

Sandy turned her attention again to the magazine, a magazine two years old with a lot of pictures. The girls did not want literature. They wanted something racy, something hot, something that breathed of everyday life.

About four the phone rang and the woman answered it. She listened for a moment, grunted and then hung up.

"That was for you," she told Sandy. "You're to go down to your cottage and wait for your parole officer." She frowned at the crossword puzzle upon which she had been working. "Too damned bad. You swept the floor and I was just going to get you to scrub it. A girl who's supposed to be working shouldn't be sitting around and doing nothing."

It was snowing when Sandy left the building—the old bitch could scrub her own floor—and she huddled down into the coat, trembling slightly because the coat was not heavy enough for winter weather. All the girls said somebody had made a quick strike by selling the coats to the school and Sandy decided that it might be true. Everybody was out for whatever he could get. You made a buck here and you made a buck there and pretty soon you were loaded.

She kept to the road, walking rapidly, wondering what the parole officer would be like and wondering if she would be lucky enough to get a weekend in town. But the last seemed a little far away for her. The town was small and there were just so many people who would take in a girl from the reform school. Sandy had talked with one girl who had been out the last weekend and the girl had said that she had had a wonderful time.

"They treated me better than my old man or old lady ever did," she had reported. "And they gave me a room all by myself. I tell you I damn near cried when I had to come back to this stinking hole in the wall."

Betty was in the office when Sandy entered the cottage. There was nobody with her and at this time of the day none of the girls were around. Wearily, she thought the call might be a trick.

"He'll be here in a couple of minutes," Betty said. "Take off your coat and wait for him."

"All right."

Sandy removed her coat and placed it over a chair in the corner. As she turned around Betty came up to her and kissed her hard on the mouth.

"I told you I would help you, didn't I?" Betty asked.

"Yes."

"And I keep my promises. If you're nice to me then I'm nice to you." Sandy was kissed again. "You were very nice to me last night. I couldn't get to sleep from thinking about you. I almost got up and came back to you."

"You're taking an awful chance," Sandy said, moving away from the other girl. "An awful chance."

"Not too much. I can always say that you were sick and that you called me. There isn't anybody who would complain about one person helping another person in an emergency."

"What if they found us—that way?"

"It's a risk we have to run." Betty laughed. "Everything is a risk. Life is a risk. You start to cross a street and a car comes along and slaps you down. This isn't as dangerous."

"It could cost you your job."

"What do I care about the job? There are other jobs. I'm a pretty fair secretary and I did the work once. I got well paid for it. The trouble is the boss expected me to stay late and play house with him. I couldn't stand that. I never could stand a man. You think of a man, what they are, and they're nothing but animals. They're all after the same thing. They give you a jolt and they knock you up and then where are you? At least, we don't have to worry about that. We take our love, give each other love, and when it's over with there's no harm done."

There was a window at the far side of the office and Sandy walked to it, staring out at the snow. Harm? A lot of harm could be done by such an association with another girl. If you kept it up long enough you would not know what you were—a girl's girl or a man's girl. But in this Sandy felt rather secure. Their whole relationship had sickened her and she was sure she would never follow that path. It was better, to her way of thinking, to be a prostitute than a lesbian. A prostitute might be a nobody but a lesbian was even less.

"There's a man coming now," Sandy said, watching a figure approach through the snow.

"Must be your parole officer."

"What's his name?"

"Jenkins. He isn't a bad sort."

"What did you tell him about me?"

"That you were ready for a weekend in town. Honestly, I had nothing but praise for you. I told him you were the best in the cottage and that you deserved a chance."

A few minutes later Mr. Jenkins came into the office. He appeared to be in his late forties and his face was red from the wind. He spoke to Betty, nodded at Sandy and took off his coat.

"Nasty storm," he observed.

Betty walked to the door.

"I'll leave you two alone," she said. "You can get to know each other and reach some decision."

As soon as she was gone, closing the door behind her, Mr. Jenkins sat down at the desk and waved Sandy into a chair alongside.

"I've been over your record," he said. "You never had too many breaks, did you?"

"Not many."

He offered her a cigarette, which she accepted gratefully, and after holding a light for her leaned back in his chair.

"Do you think you could go into a private home and conduct yourself as you should?"

"Yes, sir, I think so."

"You're in here for prostitution, aren't you?"

"That's what they charged me with."

"Do you consider that you weren't guilty?"

"Oh, no. I was guilty. I took this man's money and he was a police officer."

"What do you plan on doing when you get out?"

"I don't know. I haven't thought about it."

He consulted some papers he had brought with him. "You should think about it," he said. "You'll be able to go out on parole in a rather short time and you should start making some plans for it now."

"Maybe I'll go back with my mother."

"Is that wise?"

"Well, I don't have any place else to go."

He studied his papers again.

"We've contacted your old employer and he'll give you a steady job in the diner. That's one of the requirements that we have, that you have work. In your case this seems to be taken care of."

Sandy knew what a steady job meant. It meant that if she were to keep it, she would have to give herself away for nothing. Everything had its price on Central Avenue.

"That's nice to know," she said. "I didn't think he'd give me a break."

"A lot of people want to give you a break."

"Do they?"

"Miss Hunt is one and I'm another. Obviously the man you worked for before is interested in you."

Old Dick was interested in her all right. Old Dick was interested in getting her into the back and throwing her a fast curve. But it could not be any worse than Edgewood. It was better to have a man than a girl any day of the week, any week of the year.

"I'd like to get to town," she said. "I honestly would. It would make a new person of me."

If she could get away for a couple of nights she would not have to put up with Betty. The people might be stern and strict with her but she could stand that. This other she could not endure much longer, no matter what the reward. She was not a lesbian and nothing could ever make her become one. But, looking at it frankly, she was caught in a grip of something bigger than herself. If she wanted any degree of freedom she had to buy it with the only thing that she had—her body.

"Today is Friday," Mr. Jenkins said.

"Is it?"

He smiled faintly.

"Don't you keep track of the days?"

"Not much. The only day that's different is Sunday and then there isn't any school. I don't worry any about the days. They come and they go and I just sit it out."

"When you're up for parole you'll count them."

"Probably."

"It's a natural thing. I know I counted the days while I was waiting to get out of the army. Once I knew that I was set, the days seemed to get longer and so did the nights. And that last day seemed like a week. It will with you."

"I suppose so."

He sat staring at his hands and outside of the window the snow continued to fall.

"I could arrange for you to go into town this weekend," he said after a while.

For the first time since she had arrived at the school she felt real emotion.

"Gee, that would be swell."

"If you behave yourself and the people like you, and if you continue to show the improvement Miss Hunt says you have, you can go nearly every weekend. It all depends on you, Sandy. From here on in you make your own road. Those of us who believe that a reform school girl shouldn't be treated like a common criminal have a lot at stake every time a girl leaves Edgewood. If you get into trouble you bring discredit upon us. I ask you not to do that. I know you don't get the papers but there's a big cry about getting tough with youthful offenders. We don't believe in that. We believe that every girl—and every boy—needs help and understanding."

"I won't do nothing wrong," she assured him.

"I'm sure you won't. At this stage of the game doing the right thing is just as important to you as it is to us."

"Yes, sir."

"There's a family in town by the name of Ridgeway and I've already talked to them about you. They have a son who is nineteen and both the father and mother are very nice. They've had some of Miss Hunt's girls before and there's never been any trouble. They have a store in town and they don't close until nine so the son would have to come out and meet you. It's a rule that anybody who leaves the grounds has to leave by seven."

"What about a dress? And a coat?"

"Miss Hunt will see to that."

He wrote out a formal pass which she could submit to the main office, then walked to the door and called for Miss Hunt. He told Betty of the arrangements and Betty merely nodded. She knew of the Ridgeways—in fact, she had suggested them to Mr. Jenkins, hadn't she?—and they were very, very nice people.

"You'll be happy there," she told Sandy. "They'll treat you swell."

After Mr. Jenkins left, Sandy carried her coat up the stairs and Betty followed her.

"I'll get the clothes for you," Betty said as they entered the room. "But there's something that we have to do first."

"Such as?"

Betty's smile held a great deal of meaning.

"You know," Betty said as she pushed Sandy toward the bed. "You know as well as I do."

It was long after five before Betty left to get the clothes for her. Sandy lay on the bed and once again she was crying. She was crying for Betty and for herself and for all of the others in the world whose minds were twisted out of shape.

"I'm going to please you," Betty had promised, her voice sounding far away. "I'm going to please you and please you until you never want another man again."

Betty, however, had been wrong.

Sandy wanted a man terribly.

Hell, she wanted a man worse than ever.

10

Sandy walked to the main building shortly before seven and the walking was very difficult. The snow was still coming down, harder than ever, and it was like sand under her feet. Betty had managed to find a pair of storm boots for her—she suspected they belonged to Betty—and this she appreciated. Without them her feet would have been wet and cold in a matter of seconds. Even with the boots she had to walk around some of the small drifts piling up in the road.

"The coat is a perfect fit," the woman at the desk told Sandy when she turned in her pass. "Just like it was made for you."

The coat did fit well and so did the dress. The dress was black, without any frills, and it had a square neckline.

Sandy felt dressed up for the first time in a long while, except for the white cotton bra and white cotton underpants but, she reasoned, she could not expect everything. Besides, nobody would know what was on underneath the dress. Betty had loaned her a pair of stockings, a pair of shoes with fairly high heels, and a garter belt to hold up the stockings. Sandy just hoped she did not get a run in them. She did not want to be indebted to Betty any more than she was.

"You can wait near the door," the woman said. "One of the Ridgeways will be along for you in a few minutes."

It was hot in the building, much hotter than it ever got in the cottage, and Sandy took off the coat, holding it over one arm and walking toward the door. There was a bench near the door and she sat down, crossing her legs and feeling a tremor of excitement rush through her. She was lucky, very lucky, that she was getting away for the weekend. For two nights she would be free of Betty, of the passion in Betty's body, and for a short time she would be able to forget about the horrible things they had done together. Just the memory of them left her cold and sick inside.

She reached for her cigarettes—a girl got a full package when she was let out for the weekend—and she lit one, holding the match and staring at it until it nearly burned her fingers. She had to stop thinking about Betty. There was, she reasoned, a price for everything and her relationship with Betty was her price, a price which she would have to continue to pay and pay if she wished to get all the best the school had to offer. Her continued submission to Betty meant weekends away and an earlier parole.

Sandy glanced outside and saw it was still snowing, possibly snowing harder than it had been before. Had the same storm struck Mayville?

And, if it had, what would the gang be doing? But, of course, she knew what the gang would be doing. It was Friday night and some of the boys would have money and there would be a ball at the club. There would be whiskey to drink—not many of the kids were strong for beer—grass to smoke and some of them would mainline. As the night wore on, a lot of the couples would make love in the back room and some of them would even do it right out in front of everybody. When you were high on the broom it was very funny to watch a girl and a boy make love. Sometimes a girl would get real wild, crazy wild, and she would take on any boy who had the urge. One night she had seen a girl honored half a dozen times.

Two months later the girl had let on that she was pregnant and two months after that she had drowned herself in a tub of water. The Blue Devils had tried to go to the funeral but the mother of the girl had chased them away and she had even thrown out the flowers they had sent.

"Bastards," she had told them. "You're nothin' but bastards."

Sandy was still thinking about the past, thinking about the good times—that night with Tommy had been a good time—and the bad times—the night the cop had picked her up had been a bad time—when the door opened and a young man came in. He wore a jacket open all the way down the front and snow clung to his dark hair. He gave her a brief, full smile and continued on toward the desk. She listened while he talked to the woman. He was Bruce Ridgeway and he had come for a girl named Sandy Greening. The woman at the desk nodded in Sandy's direction and told him to sign some sort of a paper. He signed it without hesitation.

"Thanks," he said to the woman.

Sandy stood up as he came toward her and he smiled again, only this time the smile lasted. She felt as though she were being examined carefully, especially the top part of her dress, but she did not mind it a bit. There was something about him, something that reminded her of Tommy, but there was also something about him that was big and strong and fine. She found herself staring up into his face, meeting the light in his eyes, and she returned the smile.

"They grow them pretty out here," he said.

"Do they?"

"If I didn't know I was in a reform school I would think I was meeting a model."

He held her coat for her and she shrugged into it.

"Miserable night," he said.

"Terrible."

"I should have brought my father's car. I don't get much traction with mine—the tires are too smooth—and I got stuck once on the way out."

They left the building and walked through the snow to his car. She could not explain it to herself but it felt good to be near him, good to have a boy's hand on her arm. Then she smiled secretly to herself. She had not seen a boy since entering Edgewood and possibly any boy would have affected her in the same way.

It was not a new car but it was not too old, either. Inside it was warm, and she relaxed with a contented sigh. After closing the door he crossed in front of the headlights and got in behind the wheel.

"I hope we don't get stuck going back to town," he said. "There's one hill that's a bad one and this snow is like driving through sugar."

"Don't they plow the roads out here?"

"They do when they get around to it. They're supposed to start plowing when it gets to be two or three inches deep but for some reason they never do."

"It's not like it is in the city. In the city it melts almost as soon as it comes down. There has to be an awful lot of snow for it to amount to anything."

He stopped at the gate and the guard, who checked the inside of the car with a flashlight, cleared them. Soon they were on the highway.

"I'm Bruce," the boy said, driving carefully, leaning forward over the steering wheel as the windshield wipers fought to clear the snow away.

"And I'm Sandy."

He drove a short distance in silence.

"How do you like it at Edgewood?" he asked.

"All right."

"They say it's better than other reform schools."

"I wouldn't know. This is the only one I've ever been in."

"How old are you?"

"Going on seventeen."

"I won't ask you what you're in for. We aren't supposed to know."

"I see."

"They say that when a girl leaves the school for a weekend she should be accepted for what she is, not for what she has been."

"That makes sense." What would he say if he knew that she had been a prostitute? "It makes a lot of sense. Some of us get there because we've been a little foolish but that doesn't mean that we're bad."

"I know that. The folks have been bringing girls to the house ever since the school opened up and they've always conducted themselves as they should."

"I'll try to live up to it."

"I'm sure that you will." Bruce paused and glanced at her. "You're very beautiful. Do you know that?"

"Thank you."

"I'm glad I could come out for you."

"What will your steady say about driving a reform school girl?"

"My steady?"

"Sure. A regular girl, one you go with right along."

"I don't have one. I did last year but she married somebody else and that was the end of that." He reached into his pocket for a cigarette. "It didn't matter much. We were just good friends. My people thought it was a match but I knew all along that it wasn't. You can tell. I don't know how you tell but you can."

They crept down a long hill and the car slid from side to side. Once she thought they were going into the ditch but he twisted the wheel of the car and kept it on the road.

"Rough," Bruce said.

"I'm sorry I'm causing you so much trouble."

"Don't be sorry. It isn't any trouble. If I hadn't come for you I'd have had to work in the store and I'd rather be with you than be working in the store."

"What kind of a store is it?"

"Furniture. It's the only one for ten or twelve miles and the folks do pretty good at it. They pay me the same as they would anybody else and I work the same as anybody else would work. It's a pretty good arrangement. I'm learning the business and someday I can buy them out."

She lapsed into silence. Here was a boy with security, real security, a security she had never known. How did you find it? Where did you look for it? Certainly you did not find it on Central Avenue. You did not find it with a needle stuck in your arm or a puff of grass in your lungs. And you did not find it by selling yourself for five and ten dollars a trick. She felt like crying. Everything she had ever done had been wrong, all wrong.

"The next hill is a dilly," Bruce said, interrupting her thoughts. "Pray until we get to the top of it."

But they never made it. They only got part way up and then the rear wheels of the car started to spin, sending them from one side of the road to the other. By the time the car came to a stop they were off on one of the shoulders, the tires fighting to grip the snow and finding nothing.

"Damn," Bruce said. "And I don't have any chains."

He cut the lights but left the motor running and they talked about it. There was, he said, nothing to do but wait. It was too far to walk to town and sooner or later a highway truck would be along to give them a hand.

"Good thing I've got plenty of gas," he added. "We can keep warm."

They smoked and talked and she told him a little bit about herself, not about what she had done for a living but how she had lived and what awaited her upon her release from reform school.

"You poor kid," he said.

Sandy was drawn to him, and when he finally put his arm around her she did not object. It seemed to be the natural thing for him to do, the natural thing for her to accept.

"I think I like you," Bruce said.

"I hope you do."

"Do you like me?"

"There's no reason why I shouldn't."

His face came closer to her, so close that his lips brushed her hair.

"What would you do if I kissed you, Sandy?"

"I don't know," she replied honestly. "But I don't think you should. I'm just a girl from the reform school and you're—well, somebody."

"Get that out of your head, will you?"

"How can I? It's true. I know it's true and so do you."

His hand moved down from her shoulder and lay over her breast.

"I don't know any such thing," he said. "Remember what I said about being able to tell? The other girl wasn't for me and I knew that. And the other girls who came from the school weren't for me either. But you're—different. I knew it the second I saw you. All a fellow has to do is look at you and he goes nuts."

"Please—"

But she never finished what she was going to say. His mouth was there, coming down over her lips, crushing them in the fury of his kiss. She resisted for a second, not quite sure she wanted it to be this way for them, and then she was kissing him back, pushing herself up and out so that his hand rested harder against her breast.

"Somebody may come along," she panted.

"Not in this storm. Only the truck. And we can hear that a long ways off."

He kissed her lower, on the throat, and with his free hand he unbuttoned her coat. She began to shake as his hand went underneath the dress.

"You know what I want," he breathed.

"You're going to hate me," she said.

And then she did something for him that she had seldom done for a man. He gasped and clung to her, driving her over into the far comer of the car, his hand reaching for her and finding her.

"Don't tear anything," she cautioned him. "Some of the clothes aren't mine. And don't give me a baby."

He was careful and there in the front seat of the car she helped him.

He kissed her desperately.

He hurt her the first time, but it was a glorious hurt, a hurt that caused her to beg him never, never to stop. She rose to him, crying out his name, crying out her love.

It was midnight before a truck came along and pulled them up the hill behind the plow. She sat close to Bruce. Whenever he had a chance he leaned over and kissed her, not just a kiss of passion but a kiss filled with honesty.

"I love you," he said once. "I knew it the minute I saw you."

She hoped it was true....

The next morning Sandy had breakfast with Bruce and his parents, who had retired for the night before she and Bruce had come in, and she liked them right away. Martha Ridgeway was a woman in her late forties, slim and delicate and rather pretty in a dark sort of way. Hector Ridgeway was big and inclined to be fat as well as bald. He had a deep voice and he laughed a great deal while he cracked one joke after the other. Sandy laughed politely.

"I hope you like it here," he said to Sandy.

"Oh, I'm sure I will. My room is delightful and I want to thank you for having asked me."

"Think nothing of it," Martha Ridgeway said. "We're only too glad to help a girl who needs help. Aren't we, Hector?"

"Right the first time. I know I wouldn't want to be shut up in that school all the time and I don't think anybody else does."

Sandy helped Mrs. Ridgeway clear the dishes from the table and it was then that she found out that Hector Ridgeway did not go to the store on Saturday.

"We all have a day off," he explained. "And Saturday is mine."

Mrs. Ridgeway protested when Sandy offered to do the dishes but the protest was mild and she began drawing water in the sink. The water was terribly hot—probably from some automatic heater in the cellar. Sandy glanced outside. It had stopped snowing but the sky was still overcast and snow clung to the naked branches of the trees, bending some of the branches almost to the ground. After she had got into bed the night before, the memory of Bruce lingering, she thought she'd heard the snow change to rain and sleet.

"Have anything you want for lunch," Mrs. Ridgeway told her. "There's plenty in the house to eat. Hector probably won't have anything." She laughed. "He's on a diet but you can hardly tell it."

"I've lost five pounds," Mr. Ridgeway said.

"That's a long ways from fifty."

"Well, it's a start."

Bruce and his mother left shortly before nine for the store and after she had finished the dishes—Mr. Ridgeway helped her dry them—she walked through the lower part of the house. It was modern in every respect and the furniture was something out of this world. She thought of the furnished rooms along Central Avenue and she wondered how she would ever be able to return.

"You don't have to go back," Bruce had told her the night before. "If this lasts the way I think it'll last we can get married."

"But you hardly know me."

"I know enough about you. I know you're lovely and wonderful. And I know that there isn't ever going to be anybody else, not after this night."

Once in bed she had thought about it for a long time. Had he meant it? And what had been her feelings? She had never met a boy she had liked so much and so quickly but, she had cautioned herself, it might not last. They had both been hungry for love, wanting each other, but that in itself did not make a marriage. And it might just be a trick of his to gain her favors. Men did things like that. Highly confused she had at last gone to sleep, dreaming of Bruce and dreaming of Betty and dreaming of Tommy. When Mrs. Ridgeway had called her, she had been back on Central Avenue, doing what she had been doing before, looking for the end of a rainbow that never seemed to have an end.

Sandy walked up the stairs, feeling the thick carpet beneath her feet. The least she could do was make her bed and tidy up her room. Bruce had said something about them having a woman to do the housework but that the woman didn't work on Saturday.

"The man she lives with has Saturday off," Bruce had said. "They drink and live it up."

She entered the room which had been given to her and breathed deeply. It was a fine room, the best she had ever been in, and she had never slept in such a soft bed. The drapes at the windows were red and the rug on the floor was also red. The furniture was maple, not the cheap stuff but the stuff that cost money, and the cosmetics on top of the dresser were the best brands that could be bought.

It only took her a couple of minutes to make the bed and then she walked to the dresser, staring at herself in the mirror. Her face looked thinner than it had before she had entered the school but other than that there was no change. Probably some of this was due to the fact that she would go to the mess hall, sit down at the table, think of Betty and then not be able to eat. Now, however, that she was away from the school, Betty seemed to be very unreal, a monster who had existed only in her imagination. She turned away from the mirror, pulling in her breath as she saw

Mr. Ridgeway standing in the doorway watching her.

"You have a nice house," she said, unable to think of anything else to say.

"I guess it'll do."

He had changed and he was wearing a robe. It was obvious that he wore no pants because nothing showed beneath the bottom of the robe.

"Is there anything I can do?" she asked.

He smiled. "There's a lot you can do."

Sandy moved away from the dresser.

"Well, I don't mind. I'd rather be busy than just sit around. You tell me what it is and I'll do it."

Mr. Ridgeway stepped into the room and the robe parted. She could see that he had nothing on underneath.

"We should have a talk," he said. "A long talk."

"Well—all right."

He walked over to the bed and sat down. The mattress sagged under his weight.

"Bruce and you were late getting in last night," he said.

"We got stuck on a hill."

"You're from Mayville, aren't you?"

"That's right."

"And you're in for prostitution?"

She felt her mouth go dry, her head start to pound. "I didn't think you were supposed to know that," she said.

He laughed again.

"If you listen to the preachers at the school, I'm not supposed to. But it so happens I do. You're going on seventeen and you lived in the slums of Mayville. You took on a cop for money and he nailed you. That's why you're here. You can get out in a few weeks if you play it smart and don't cause yourself trouble. It's up to you, Sandy. You follow through and you'll be out in no time. Get stubborn and you'll serve your time, serve every bit of it. Miss Hunt will see to that."

Sandy was up against something here, something bigger than she was, and she did not know whether or not she would be able to handle it.

"I'm listening," she said tightly.

"It wouldn't do you any good to repeat what I'm going to tell you. Nobody would believe a reform school girl."

"Nobody has to tell me that."

"You've seen my wife?"

"Of course."

He leaned back, his elbows on the bed, and now she could see all of him. She glanced away, staring down at the rug, trying to think that this was not happening to her.

"Well, she's a wife in name only. I haven't had a physical relationship with her in over ten years. You know what that means to a man, don't you?"

"No."

"It means a lot. Sex is a part of our lives and when that stops part of living stops. Hell, I'm only forty-nine. But I was up against a brick wall until the school opened up. This is a small town and you can't move without somebody knowing about it. Then the school came along and later I met Miss Hunt. All her girls are prostitutes and most of them want a weekend away from the school. I made a deal with her that I would pay her twenty-five dollars every time she sent me a girl who took care of my needs. So far it has worked out very well but I must say that none of them have been as pretty as you are."

Sandy broke out laughing. This whole thing was so funny, so tragically funny. The law stuck you into a reform school because you sold yourself to men and then the house-mother not only forced you into a lesbian relationship but took in money for your charms.

"You needn't laugh," Mr. Ridgeway said. "This is serious enough. If you don't come across I pass the word along and you'll live out the rest of the next year behind bars. You want that to happen?"

She thought of parole, of getting out, and she decided that no price was greater than the one she had already paid. And it was no worse than the price she had paid on Central Avenue. In fact, it was the same price, only this time she was not the one collecting the money.

"No wonder you take Saturday off," she said, flinging the words at him. "You can play house while your wife works."

"Smart girl."

She had no choice but to go through with it. She wanted out of that school so badly she could not see straight. But this, this trap into which she had fallen, made her hate everybody. She hated the cops who had put her away, hated the judge, hated Betty Hunt, hated this fat slob on the bed in front of her, hated everybody she had ever known or met. Her hate even went as far as Bruce. He probably knew what his old man was doing and he had only got in his lumps ahead of time. Men were nothing but filth on the face of the earth.

"You're going to get yours," she said savagely, reaching for the zipper on the dress. "You're going to get yours like you never had it before."

"You get smarter all the time."

It only took her a few minutes to undress.

"You got a pair," he said, sitting up straight.

She laughed, still hating everybody, hating everything.

"Fasten your hands on them," she said. "Isn't that what you want to do, you goddamned slob?"

"Don't call me any names."

"You goddamned slob."

He got up, removing his robe, and then he flung her to the bed, his huge weight coming down to crush her on the mattress. The breath was knocked out of her and she turned her head to avoid his kiss.

"You forgot something," she said.

"No, I didn't."

It was hell after that, a living hell. He was like a savage. Mr. Ridgeway did not leave her until late in the afternoon and Sandy lay on the bed, naked and crying.

There seemed to be nothing to live for.

Nothing at all.

11

Every day was the same for Sandy. Every night from Monday through Thursday was the same. Every weekend was the same. It was for the most part, except for her stolen moments with Bruce, a period of her life which she would rather not have lived.

School was boring. Some teachers kept her after class, pointing out the advantages of learning all she could, but no matter how hard she tried to improve she continued to fail. She could not type without looking at the keys, and the English and the history were beyond her. She just went on from day to day, going from one failure straight into another.

"You should have been assigned to a job on the grounds," one of the teachers told her. "You don't have the capacity to learn."

But that was not true, not exactly. Sandy had too many things on her mind, too many things pulling her in various directions, and her mind was never clear. When a teacher was talking about the work for the day she was thinking of Betty—oh, God, how she hated Betty—or of the weekend and Bruce and Bruce's father. Sandy was, to be frank about it, totally confused.

"Nuts to them," Fran Peters told her. "You don't have to pass no school to get a parole. All they want is a good record and they don't care about anything else."

Fran was one of the girls in the cottage who never became angry with Sandy because she was permitted to be out every weekend. Most of the girls insulted her, called her rotten names, and some stopped speaking to her altogether.

"You've got it made," one girl told her, the words sharp and cutting. "Who the hell do you go to bed with so you can get outa this dump?"

"Nobody."

"Don't hand me that bull. Who does things at Edgewood out of the goodness of their hearts?"

"Maybe I was just lucky."

"You make your own luck."

Nights Sandy spent in the recreation room, watching television, playing a game of cards once in a while, staying in the recreation room as long as she could, hoping, desperately hoping, that Betty would find somebody else. Which never happened. Each night after the others were in their rooms, Betty came to her, making love, remaining with her hours at a time.

"I'm going to miss you," Betty kept saying. "I'm going to miss you when you're let out. I've had some fun in my time but never as much fun as I've had with you. You're all body, all sex. I see you in the recreation room and I want to rip the dress right off of you and take what's mine."

"That didn't stop you from selling me, did it?"

"Oh, that. Well, you aren't a true les. You never will be. You've got some kind of a complex that won't let you become one. I'm no fool. I can tell. When I make love to you you hate me and when I have you make love to me you hate me all the more. If you were like me, loving me as much as I love you, you'd never get out of here. I'd see to that. But you're a guy's girl and I can't change you. When you're gone I'll find somebody else. It isn't hard. Then there's that business with Mr. Ridgeway. I don't get rich on this job and twenty-five bucks a week isn't anything to overlook. Most of the girls I send him don't mind and they get away from here for a weekend. He gets his ashes hauled and everybody is happy. What's so wrong about that?"

As far as Sandy was concerned there was a lot wrong with it. A girl was sent to a reform school to pay her debt to society, and a house-mother had the power to make her a bigger prostitute than she had ever been. Was that right? But the people in power did not know. There was no way they could know. If a girl wanted her parole she did what she was told to do, regardless of what the act might be, and she kept her mouth shut.

"You're doing well," her parole officer told her during an interview. "Mrs. Ridgeway likes you, says you're very helpful around the house, and the rest of the family thinks you're quite a girl. Add to this the satisfactory report by Miss Hunt on your conduct in the cottage and you have every reason to expect that you'll soon be out of here."

"What do I do then?"

"Well, I spoke of that job waiting for you and you should take that.

Stay away from the people you were running with before you got into trouble and report to your local police station once each week. That you must do until your parole is up. By that time you should have both feet on the ground and be well on your way to making something of yourself."

That was a joke. What could she ever hope to make of herself? She was just a bum, a seventeen-year-old bum without any particular aim in life. The reform school had done more harm than good. Sandy had less respect for convention than she had ever had.

"Don't let your poor standing in school bother you," the parole officer assured her. "When you get to work in the diner all you'll have to do is add up checks and you're capable of doing that. You know enough English to get by. A lot of girls aren't any better equipped, even some of them who graduate from high school. All you have to do is give yourself a chance. Eventually you'll meet a nice boy and get married. If you're wise you'll guide your children so that they don't make the same mistake that you have made."

He made it sound as easy as swallowing a glass of water but Sandy did not believe him. She had already found Bruce and she thought a great deal of him but nothing was possible for them. On Saturday she was his father's private whore and you could not build a marriage out of a situation like that.

Bruce came out for her every Friday night and on the way back to town he always parked with her. She never refused him. She gave him her body, gave him her love, knowing it would soon end and that she would never see him again. She told herself that she would forget, that he would find somebody else, but she knew that she would never forget. It was not just a physical love she had for him. It was something deeper than that, something that dug down into her heart and filled her with pain.

"You'll soon be out," Bruce told her one Friday night as he parked the car in the familiar place near a high shale bank. "Once those gates swing wide for you for good we can talk about what we're going to do."

"Don't say anything about it to your family yet."

"Oh, I won't. You asked me not to and I won't. The main thing is that we know where we stand. I'm sure the folks will see it my way—our way."

It was dark in the car and Sandy was glad he could not see the gathering tears in her eyes. It would be fine to be married to him, simply fine, but there was so much he was unaware of, so much she could not tell him.

"Kiss me and don't worry," she said. "Just kiss me and hold me tight."

The parole officer had told her she would be released before the end of the next week and this was the last time she would see Bruce. These were their final moments together, moments that would have to last her for the rest of her life. The previous Saturday night they had stayed at the house, had watched television and just enjoyed being together. But on Sunday they had had no opportunity to be alone—not even on the trip back to the school, because Mrs. Ridgeway had accompanied them. We must make the most of tonight, Sandy thought miserably.

Bruce kissed her as he usually kissed her, the kiss teasing at first and then growing in intensity, his arms hard around her, straining her to him. She returned the kiss, blinking back the tears, her arms going around his neck and bringing him even closer to her.

"You drive me out of my mind," he said, kissing her on the lobe of one ear. "All I do is think about you the whole week long."

"I want you," she whispered, clinging to him.

"That goes double."

Sandy turned his head so she could kiss him on the mouth.

"But I want you all the way. I don't want you to be careful."

He was silent for a moment, running his fingers through her hair, pushing her head back and kissing her low on the throat.

"You could get pregnant," he said.

She kissed him on the forehead, taking one of his hands and putting it inside of her coat to rest on one of her breasts.

"I want something that belongs to you," she told him. "I want it bad. I want your seed inside of me and I want to get big with your child."

She had thought it over, thought it over carefully. If she took his baby back to the city with her it would be tough on her to get along but she would somehow manage. She could not have him, not for keeps, but she could have his child, perhaps a boy, and in the child she would see and remember Bruce Ridgeway. It was wrong—she knew it was wrong—but the longing and the need were so great that she could not control herself.

"You sound serious, Sandy."

"I am serious."

"Most girls would be afraid of getting in that condition."

"I'm not."

His mouth returned to her lips and this time he kissed her so hard he hurt her teeth.

"I wish we could go to a hotel," he said.

"So do I."

"Or that the folks would get out of the house long enough for us to be alone. I've never seen you—well, undressed. But I know how you must look. For my money you're the loveliest creature in the world."

They kissed and kissed and soon the flames of passion claimed them. They were wild in the front of the car, each seeking the other, each wanting the other with a want that was a blind and terrible hunger.

She felt him, and a long moan escaped her.

It was the best they had known, better than ever before. She cried out, responding to him as he responded to her, giving as much as she received in a torrent of desire.

"I won't let you down," he said later as they drove toward town. "I'll never let you down, Sandy."

Again the tears were in her eyes. Had she made a mistake? It would be hard to go it alone and support a child. But, she consoled herself, it would be his child and that was all that mattered. If he had made her that way he would be with her always.

The next day, Saturday, was the same as every Saturday. Bruce and his mother left for work and old man Ridgeway had her in bed, the fat slob getting from her what he could not get from his wife.

"You bring out the man in me," he said later, lying on the bed.

"Thanks for nothing."

"Maybe I should give you a present."

"Keep your presents to yourself."

She started to dress and he rolled over and sat up on the edge of the bed. It was a waste of time to dress. He would have her out of her clothes again before noon but she figured the effort was worth it. She could not bear being nude and having him examine her.

"Maybe my son already gave you a present," he suggested.

She slipped into her dress.

"Bruce is all right," she said.

"Bet he gets his on the way down when he drives you in on Friday nights."

"No, he doesn't," she lied. "Whatever gave you that idea?"

"Because of the way he sticks around the house over the weekend. He never did that when any of the other girls were here. He always went out with his regular girl."

Something crawled at her insides and she fought with the zipper on the dress.

"Regular girl?"

"Sure. He's got one. Why wouldn't he have one? He's nineteen and the girl is the same age. She's the daughter of a lawyer and quite a looker herself." Mr. Ridgeway laughed. "My guess is he scores with her whenever he gets the notion."

She felt sick, so sick that she could have thrown up. Bruce had never mentioned the girl to her but, looking at it logically, there was no rea-son why he should have told her. She was just a reform school girl and she was good for only one thing. He had whispered sweet nothings in her ear and she had fallen for them. How dumb could you get? And she had taken a chance with him the night before, a long chance. If she had a child because of it she would not only remember Bruce but she would remember the lies. Something died within her just then, something that had been big and important and fine. A girl, she decided, who was no-body did not have a chance. A girl, she further decided, was a sucker to believe anything a man told her. A man was out to gain physical satis-faction from a girl and nothing else.

That Saturday was as bad as most had been. Four times she undressed and four times she went to the bed with Mr. Ridgeway. She was like a piece of wood being carved up with a knife.

"I'm starved," he told her.

"You can say that again. What the hell do you want from me anyway? When you want to play for the jackpot why don't you do it with your wife?"

"I told you how she was."

"Then soften her up. Give her a little love. You ever try that?"

And for that Mr. Ridgeway had no answer.

At four o'clock she dressed for the last time and Mr. Ridgeway went to his own bedroom to put on his clothes.

She had just finished when he returned.

"Not again," she sighed, combing out her hair.

He grinned.

"No, not again. But I want to give you something."

"You already gave me something."

"I mean money. Here."

He put some bills on the dresser and after he had gone she counted them. There were five twenties, a hundred dollars. She shrugged and hid them in her bra. Well, why not? His son had given her a line a mile long and a yard wide and the old man had had his fun. Besides, it would help when she got out. The school gave a girl some clothes and twenty-five dollars upon her release but what was twenty-five dollars? One night of playing around, of drinking away the memories, and it would be all shot.

Somehow she endured the rest of the weekend. There was television that night, and on Sunday there was a big dinner. She was glad that she had little time alone with Bruce because she did not know what to say to him. After thinking it over she could not blame him for wanting a de-cent girl. Most boys did. But all she needed was a break and she could be as good as any girl, not just in bed or in a car but in the sense a girl was supposed to be good. But everywhere she turned the doors seemed to be locked against her. She was going back to a crummy job in a crummy neighborhood and she would never amount to anything. The knowledge gave her a reckless and restless feeling, a feeling of not giving a damn about what she did or what happened to her.

Late Sunday afternoon Bruce drove her back to the school. For the first time his mother did not come along.

"We can park," Bruce said. "You don't have to be in until seven."

"No. I've got a headache." This was a lie. "I had it all day yesterday and now I feel like my head is going to split open."

"You should have taken something for it."

"It's too late to think about that now."

It was too late to think about a lot of things and she was glad when he let her out in front of the main building.

"I'd kiss you," Bruce said, "but somebody might be watching and it would look funny." He reached across her and pushed the door open. "See you Friday night."

"Sure."

She walked up the steps and stood watching his car as he drove away. She would never see him again.

Never.

12

Sandy was supposed to leave the school Thursday but there was a car going into Mayville on Tuesday and they let her go then.

"No use making two trips," the woman at the desk told her. "And what's two days?"

She was issued a gray coat, a blue dress, a pair of shoes with fairly high heels, two pairs of stockings, and twenty-five dollars.

Back in the cottage and up in her room Sandy dressed quickly, humming to herself as she did so. In a few hours she would be free, walking the streets of Mayville, leading her own life again. Nothing could stop her now. Nothing.

"I'm going to miss you," Betty Hunt said as she came into the room. "I'm going to miss you like the devil."

"It'll be a one-way miss," Sandy retorted.

"Perhaps."

"No perhaps about it. You had me up a tree and there was only one way for me to run. You run up to the top of a tree and you fall off. I ran down. I ran down and buried myself in muck."

"Who made your parole possible?"

"That's beside the point. You made money off of me and you had your pleasure. I feel sorry for the next girl you trap."

Betty smiled.

"I've got one in mind. She came in today and although she isn't as pretty as you are she'll do. She looks dumb and that's a help."

"Well, I was dumb."

Sandy had not much to carry, just a paper bag with her uniform in it, and she walked to the main building. Three girls were making the trip with her and they joined the deputy sheriff out front. Unlike during the trip up, no matron was present now.

"Good driving day," the deputy said, his eyes shielded from the blazing sun on the snow by dark glasses.

"Any day is a good day to drive out of here," one girl said. "I'd go out with a broken back if I had to ride a mule."

"Oh, it isn't that bad."

"No, you just go nuts from doing nothing."

Sandy sat in back with two of the girls and the other girl sat up front with the deputy. Sandy was on the outside, next to the window, and the fat girl beside her had a lot to say.

"What if we have to go to the john some place?" she wanted to know. "You go in with us?"

"Nobody figures on you running away now," the deputy replied. "What have you got to win?"

They were passed at the gate and they moved down to the highway. The highway was covered with water and slush and the car picked up speed.

"God help my boy friend this night," the fat girl said. "He'll get jacked up off the ground for sure."

"Me, too," the girl on the opposite side of the seat declared. "You spend three months in a cage—three months and ten days to be exact—and you'd take on a guy with one leg and no eyes."

"Who cares about his legs or his eyes?" the fat girl wanted to know.

The driver made no stops on the way to Mayville and they were there in about two hours. There was no snow in the city and the streets and sidewalks were dry.

Two girls had to report to a police station uptown and the driver took them inside, returning to the car in a few minutes.

"Almost done," the driver said.

The police station to which Sandy and the fat girl went was on Fourth Street bordering the park.

"You'll meet your parole officer," the deputy told them as they went up the steps. "You do what he tells you to do and you won't have any trouble."

The fat girl was admitted to the parole officer's office first but she soon returned.

"A lotta bull," she told Sandy when she came out. "You gotta get permission to breathe even."

Sandy entered the office and the man told her to sit down. He told her his name but she made no effort to remember it and she kept watching the nervous twitch he had over one eye.

"Where are you living?" he asked her.

"I don't know. I've got to find a room."

"On Central Avenue?"

"Well, I won't make a fortune in the diner. Five bucks a week for a room is about all I'll be able to afford."

He explained the rules to her and they were simple enough. As soon as she had found living quarters she was to leave the address with the police. Once a week, on Friday, she had to report to the parole officer in his office at four in the afternoon and she was to be off the streets before ten o'clock at night. She could not drink, nor use dope nor associate with any members of the Blue Devils. If she changed her place of employment she was to notify him immediately.

"You used to run with a tough crowd," he said. "Stay away from them. If you don't do that you'll be back in reform school again."

"I get you."

The twitch over his eye became worse.

"They let you out too soon. They let all of you out too soon. They send you away to cure you and then they shove you back on the streets. It doesn't make much sense to me. And that Edgewood school makes less sense to me. You break the law and you should be punished."

He gave her the business about dope and prostitution, saying that sooner or later she would return to one or both, and then he let her go. She was glad to get away from him. That twitch made her nervous.

Since it was mild outside, Sandy walked slowly toward Central Avenue. Everything was pretty much the same. The houses were old, the street dirty, and the people she met looked as though they were living on refuse. She thought of the hundred and twenty-five dollars she had and she considered herself lucky.

The diner was as shabby as it had been before and the door, when she pushed it open, had the same squeak to it.

"Well," Old Dick said, smiling at her. "Well, for Christ's sake."

She walked up to the counter and sat down.

"Coffee," she told him.

He rubbed his fat hands on his dirty apron.

"Is that all you can say?"

"Thanks for the job." It was hot in the diner and she unbuttoned her coat. "I couldn't have got out of there without a job or having somebody to look after me. You have to have one or the other."

Old Dick drew a mug of coffee and placed it in front of her.

"The strike's over," he said. "Guys have been askin' for you. Lots of guys."

She tasted the coffee and her lips curled. Sure the guys had been asking for her. Five and ten dollar guys, guys who acted like big shots because they gave a girl a few dollars.

"How much are you payin' me?" she wanted to know.

"Thirty a week and one day off."

Her lips curled again.

"Don't break your heart."

He leaned on the counter and she could smell his breath. He ate onions raw and he never did anything to curb the odor. Immediately she lost her desire for the coffee.

"You'll be shackin' up," he said. "The guys come in and they eat and you make dates with them. You'll do all right."

"I'm on parole," she reminded him.

Old Dick waved this remark aside.

"Parole don't mean nothin'. You just report when you have to and you do what you want other times. The only reason the guys keep comin' in here is that I told 'em you're gonna come back and every last one of them wants to be first."

"As if you didn't."

"First or last don't make no matter to me. I'll take what's left of you any day of the week. Or night," he added. "I'd bounce the hell outa you."

They were interrupted by the door opening and closing and then somebody was sitting beside her. It was Tommy Forbes.

"When did you blow in?" he inquired.

"I just got here."

"How was it up there?"

"Hell."

Old Dick said he had to look at some stuff in the oven and left them. He had no sooner disappeared into the kitchen than Tammy reached down, pushed her coat aside and felt of the inside of her leg.

"I've been waitin' for you," he said. "I didn't forget what you done for me with the cops and I didn't forget that fun we had down at the club."

She reached down and pushed his hand away. "What about Ruth?"

He unzipped his jacket and made a sour face. "Ruth ain't around no more."

"She move away?"

"She did but her folks didn't. She's gonna have a kid and her old man had her sent away to some home. She took the pills, all the pills that she had, but this time they didn't do no good."

"You should have married her."

"Me? Why should I marry her? After you left she went into it for the dough and somebody scored. I didn't touch her none after that night she got taken care of in the park. Why should I marry her and give a name to somebody else's brat?"

She found it hard to believe of Ruth but it was probably true. Just the thought of Ruth's condition left her slightly numb. Bruce could have made her that way.

"I never heard from my old lady," Sandy said.

"She's gone, too."

"Gone?"

"Some place uptown. She's gettin' a divorce from your father and she's gonna marry this guy who worked in the factory with her. I seen the guy a couple of times and he seemed regular. She was off the wine, just suckin' on a bottle of soda pop, and she seemed to be nuts over him."

"What about Marty White?"

"I guess you didn't get much news where you were."

"Hardly any."

"The cops got Marty and they got Phil Landers. They got almost everybody who was pushin' dope but you can still buy grass. Horse is out until this new guy gets established."

"Who's the new guy?"

Tommy hesitated a moment.

"Me," he said.

"You!"

"Well, why not? The kids want a lift and they're gonna get a lift from somebody. I can clean up plenty of dough every week and I ain't about to let it slide by me." He hesitated again. "You want a stick? You need a stick, baby?"

"I kicked it in reform school."

"That don't mean you have to keep it kicked."

Sandy thought about it, about riding through the sky on a cloud, but she also thought about the pains she had suffered during the withdrawal period. Maybe the grass was not habit-forming but the grass only led to something else that was. Then, if that happened, it would be the same thing all over again. She would be hooked and the second time might not be so easy.

"I don't want none," she said, pushing the coffee away from her.

His hand returned to her leg, higher than it had been before.

"I know somethin' else that you want. I know somethin' else that you must want bad."

She tried to make him let go again but his fingers dug into her flesh, hanging on, hurting her so much she could hardly get her breath.

"You've got me all wrong," she managed.

"Nuts to that. All dames are the same. All dames go for it in a big way."

"You ought to know. You've most likely had your share."

"Not since I was with you."

"Expect me to believe that?"

"Believe what you want. It's the truth. In the club you're still my chick. And now you've done time you're somebody to look up to. Once you've done time you're somebody with a gang. Somebody important."

She knew that was so and in a way it thrilled her.

"I got a new room," Tommy said. "Real nice. And booze. We could go there and break out a bottle."

"And then you get your roll in the hay?"

"I won't touch you if you say not."

Part of her refused to believe him but the other part of her needed a drink, needed one terribly. If she could get a little high, take on just a few, she could forget about Edgewood and all that had happened to her there. More important, she could forget about Bruce—and this she had to do.

"All right," she said. "I could use a couple."

They went outside together. It was about four; they could see some of the dock workers coming up the street. Well, they could wait until the next day. The next day she would be back in business again. She could not live on thirty dollars a week and if she used her head the parole officer would not be able to prove anything against her. If only Bruce had told her the truth, things might be different. But he had lied to her and everything had changed. For a while she had dreamed of something better out of life but he had only gone after her body and nothing else. Now she was back where she had started, worried about being pregnant, stuck in a part of Mayville that should be buried and forgotten. In several respects her mother was better off than she was. Her mother had escaped and if the man Flora Greening had married was regular she would make something of herself.

"The gang's gettin' bigger," Tommy said.

"Is it?"

"Every day. And the new kids go on the grass right off the bat. By the time I get the H they'll be ready to mainline and before I know it I'll have a lot of pushers. The good part is that some of them are in schools and

I can get in there. Give me a year and I'll be drivin' a Caddy."

"Think so?"

He nodded as they turned in at a brick building.

"And you can be ridin' in the Caddy. You play it smart and you work with me and there ain't nothin' that you can't have."

His room was on the first floor, to the rear, but it was more than just a room. There was a small kitchen with a refrigerator and he had his own bath. The furniture was much better than the junk in the room she had shared with her mother.

"Take off your coat," Tommy said.

He had rye and scotch and they made their drinks in the small kitchen, using the rye with soda and ice cubes.

"Here's how," he said, lifting his glass.

She clinked glasses with him.

"And how," she agreed.

They had a couple drinks in the kitchen and he asked her about the school. She told him it was okay if you went in for that sort of thing and let it go at that. On the third drink they moved into the living room, taking seats on the davenport and sitting rather close together.

"I've got it all figured out," Tommy said, stretching his legs. "Once I get eight or ten guys really hooked we can cover the city, picking up where Marty and Phil left off. Those who've been on the junk are going nuts to get the stuff and I can't be everywhere at once. It's a cinch we'll clean up big."

She lit a cigarette and watched the smoke curl toward the ceiling.

"I don't know where I fit in, Tommy."

"You must be blind."

"Well, I don't. If you gave me a bunch of grass to sell I wouldn't know where to start."

He left to get more drinks and when he came back he was grinning.

"I'm not talkin' about the weed or H. I'm talkin' about the girls. We got some good-lookin' dolls in the club and most of them are on their way to gettin' hooked already. Once they've gone that far they'll do whatever they have to do to get what they need. You'll be in the diner and you can make the contacts. Five dollars for the girl and five dollars for you. Once we get some rooms where the girls can take the men we'll branch out uptown. We'll set up the bartenders and the cab drivers, makin' the sucker pay an extra five for the information, and before you know it you'll be in clover." He laughed. "Most of the girls are young—say, your age—and the guys go for the ripe stuff. You take a guy who's forty and who can make time with a sixteen-year-old piece of fluff, why, he'll pay through the nose for it. The deal works both ways. You get your cut for linin' up the girls and then they turn around and spend it with me for their kicks. You know of anythin' sweeter?"

"What about my parole officer? I gotta watch out for that guy. He catches me in one bad move and I'm in for another trip."

"How can he catch you? You only make the appointments. I don't intend for you to be goin' to bed with no guys for money."

"Think you're saving it for yourself?"

"Sort of."

"Don't be too sure," she warned him. "You haven't gotten anything yet."

"Well, you ought to be able to see what I've been talkin' about."

"I see all right. The guys get the yen and they have to go out and sell for you. The girls get the yen and they have to go to bed to earn enough to buy the junk."

"You're on the stick, baby."

They drank and talked and after a while it got so dark in the room he had to turn on a light. She had been off the liquor for quite a while and it hit her and hit her hard. She tried to think of Edgewood and Bruce but both were just distant memories and they died in the dark recesses of her mind. She was on her own and she would be able to live again. Nuts to that parole officer. Nuts to the cops. She could fool the parole officer and she could fool the cops. Hell, if she put her mind to it, there was nobody she could not fool.

"Where you stayin'?" Tommy asked her.

"Beats me. I didn't have no chance to find a room." Sandy started to get to her feet. "Maybe I better go out and look for one now."

He grabbed her arm and pulled her down beside him.

"You can stay here," he said. "That davenport gets awful lonesome."

The dress rode up over her knees but she left it that way. Tommy had seen her knees before. Just her knees? That was a laugh.

"There's gonna be a rumble," he was saying. "A hell of a rumble this time."

"Who is it this time? You fight with the uptown gangs?"

"Naw. It's the Black Cats again. Ever since Slim got his in the belly they been jumpin' our guys in the park. Not four or five guys but one or two. They beat hell out of some of our guys, cut one so bad he had to have sixteen stitches in his head. Or maybe it was eighteen. I don't know. But I do know there's gonna be a rumble. I don't want it and I tried to talk 'em down but you know how they are. They want blood for blood. I guess you can't blame 'em none. Somebody has to put the lumps to 'em. And the park belongs to us. We got a right to the park. They got Cannon Street and we don't go over there. We stay in our territory and they should stay in theirs."

He went on talking about the rumble. It was going to be Saturday night, as soon as it got dark, and they were going to hunt down every Black Cat and give each a going over. The Cats met one night a week in the park, Saturday night, and that was the best time to go after them.

"You carry my tools," he said. "You do the same as you did before, huh?"

"I'm not supposed to be out late."

"Who's gonna know? There ain't a parole officer in the state that works Saturday night. You think they don't wanta go home and crawl in the sheets with the old woman?"

Sandy remembered the body of Slim Jefferies lying on the ground.

"You'll gut somebody," she said.

"So I gut 'em. So what? The Blue Devils fit in with my plans and I've gotta keep control of 'em. And if somebody gets gutted they got it comin' to 'em."

She shuddered. This was violence, raw violence, brutal and terrible. A life meant nothing. Yet if she wanted more out of living than she would find on Central Avenue she had to stick with Tommy. He was brash enough to go far and if she trailed along she could have all the things she had always wanted. The thought of arranging dates for young girls did not disturb her. If she did not cut herself in on the cake somebody else would. By the time she was twenty, possibly before, she would have it made, have it made in a big way.

"It's sure hot enough in here," she said.

"It's always hot. The knob on the radiator is busted and you gotta have a pair of pliers to turn it off." He took the hem of her dress and lifted it high on her thighs. "You oughta get out of that crazy thing. It looks like a rag somebody threw in the dump."

She turned her head and gave him a drunken smile.

"You want a free show, huh?"

Tommy nodded, very slowly.

Several drinks later Sandy did get out of the dress. As long as she was a tramp she might as well be a tramp. There had been nights at Edgewood she had dreamed of being married to Bruce, of being somebody, but when she had awakened she had known it impossible. She was a prostitute, both in and out of the reform school, and no amount of dreaming or hoping could change that.

Sandy could not be sure what time they went to bed but it must have been late. She tried to help him open up the davenport but she slipped and fell on the floor and they both laughed.

"Shook me up," she said as she got to her feet.

"I'll shake you up more," he promised her.

"Let's not run any risk," she said as he pushed her down on the bed. She moved her lips against his mouth. "You know what I mean?"

"Shut up."

The only thing she remembered after that was that he had his way with her. But she had felt nothing, nothing at all.

"Bruce," she said after he stretched out beside her. "Bruce."

"Who's Bruce?" Tommy demanded.

"A rat."

"Well, shut up and go to sleep."

She did.

13

It was not easy for Sandy to get away from her parole officer. He checked on her at the diner almost every day and several times he stopped at the room she had taken in the rooming house where Tommy lived.

"We just want to see that you get off to the right start," he explained. "We want you to work steadily and live like a girl should."

"I'm doing okay."

"How much are you earning?"

"Thirty dollars a week."

"That isn't a great deal. The factories pay more than that and you'd only have to work five days, not six. I know some people and I'll see what I can do for you."

"Thanks."

She saw Tommy every night after it was late and she was reasonably sure that the parole officer would not be looking for her. Sometimes they went down to the club, mixing with the other kids, drinking if there was anything to drink, and horsing around. A lot of kids were on the grass, both girls and boys; one girl who wanted to be a stripper usually put on a show. She had a tall, slim body, not quite fully developed, and some of the boys laughed at her. But when she took them into the back room, still naked and panting from her efforts, they no longer laughed. They took their turns and they all said she was good, that she did not care what she did or how she did it.

"I oughta haul my freight with her," Tommy told Sandy one night. "A lot of good you do me."

She had not let him touch her since that first night she had returned to the city, nor had she been with any men from the docks. Her first day at the diner she had made a date with a foreman who had money to blow away but she had stood him up. She had not known why and she had not tried to explain it to herself. All she had to do was look at a boy and she saw Bruce and then she was scared. This would cause her to put her hands over her stomach, pressing in, thinking that he might have put her in a family way and not knowing what she would do with the kid if he had. She had heard along the avenue that Ruth was being treated swell where she was, not wanting for anything, and she wondered constantly if she might wind up in the same place. The hell of it was she would not know if the kid belonged to Bruce or to Tommy. Tommy had had his fun with her that first night and it did not seem to bother him any.

"You ain't gonna have no kid," he told her more than once. "Why spoil everything with all your worryin'?"

But she could not help worrying and it showed in her work at the diner. Mornings and afternoons were all right, because there was not much doing, but when the men came in from work she found it difficult to smile and joke with them. Some complained to Old Dick about her attitude and Old Dick jumped her about it.

"That school didn't do you no good," Old Dick said. "That school took all of the zing outa you."

"Just give me time."

"How long you want? The rest of your life?"

Quite often when Sandy had to go into the kitchen for something Old Dick would shove her into a corner or against the wall and run his hands down over her.

"You better be nice to me, kid. I let the other woman go just so's you could have the job and it helped get you out of that reform school. All I've gotta do is fire you and shove you back onto the street and there's a good chance you'll be put away again."

"Some night," she would promise him, not meaning it.

"What night?"

"Some night."

The touch of his hands made her feel dirty, as dirty as she had ever felt before, but she put up with it. She had no other choice. If the parole officer followed through, as he had said he would, she could tell Old Dick what to do with his job. The only reason Old Dick had hired her was so that he could make time with her. And she would rather die than have anything to do with him that way.

Friday night was a big night at the club and everybody boozed it up. Those who had enough money bought their sticks from Tommy and hit the grass, passing the sticks from one to another and trying to get a lift.

"I gotta have money," one girl said. "I gotta have a smoke and you can't get no smoke without no money."

She was fifteen, maybe sixteen, and she had a well-developed shape. She was with a boy who had no money and she kept telling him to go out and snatch a purse or something.

"Sell it," the boy told her. "You sure as hell give it away enough."

Tommy had been after Sandy to approach the girls and make dates for them with the men from the docks but so far she had done nothing about it. The night they had talked about it, the night she had been drunk, the idea had seemed all right but now it did not. She asked herself why and she did not know. It was an easy way to pick up some fast money.

"You work in the diner," the girl said to her. "You got connections. You could fix me up."

"With what?"

"With a man, you crazy fool. How else you think I'm gonna earn any dough? The last time I snitched five bucks from my old lady she beat me so much I couldn't hardly walk."

"You'd only get five from a man."

"That's five sticks."

"And where would you take him?"

"For a stinkin' five the guy could rent a hotel room. What do I care? If he can stand the cold in the park I can, too. All I gotta have is a blanket and five minutes of his time."

"It takes me longer'n five minutes," the boy beside her said.

"Yeah, and you don't pay. What's the percentage in that?"

"I'll see what I can do," Sandy said, moving away. "I'll let you know."

The girl who wanted to be a stripper was already drunk and in the back room with some of the boys who were giving her the works. Sandy looked for Tommy, could not see him, and decided that he had dealt himself in. She did not blame him. Any girl in the club was supposed to put out and Sandy had not been doing it.

About an hour later the boys got together and began discussing the rumble for the next night. Everybody, including the girls, was in on it and they were going to show the Black Cats. They were going to show them good.

"We won't let any of 'em get away," Tommy said, his voice filled with authority. "We've got enough guys to go two for one and we smash them down. They gotta learn they got no business in the park."

"We'll stomp the hell outa them," a big boy said.

"And gut them," another boy added.

Sandy was tired; she was glad when Tommy was ready to leave. On the way out the girl who had been dying for a puff of grass stopped Tommy.

"Gimme a stick," she pleaded. "Just one."

"You got money?"

"No."

"Then no stick. Get some money and you can have a dream."

"How'm I gonna get money this time of night?"

"Don't ask me. I'm just tellin' you. It costs money to dream, baby."

Once outside the club Sandy and Tommy walked along Central Avenue.

"You could have given her one," Sandy said.

"For what? She's got somethin' to sell. Let her go out and sell it."

Tommy wanted to come into her room with her but she refused.

"You got yours for tonight," she told him. "You got it in the back room."

"Yeah," he admitted. "And she wasn't bad. She may have been drunk but she knew what the score was."

Once inside of her room Sandy undressed and went to bed but it took her a long time to go to sleep. Within twenty-four hours there would be a rumble and she had the feeling that somebody would be hurt bad.

She was happy the next morning when she went to work, though she had had to go to the drug store first and she was late. She was not pregnant. It was as if a black cloud had been lifted from her eyes.

"You've gotta be on time," Old Dick said when she checked in.

"I'm on time," she said, smiling, though there was no possible way he could know what she meant.

It was a slow day. The parole officer did not bother her and there were only a few men working the docks. Saturday was a day for time-and-a-half and dock owners did not like to shell out money that way. Maybe a dozen men came in for lunch, most of them soup and coffee customers, and after that business died down. A few men had tried to date her. She just laughed and told them to come back another day.

"You take tomorrow off," Dick told her as she was getting ready to leave. "I'm gonna start closin' the diner on Sundays. I don't take in enough money to pay me to get outa bed."

"All right."

"But that wouldn't stop me none from comin' around to see you. I got the time Sundays and we could have a little party. I'll bring a bottle and we'll kill the thing."

"Forget it."

They were out front, where anybody could see them from the avenue, but he put his hand over one of her breasts and shoved her back against the counter.

"Don't keep me waitin' too long," he said. "I got no patience for little girls who stall. You play it square with me and I'll play it square with you. Play me for a sucker and you can go to hell."

Sandy left the diner and walked toward her rooming house, determined she would have to get away from him; if the parole officer could not find her another job she would have to get one herself. Still, if she went along with Tommy, if she did what he wanted her to do with the girls from the club, being at the diner was important. Later, after they branched out up-town, she would not need Old Dick.

"Hello, cutie," a man said to her.

She stopped and stared at him.

"I don't remember you," she said, looking up into his face.

A cigarette hung out of one corner of his mouth and it jumped up and down when he talked. "You did it for five one night."

"Did I?"

"Yeah, and I got ten that says you can do it again."

"Drop dead."

Sandy moved down the avenue, leaving the man standing there, saying something under his breath she did not catch. Maybe he was younger than Old Dick but he was in the same class. They were all in the same class. Some wanted it for free and some wanted it for money but that was the only difference.

Sandy left the rooming house with Tommy a few minutes before eight and they joined the gang on the corner. The boys were shuffling around, slapping their bare hands to keep them warm, talking low. The girls stood in a tight little group, saying nothing, their faces white and wondering in the shadows.

"A police car just went up the avenue," one of the boys told Tommy. "It was going real slow."

"Nuts to them," Tommy said. "All they do is put their fat cans on soft cushions and see nothin'."

Tommy outlined the plan of attack and it was pretty much the same as it had been on the night Slim was killed. They would sneak up on the Cats from three sides—the wall would be behind them—and the Cats would be cut off from escape.

"Everybody here?" Tommy wanted to know.

Everybody was present except the girl who had asked Tommy for a stick the night before. The boy who had been with her then said she did not count, that probably her old lady would not let her out.

"I ain't seen her all day," the boy snickered. "Maybe she did get out but if she did she's tryin' to get money for sticks."

Some had been to the club before coming up to the corner and they were high. They were indifferent as to what they would do or who they would do it to. All they wanted was blood.

"The girls carry the tools," Tommy said. "Once we're in the park we take over and the girls stay out of the way."

The boys—all were wearing jackets—began bringing out weapons and the girls started hiding them under their coats, shoving pieces of iron pipe up their sleeves and hiding other things in their pockets or inside of their sweaters. Sandy was wearing the dress given her at reform school, and she put Tommy's brass knuckles in the pocket of her coat.

"I'm glad you haven't got a knife," she said. "I don't want anybody else killed."

"You chicken?"

"No, but why kill?"

Tommy laughed at her.

"Those knuckles could. You hit a guy right and he's done."

"Well, don't."

The boys began moving across the street, going in pairs, passing under the light and disappearing into the darkness of the park.

"This is the last rumble," Tommy said.

"I hope so. I think of the other one and it gives me the willies."

"Slim had it coming."

"Maybe, but there ought to be another way."

It only took a few minutes for the whole group to cross the street and then they were in the cold stillness of the park. The boys sought out the girls and weapons exchanged hands.

"It isn't too late to stop," Sandy said as she gave the brass knuckles to Tommy.

"It is now."

"But if you talked to them—"

"What's the use of talking to 'em? They don't understand a word you say. The Cats just beat up our guys and they'll keep it up until we stop 'em. And the gang wants the rumble. You can see that. I don't have to tell you. Some of the guys have accounts to settle and this is the only way to do it."

The boys moved out like an army searching for the enemy. The girls followed, keeping close together, some of them whispering.

"This'll rock the city," one girl predicted. "This'll rock it from one end to the other. Tomorrow's papers will be splashed with it."

It happened fast when it happened. One moment the night was silent and the next moment the silence was broken by screams and shouts and curses.

Sandy broke away from the girls, plunging forward and racing through the darkness. She rounded a turn in the path and saw that the Cats had had a big fire going at the base of the wall. The glow from the fire revealed the struggling figures and cast weird shadows over the ground.

"Don't!" she yelled, finding Tommy and throwing herself at him. "For God sakes, don't!"

He had a small boy backed against the wall and was hammering him in the face with the brass knuckles. The boy's face was covered with blood.

"Get away, you bitch," he breathed, flinging her aside. "You wanta ruin the whole show?"

Sandy struck the ground, rolling over twice, and a boy—she could not tell whether he was a Cat or a Blue Devil—stepped on her, driving his foot deep into her stomach. She rolled away, getting to her knees, and then she heard the police whistles.

"Tommy!" she managed. "Tommy, the cops!"

Tommy cursed, turning away from the wall. The boy he had been working over sagged to the ground, sobbing.

The cops were all over. They came from every direction, yelling at the kids, their flashlights probing the night.

"Halt! Everybody stand right where they are!"

She stumbled to her feet and Tommy brushed up against her.

"I gotta get outa here," he breathed. "I'm loaded with sticks and if they catch me—"

"Tommy—"

Then he was away from her, running straight at a cop with a drawn gun. The cop hollered something, waving the gun, but Tommy refused to halt. He threw himself at the cop, clawing for the gun, and there was a terrific explosion.

"Tommy!"

Horrified, she saw him stop abruptly, turn part way around, his hands going to his stomach as he bent over and sank to the ground.

"Tommy!"

She ran to him, kneeling beside him.

"Tommy!"

The cop was on the other side of Tommy, rolling up the sleeve of the boy's jacket, obviously feeling for his pulse.

"He's dead," she wailed.

The cop was silent for a moment and then he stood up slowly.

"Yes, he's dead," he said. "I didn't want to do it. I've got a kid of my own. But if he'd ever gotten my gun there's no telling what he might have done."

The shooting of Tommy, coupled with the presence of so many policemen, completely subdued the members of both gangs. Some boys were protesting their innocence, trying to get rid of weapons, and nearly all the girls were crying.

"Lock me up," one boy sneered. "Lock me up, you big fat slob."

"That's what I'm going to do," the officer said gently. "This stuff has got to stop."

The policemen herded them into groups and led them out of the park, making them walk the entire distance from the park to the police station. People stopped to stare at them.

"Hoods," one man remarked. "Young hoods."

It was not bad in the police station. Those who had been cut up were given first-aid and the boy Tommy had been pounding was sent to a hospital in a patrol car, along with two other boys.

The boys were put in one room and the girls in another.

"You'll be called out when we need you," they were told.

Sandy sat numb and frightened. Tommy was dead, dying as violently as he had lived, and she was in trouble again. Miserably she stared at the floor and wished she could cry but she could not.

She was the last one taken into the small room across the hall. Both officers had questioned her at the time she had been arrested for prostitution.

"Sit down," the older man said.

She sat down.

"What's your name?"

"Sandy Greening." Her mouth was dry, her throat aching.

The two men exchanged looks.

"You were in here before," the younger one said. "For prostitution, weren't you?"

"That's right."

"When did you get out of reform school?"

"This week."

"You know what this means, don't you?"

"Yes. That I go back."

"Where were you?"

"Edgewood."

"Well, you won't go back there. We'll send you to a place that will do a job on you."

"Yes—sir."

They kept her a long time. They dug up old records and they asked her about the death of Slim Jefferies again. There was no use lying. She could not help Tommy. Tommy was beyond help.

"He did it," she said at last. "He did it with the knife you had. I only lied for him because Slim had raped a girl—raped her three times in the park."

"Why didn't she come to us?"

"Because she didn't think it would do her much good."

"Do you know a girl by the name of Cindy Walker?"

"I couldn't tell you. I might know her but I don't know her name."

"You were at the club last night?" The older officer was doing most of the talking. "You were with Tommy Forbes?"

"That's right."

"And a girl asked Tommy for a free smoke of marijuana?"

"Some girl did."

"Well, that was Cindy Walker. When she got turned down she came here. She told us about the rumble tonight. That's why we had the park covered."

Sandy said nothing. It all fit, fit perfectly. Tommy had been cheap and brutal and he had brought this upon them. For his greed he had paid with his life, paid with the most precious thing a person could possibly own.

She continued her silence when the matron—the same one who had had charge of her before—came and led her away.

What, she asked herself, was the use of words?

Words did not add up.

14

Sandy was kept in Mayville three days to await transportation to a reform school upstate. On the second day her mother came to see her.

"You look good," Sandy told her mother. "Your face is fuller and your don't have red eyes from so much wine."

"That's because I'm not touching it."

"I hear you're living with some man."

"You heard wrong. I've got a better job in another factory and I'm living by myself. There was a man I liked quite a lot but your father is getting out soon and I've never forgotten him. I drove him where he is and it's up to me to save some money and help us get started again when he gets out. I owe him that much and if we work together, with me not wanting too much, we ought to be happy."

Sandy was glad to know this and happy for her mother and father. After Flora Greening left, Sandy cried because she was so pleased. People could go a long way down and they could come a long way back. With half a chance they would be able to pick up the pieces.

Later that day a minister called on her. He was not from her church— she had never had a church except when she had been going to Sunday school and she could not remember its name—but that did not perturb the minister.

"Do as they tell you to do," he said. "Resolve that you will return to your freedom a better person. You aren't old. You're young. Life isn't behind you. It's ahead of you."

The next morning, just a few hours before Sandy was scheduled to leave for another institution which would shut her away from the world, the matron came and told her she had a visitor.

"Who?"

"I don't know. A young man. He seems very nervous and very tired."

Sandy followed the matron down the wide hall to the room reserved for visitors in which one could talk in private.

"Ten minutes," the matron said as she opened the door.

Sandy stepped into the room and then she stopped dead. Nights she had dreamed of him, days she had thought of him—and here he was.

"Bruce!" she whispered, unable to move further.

He came to her, looking as tired as the matron had said, a smile pulling up the corners of his mouth.

"I thought I might miss you," Bruce said.

"You almost did." She tried to match his smile. "Perhaps it would have been better for if you had."

"Not for me. Not unless you don't feel the same way about us as I do."

She found herself unable to meet the honesty in his eyes.

"You don't know what I am," Sandy murmured.

"I know. I wouldn't be here if I didn't know. And I know what went on at Edgewood."

"I doubt if you do."

Bruce held out a cigarette but she shook her head. Sandy could not smoke. She could not think.

"We had the store's checkbook home Friday night," he said. "When my mother and I went to the store Saturday morning we forgot it and I returned for it. I found my father and a new girl from the school in the living room and I don't have to tell you what they were doing. I raised all kinds of hell, and then he told me what you two had done when my mother and I had been away on Saturdays. He even bragged about the arrangement he had with this Miss Hunt. The short of it is I didn't go back to the store right away. The girl told me what Miss Hunt had done to her, what Miss Hunt had made her do, and I went right to the school. I started at the top and I got action. They called in Miss Hunt and they gave her the business. She broke when they threatened her with a jail term for what she had done, not only to you and to the girl with my father, but to lots of others. She got her final pay in a hurry."

Bruce knew what she was, and Sandy felt as if she had been undressed in public for everybody to see.

"I don't know why you came here," she said. "If it had been me I'd have run the other way."

"Not when you're in love," he disagreed gently.

This time she accepted the cigarette he offered and her hand shook.

"You can't be in love with me," she said. "It just isn't possible."

He leaned down and kissed her on the mouth.

"You could say that of my mother. How do you think she felt when she heard about what my father had been doing? She was stunned at first, but she was smart enough to realize she hadn't been a wife for a long, long time. Now she's going to hire somebody else for the store and settle down to making a home."

"That has nothing to do with us."

"Yes, it has a lot to do with us. Everybody makes mistakes and you've made your share. I knew you weren't perfect when I fell in love with you. You weren't in a reform school for your health."

"And I'm going to another one," she reminded him. "The judge told me it would be nine months this time. Some of the others picked up with me who had dope on them got longer terms. The rest are on probation."

This time when Bruce kissed her there could be no doubt about the love he felt. At first she could not respond, thinking she was being unfair to him; but then, from a deeper urgency, she rose on her toes, wanting his lips more than ever, wanting him in the clean way a girl should want a boy.

"I'll write to you every night," he said. "And when I can come to see you I will. Other times I'll be working in the store and I'll be building a house you'll be proud of."

"I'd feel funny seeing your father again."

"Why? It was his fault. Just as much as it was Miss Hunt's. You learn by living and nobody can change that."

"What about the girl you were going with at home? The one your father told me about."

"Would I be here if it were important? She was just a friend and nothing more. I won't say we didn't go too far once or twice—it would be a lie if I did—but nobody is perfect. Get it out of your head that they are. If you hadn't come along I might have married her but you did come along and I wouldn't marry anybody else in the world."

His insistence on marriage was too much to hope for, too much to dream for, but here it was, and Sandy was the girl. She smiled as she gazed up into his face. He was a fine boy, very fine, and she had no right to him.

"I love you," he said before he kissed her.

"And I love you," she said. "Somehow, someday I'll make you proud of me." Her lips blazed as they touched his mouth. "I don't know how, but I will. I promise you that."

The boy and girl were still kissing when the matron opened the door and told them their time was up.

"Not for nine months," Sandy said.

Bruce squeezed her close and she joined in with his laughter.

They could afford to laugh.

Nine months was not much.

Not when they had their lives ahead of them.

THE END

The Widow

By Orrie Hitt

PART ONE

Old man Sparks fired me the fourth day on the job, and since there wasn't any transportation going down to The Dell until noon I decided to walk rather than wait for somebody to do me a favor. The road was plenty rough where the cats had been bucking the rocks but the air was filled with early morning dampness and sunshine and I didn't mind it at all.

The Dell was one of those out of the way places that often gets caught in the middle of a construction project and prospers as a result. Before the work had started on the highway it had just been a gas station and sandwich joint with some ancient cabins scattered around in the back. Now that about eighteen miles of the highway were ripped up, traffic had stopped using this part of Route 6 and was detouring through Monticello and north that way. On the surface this should have put The Dell out of business, but since few people stopped there before, and since the construction workers had to have a place to stay, old lady Sprague's bank account had been given a healthy transfusion of green plasma.

I entered my cabin, wrapped my tooth brush and shaving stuff in some clean underwear, threw the whole mess into a paper bag and sat down on the bed for a couple of minutes, looking at the five twenties in my hand and wondering if I should settle with the old lady or if I should play it smart and just fade off down the road. Old lady Sprague had more money than I did; besides, she was getting a break. I wasn't taking her sheets or anything like that with me and I didn't intend to haul the mattress out and sell it. I had done that once before, sold a mattress on a dame in Easton, but this thing I was sitting on, wouldn't even give a good nap to a tired drunk.

My cabin was the smallest of the lot, a lean-to kind of affair with boards on the sides, which featured just enough room for one guy. I looked around very carefully but there wasn't anything worth carrying away so I picked up the paper bag and walked outside.

Five steps past the cabin door and I didn't know if I would ever get started.

It was one of those things that hits you fast, like a sneak blow in a fight. I'd had this feeling once before, in the French Quarter of New Orleans, but the girl had a knife and she was hanging to the handle that was sticking out of my shoulder. I didn't have a chance to find out what she was like; she was fast and I hadn't gotten any closer than the sharp blade of that knife.

"Hello," I said to the girl who was hanging up the clothes.

She had her back to me but now she slowly turned around, and I got a good full side view of her. She was like something you see drawn by an artist. Her dungarees were tight and rounded and the man's shirt she was wearing was so loose and alive that I could tell she didn't have anything on underneath it.

"Oh," she said, dropping a clothespin out of her mouth. "You sort of scared me."

"Sorry."

But I wasn't sorry at all. The only people I had seen at The Dell had been the Sprague woman and the men who worked on the job. The bars of Sayville were seven miles away and I didn't have any money until they paid me off on the job. As soon as I hit the bars I would be broke again. Things had gone that way for twenty-six years and I couldn't see any reason why they would suddenly change.

"Nice day," the girl said.

"Fine."

She had beautiful black hair and soft gray eyes and a bright red mouth. I could see her face just by glancing up and I had an idea that she should do something about the way the shirt hung open at the top. A couple of buttons were gone from the shirt and where it parted she was all cleavage, dark and warm and deep.

"You leaving?" she wanted to know, nodding at the paper bag in my hand.

"Not by choice."

"How come?"

"Simple. I got fired."

She hung up a pair of panties, blue things that the sun shone through, and I liked the way she had to stretch. "I thought they needed men."

"Maybe they do. Only the boss can't stand for guys belting him around."

"You did that?"

"He took the first swing but he missed."

"And you finished it?"

"I finished it all right."

"What were you fighting about?"

"I didn't like the way he wanted me to dig."

"In the ground?"

"Where else would I be digging?"

She took some other things from the basket on the ground and hung them on the line. I stood watching her, wondering if Sparks would be able to run the shovel. Frankly, I didn't care if he had to dig the stumps out by hand. But then I decided that he might have been right after all. All the operating I had ever done was in Arabia and there hadn't been any tree stumps over there to get in my way.

"Your husband working around here?" I asked.

"Not if he can help it."

I shifted the paper bag from one hand to the other.

"Nice work if you can get it," I said.

"His mother owns The Dell."

"That's not enough to retire on."

"It is for Frank."

She bent over, looking into the basket, and what I saw made my head throb. Then she closed the gap in the shirt. Still holding the shirt she straightened and smiled at me.

"Got a cigarette, Mr.—"

"Rebner. Jerry Rebner." I dropped the paper bag to the ground and took a package of cigarettes from my shirt pocket. "Yeah, I've got a cigarette."

She came toward me. Her hand was away from the top of the shirt and the thing was all open again.

"Thanks," she said after she had inhaled the smoke. "The old bag in there doesn't like these things."

I knew she was talking about her mother-in-law and it kind of drew me up tight. It wasn't what she said so much as the way she said it, sort of disgusted and dirty.

"You just get here?" I asked her.

"Last night."

"From where?"

"All over."

"I see."

She smiled and rubbed the sole of one shoe in the dry grass.

"Frank and I have been married two years and we've lived in nine different places. Can you tie that?"

"Just about."

"So you're another one?"

"Another what?"

"Wanderer. No sooner do you light than you want to go."

"Something like that."

"It's different with a man."

"Is it?"

She watched me through the smoke and wet her lips with the tip of her tongue.

"A man can make out any place but a woman wants things. She wants a home and friends and—well, kids. You can't have any of these when you're moving around all the time."

"I guess not."

"Frank had some good jobs," she said, "but he never stayed at any of them."

"What does he do?"

"Work in garages."

"Pumping gas?"

"No, he's a mechanic."

"That ought to be a good racket."

"It is if a man sticks to it. But Frank is hot rod nuts. All he wants to do is work on his old Ford. You'd think he was married to the damned car, the way he spends money on it. First it's something in the motor—a cam—then it's a manifold or whatever you call it. I don't know. It's beyond me. The more he works on it the worse it sounds, as far as I'm concerned."

I picked up the bag and stuffed it under my arm. The sun was hot but it wasn't only the sun that was making me sweat. I was used to taking what I wanted, if it was pretty and willing, but it didn't look as though I'd have time for this one. In that second I was sorry I had fought with Sparks. Here was a number who wasn't happy with her marriage; those are the best kind.

"I'm Linda," she said.

"That's a pretty name."

"I hate it."

So did I but I liked what bore the name.

"What are you going to do now?" she asked, staring up into my face.

"I don't know."

I knew. It would be Sayville and the bars and when I was broke—which wouldn't take long—it would be the road again. It didn't bother me any. I expected it. I had long accepted the fact that I was a bum. I had been since Mary's death.

"I know where there's a job," Linda said slowly.

I looked her over again. It wasn't gray smoke I saw her eyes. It was raw fire.

"Tell me," I said.

"Well, it isn't much. Just washing dishes and things like that inside." She flipped the cigarette into the grass and stepped on it. "The old lady's running out of gas," she said. "like a leaky scow going upriver."

"She has got a lot to do."

"And I'm supposed to help her."

"What about your husband?"

"He'll fuss with the car. I told you he's a nut about it. While I'm breaking my back he'll be blowing our money on parts."

"Don't give it to him."

"Tell his mother that. He already got a hundred from her and the last I saw of him he was going to drive a hundred miles to spend it."

"Leaving you behind?"

"That's where he always leaves me,"

I hadn't met Frank Sprague but I decided that he must be a jackass. If I had a woman like this I wouldn't let her out of my sight long enough to take a bath.

"She wouldn't pay much," I said.

"I don't know."

"Peanuts."

"You'd have to ask her."

I kept looking at Linda Sprague and wondering if maybe I could find a job on the throughway. She was a ripe dish but if I could just get down the road and around the first turn, she'd pass out of my life faster than Mary had died in that car accident. I had met her kind before, because that kind inhabited the world which I had made for myself. They had been along the docks and they had been in the tiny, shabby rooms on darkened side streets. And they had all been smarter than I could ever learn to be.

"I'll see you," I said, turning away from her. My legs felt weak but the gravel in the driveway was good under my shoes. "I'll see you, Linda."

She was silent for a moment.

"You will—if you take the job," she said.

"Yeah."

"Otherwise, so long."

I spit in the grass and walked around to the front of the building. There was something here that frightened me, but there was something here that beckoned me, too. I didn't know what it was. She was married to a man who didn't give a damn, but it went beyond that.

I turned right.

And then I turned back.

What did I have to lose?

Old lady Sprague was inside, scrubbing the floor with a worn-out mop. She looked up when I came in, halted her work and wiped a fat forearm across her face. She noticed the bag in my hand, stood the mop against one of the tables, and limped behind the counter.

"You finished, Mr. Rebner?"

I nodded and sat down at the counter. She found my bill and put it in front of me. I didn't bother even to look at it.

"I hear you've got a job open," I said.

She drew half a glass of water from the tap under the counter and gulped it down.

"Dishwashing," she said, and the wrinkles on her neck moved. "Dishwashing and helping me keep this place clean. It's not much."

"It wouldn't be."

"I'll pay forty a week and your room and board. Eight in the morning until ten at night, two hours off in the afternoon, with Monday free."

"You said a mouthful," I told her. "It isn't much."

She was offended.

"Did I tell you to ask me?"

"No, you didn't."

She took some more water but this time she drank it slowly.

"It's up to you," she said, putting the glass down.

"So it is."

"And no drinking, not on the job."

"With those hours I'd always be on the job."

"It isn't hard work, only the dishes. They have to be done by hand."

"And dried?"

"And dried."

"They shouldn't be dried," I said. "You scald them with hot water and let the air do the drying. That's what they told us in the army."

"This isn't the army."

I thought about it. I had seldom made less than two hundred a week running a shovel but this job might have a bonus with it that would make up for the difference. I made my decision.

"When do I start?"

Mrs. Sprague pushed a gray hair out of her eyes and stared at me.

"You don't look very busy right now," she said.

"I'm not."

"So you can take the mop and finish up."

I was almost finished with the floor when Linda came in.

"You're tracking it up," I said,

"Am I? Do you mind?"

"Not much."

She walked on through to the kitchen and I followed her every movement with my eyes. For forty a week and that body, this was a good job.

2

Mrs. Sprague sent me into Sayville that afternoon to pick up groceries from the store and Mr. Sparks' daughter Norma from the bus station.

"I don't know what she looks like," Mrs. Sprague said. "But I told Mr. Sparks that I would send you to get her."

"Okay."

"She's to have cabin seven."

"Will do."

I asked her about money to pay for the food but she said she had a charge account at Bertie's Store.

"That's part of your job," she said. "Doing the shopping. Since the road has been torn up, Bertie won't deliver out here and I can't drive."

"How come you've got a car?"

"Well, it was my husband's. I never did sell it. It hasn't been driven much."

That trap had been driven plenty. The speedometer registered over seventy thousand, but if it hadn't gone over the top more than once I didn't know anything about cars. It rattled and the doors wouldn't close and the window on the driver's side couldn't be put down. Quite a heap, that car.

It was only seven miles in to Sayville and I drove slowly. The road was torn up for about three miles and I had noticed that the tires on the car were smooth. The chuck holes were deep and the Plymouth rattled and creaked in every joint.

Bertie's was a market on the main street and easy to find. Using my list, he helped me get the stuff together. The bill came to almost fifty bucks and he had me sign for it.

"She's as good as gold," he said.

"Yeah."

"When did you start working for her?"

"Just today."

"Then you can buy where and what you want to buy."

"She didn't say that."

"She will. She seldom gets to town and if you can pick up any specials she'll pat you on the back. But don't be fooled with these supermarkets. They give you a bargain in one direction and they screw you on something else. You just keep coming in here and I'll see that you get ten percent at the end of each month."

"Not bad."

"Money is money."

"Somebody said that before."

The bus was late because of the detour, and I had about thirty minutes to kill. Mrs. Sprague had told me that I shouldn't drink on the job but I wouldn't be on the job for half an hour so I drifted into a bar.

"Double rye."

"Water or ginger?"

"Straight."

I sat at the bar and drank and looked at myself in the mirror. My hair was brown and my face tanned, with a rugged, outdoor appearance. Some women told me that it was a hard face, others said it was a handsome face. I tried to judge that and couldn't. There was a scar on the right side under my jaw, but that didn't show. The doctor had done a good job of sewing up the slash; about the only time it was visible was when I didn't shave for a couple of days.

"Another?"

"Another."

I wondered what I was doing in such a lousy town, what I was doing with such a miserable job, and where it would end. Or had it ended already? Had it ended that frightful moment when they had pulled Mary's body from the wreckage of our car, broken and smashed?

Whenever I thought of it I felt cold all over. We had been happy, a couple of crazy kids in love, and I had made good money running a dozer for an outfit building a housing project. I had met her in Philadelphia during one wild weekend there, and I had married her less than a month later. Her parents hadn't approved of me—her father was a doctor with big ideas for her—but that didn't bother Mary in the least.

"It's love that counts," she always said. "It isn't money. Without love you don't have anything."

She was petite and dark; it had been good to come to the apartment each day after work and find her there. That was the only real home I had ever known, the only real home I'd ever had. My father hadn't married my mother and she had left me to be raised by an aunt. The aunt tried to be nice to me but she didn't understand a growing boy. I left her right after becoming sixteen. I quit school, got a job—and found my first woman. She had been a widow in her late twenties, and she laughed at me because I was clumsy and careless.

"Another one, mister?" The bartender interrupted my thoughts.

"Why not?"

"Cripes, you can really put them away."

"Time is short."

I kept on drinking and thinking about Mary. The night she had been killed we were going home from a party at a friend's house. We had left at midnight, neither one of us feeling our drinks, and at a blind intersection a wild kid had come storming out at us in an old junk. I tried to miss him, tried to stop, but it was too late. He hit on her side of the car and piled us on the sidewalk. I knew, even before they told me, that she was dead. Later, after the funeral, I went to a lawyer but she hadn't been insured. Three weeks later I had closed the apartment and left Philadelphia. I had been on the move ever since, ripping from life what I could take, trying to forget the shreds of the past. I had made good money and tossed it away, met good girls and pushed them aside. And now I had nothing to show for any of it.

"The bus is coming in," the bartender said.

"Thanks."

"You new around here?"

"As new as they come."

"Well, thanks, and stop again."

I walked outside and down the street to where the bus had stopped, feeling the heat of the sun.

Only one person got off.

And she was a honey.

She had long white-blonde hair, and the red chemise she was wearing didn't hide the lush, full lines of her figure. She was tall, about five-seven, and from where I stood I thought her eyes were blue.

"Are you Norma Sparks?"

Her eyes were blue, a lazy blue that moved from my face down over my body.

"Who are you?"

"I asked you a question."

The bus driver got her things from the luggage carrier and piled the two suitcases on the sidewalk.

"Yes, I'm Norma Sparks."

"I was sent out to meet you."

"And who are you?"

I told her.

"It's funny my father didn't come himself."

"Your father's busy."

She seemed to accept that and she searched in her pocket for a cigarette.

"They won't let you smoke on the bus," she said.

I walked over to the suitcases and picked them up.

They were so light they didn't feel as though there were anything in them.

"The car is up the street," I said.

She walked beside me and I could smell her perfume. I could tell that it was really expensive stuff.

"Do you work for my father?"

"I did but not now."

"What happened?"

"We had a slight disagreement."

"My father is a good man," she said, "He knows his work."

I let it go. There was no point in arguing with her. We reached the car and I put the suitcases in back on top of the groceries. The interior of the car smelled of onions and celery.

"It's no Caddy," I said.

She opened the door, paused, and looked toward the bar.

"Do we have to hurry?"

"Not particularly."

She closed the door.

"I could use a drink," she said. "I never had such a hot ride in all my life."

"I thought some of the busses were air-conditioned."

"This one wasn't."

We walked up the street toward the bar. I was feeling the doubles but I could always go for more. I have a middle initial and it doesn't mean Lewis. It means "Liquor." Take a liberal amount of liquor, a whale of a lot of woman, and you can have yourself a sensational time. I glanced at her as we entered the bar and felt something surge through me. Maybe she was one of them. Maybe she was as easy as picking daisies in a farm yard.

"Back again, I see," the bartender said.

"Same day, same thing." We sat down on the stools and I looked at the girl. "What's for you?"

She opened her purse and she put a ten on the bar.

"Rum collins," she said to the bartender, Then, to me, "I'm buying this one."

"Suit yourself."

"You don't mind?"

"Why should I mind?"

"Most men do."

She crossed her legs and I watched her. She had long legs and they were well-formed.

"I'm not most men," I said.

Her smile was amused.

"Something special?"

"No, not that either."

We had two drinks and I paid for the second round.

"You a model?" I inquired.

"How did you guess?"

Our glasses were empty and I ordered a third set.

"It follows. You've got the equipment and the face and the style. If you weren't a model you'd be a singer or a dancer."

"I don't sing."

"Dance?"

"I used to. I took tap and ballet but you have to have more than just looks to get along in the modeling field."

For a second, as I listened to her, I closed my eyes. She had a sexy voice, deep and throaty, and it reminded me of Mary. Mary had a bedroom voice and it had always fascinated me.

"You staying long?" I asked.

"A couple of weeks, maybe longer. Things are slow right now and I like to visit my father whenever I get the chance. When she was alive, Mother used to travel with him but now there are just the two of us."

"Where do you work?"

"New York."

"You won't find much here in the sticks."

Her eyes were frank. "I'm not looking for anything. This is just to see my father."

"The Dell is pretty lonely."

"Is it?"

"You could get lost in the silence out there."

It was getting late and I knew that I should get back, but I didn't want to go. So I was getting forty bucks a week and my room and board—that wasn't anything that couldn't be replaced.

"Have another?"

"I'd better not. Daddy hates the smell of liquor on my breath."

"Chew up one of the onions in the car," I said. "He'll never know the difference,"

"You're not very funny."

But we had the fourth drink and took it slow. I found out she was twenty-one, had gone to college and, after quitting, went to a modeling school. She did most of her work for artists and I wondered if she posed draped or undraped. I didn't ask her and she didn't tell me. I could imagine how she would be without her clothes on and she was a pretty cool picture.

We left the bar about four-thirty and drove toward The Dell. She managed to get the window down on her side of the car and the smell of the onions wasn't quite so bad. After a couple tries I got the ventilator open and the air rushed in around our legs. The wind lifted her skirt and she pushed it down. Finally she folded the material and sat on it. But her legs were out straight and I could see a little of what I wanted to see.

"You work out here?" she asked.

"I wash the dishes and scrub the floors."

"A young man like you?"

"It's better than nothing."

We came to the detour and I continued right on through, slowing the Plymouth and listening to the springs squeak.

"You could make more working for Daddy," she said.

"I could but we don't see things the same way. I was running the shovel and what I was doing didn't suit him." I applied the brakes and crept through a deep hole. "You'll hear about it sooner or later so I might as well tell you. He got sore, boiling mad, and made a pass at me. He missed but I didn't."

"You hit him?"

"I sure did. Right smack in the eye."

"But he's so much older than you are!"

"I don't care if he is. A man who isn't too old to swing isn't too old to get hit."

We didn't talk much more for the rest of the way and I knew she was angry at me. I didn't blame her very much. I should have told Sparks to go to hell and walked off the job.

The Sparks girl wasn't the only one who was angry at me; Mrs. Sprague was hopping, and she came out to the car as soon as I stopped in back of The Dell.

"Where have you been? Don't you know you've got the meat in there for supper? You think I cook those prime ribs in a couple of minutes?"

"You get what you pay for," I told her, "and you don't pay much."

I unloaded the groceries and meat from the car, carried them into the kitchen, and piled them near the door that led into the storeroom.

"Get Miss Sparks settled," the old lady told me. "And then come back here and get to work."

"Okay."

I took the suitcases down to the empty cabin and the girl followed me.

"I'm sorry if I got you in any trouble," she said.

"That's all right."

"I wish there were something I could do to straighten it out."

I opened the door to the cabin and held it for her. She slid by me and the perfume crept up into my nostrils.

"Forget it," I said. "She has to complain about something."

The cabin wasn't much, about the same as mine. There was a big double bed, a couple of chairs and a desk without a lamp. Somebody had painted one of the walls blue and the other three were white. A picture hung over the bed, one of those modern things which looks just as well upside down as right side up.

"Thank you," she said.

She wanted to give me a tip but I wouldn't take one from her. There was only one thing I wanted from her and she wasn't ready to come across with that yet.

"It was a pleasure," I told her.

She was unzipping her dress when I left.

Pity. I could have done it for her faster and better.

3

The next morning the old woman rode my back because I was half an hour late.

"This is no game," she told me, "You either do what I want you to do or you can pick up your pay."

There was a mountain of dishes and it took me until nine-thirty to get them done. No sooner had I finished them and started scrubbing the kitchen floor than Linda Sprague came in with her husband. They sat at a little table in one corner and Frank began yelling for a couple of eggs.

"Your wife can fix them," his mother said. "I've got to look at the sump pump in the cellar."

The night before she had been down to the cellar twice, fooling with the float on the sump pump. Water seeped down from the mountain, collected in a barrel and the pump pushed it out into a drain. I told her that I would do it, because the stairs were so steep leading down to the basement, but she promptly told me that she knew more about it than I did and that I should tend to my own work.

I scrubbed the floor, working around the table and where Linda stood at the stove, and I got a good look at this Frank. He had a thin face, long, skinny arms and his eyes were so pale there was hardly any color to them at all. He smoked one cigarette after the other and when he finally got the eggs he said they weren't the way he wanted them.

"You're a hell of a cook," he told his wife.

She sat down and drank her coffee and said nothing. She was wearing tight pink shorts and a halter that wasn't any bigger than the law allowed.

"You know Frank?" she asked me.

I said I didn't.

"Frank, this is Jerry."

He stuffed half of an egg into his mouth and chewed it up.

"Glad to know you," he said.

"Same here."

"You know anything about cars?"

"Not much."

"Superchargers?"

"Nothing."

"Hell," he said.

He finished his breakfast, pushed the plate aside and said he was going out to work on his car.

"I got this charger at a steal," he boasted, looking at me. "You know how much a new one costs?"

"No."

"About three hundred. And I got this for a hundred. Secondhand." He stood up. "It'll make the Ford hum. She'll do ninety in second with that thing on it."

He walked out of the kitchen, slamming the screen door shut behind him, and Linda picked up the dishes from the table.

"More work for you," she said to me.

The old woman had just come up from the cellar and she was breathing heavily.

"You do them yourself," she said. "What do you think this is around here?"

Linda made a face and ran some water in the sink.

"I wouldn't know," she said.

"You can't just park here and not do anything."

"What about Frank?"

"You leave Frank out of this. Frank is working on his car and trying to learn things."

Linda shrugged.

"What about me?"

"You can help me wait on tables at breakfast and at noon and at night. I can't do everything."

"I didn't say you could."

The door opened and closed out front. Mrs. Sprague wiped her face on her apron.

"I'm getting older," she said. "You ought to understand that."

She limped toward the front of the building and I squeezed the dirty water out of the mop into the scrub pail.

"You've got a job," I said to Linda.

"Lucky me."

"The tips you'll get you can put in your ear."

"And the pay I'll get I can stick in the same place."

"Somebody in your family has to work."

"Don't remind me."

The dishes required only a few moments and she left the kitchen heading in the direction her husband had gone. Pretty soon I could hear them talking and arguing, but I couldn't hear what they said. I walked to one of the windows and looked out. He had the hood up on the car and he was doing something with the motor. She was standing in the sun near one of the fenders, and all I could think of was a ripe, red berry that somebody should pick.

Mrs. Sprague kept me busy for the rest of the morning, peeling potatoes and carrots and doing the floor in the dining room. By the time I was through the men had come down from the job, all of them hungry. Some of them kidded me about what I was doing, but I didn't pay any attention to them.

Norma Sparks ate sitting with her father. She spoke to me when I passed near their table, but Sparks didn't speak. His right eye was black and part of the cheek below it was swollen.

The men stayed longer than usual, fooling around with their food, and I guess it was because of Linda. She hopped tables in her shorts and halter and she got the orders mixed up.

"I hate this," she told me.

"I don't blame you."

"Frank is the one who should work, not me. All he does is mess with that car. Now he's got it apart so that you couldn't start it with a team of horses."

"Wait until he's finished with it."

"I can't wait," she said crossly. "Honest to heaven, I can't wait. What do I care about an old supercharger, or whatever that is?"

"Isn't he going to eat?"

"Eat? Are you kidding? The only meal he eats is breakfast and after that he drinks beer. By the time the afternoon is over he won't know where he is."

She didn't have to help me with the dishes, but she did. I argued with Mrs. Sprague again about putting them on the drainboard and scalding them but she said they had to be dried, so we dried them.

"You can't change old ideas," Linda said.

"Not easily."

"It's like that pump down in the cellar. You'd think she was going steady with it."

I got out of the kitchen about two o'clock and stopped to see how Frank was coming along with the car. He was covered with grease and sweat.

A small tub of partially melted ice containing several cans of beer sat on the ground by the left front wheel. Several empties were also scattered around on the ground.

"Have one?"

"Thanks."

"Help yourself."

I opened a can and drank some of the beer. He had removed the manifold from the motor and the charger was nearly in place.

"She'll hum," he said.

"Probably."

"She'll go like a shot out of a gun."

He put the tools aside and went for the beer. He drank three cans while I was standing there.

"Another?"

"No, thanks."

"Nice and cold," he said. "Anything I hate, boy, it's warm beer."

He was on his fourth can when I departed. His wife was probably right—he would get plastered to the ears and wouldn't know up from down or right from left.

I rounded the building, started for my cabin, and came up short. She was on the grass just off the road, and she was lying on her stomach. She was wearing a black bathing suit, a one-piece thing that was low in the back, cut almost down to her hips. At first I thought her eyes were closed but then I saw they were open and that she was staring at me.

"You like the sun?"

"Like a cat," Linda said.

She rolled over and sat up and I saw that the suit was just as low in front as it was in back. She hitched at the straps and pulled it up, but it didn't go very far. She was too big for the suit, and she must have known where I was looking.

"The slave get a break?" she asked.

"Two hours. Big deal."

"Sit down."

I sat.

"Got a cigarette?"

I gave her a cigarette and held a match for her.

"I never thought you would take the job," she said. "It was just a gag."

"A guy has to work somewhere."

"But washing dishes?"

"It's no worse than you waiting on tables."

She frowned.

"I guess you're right," she admitted. "Neither of us got much of a bargain."

"You can't say that about your husband."

"Oh, him."

"He has his beer and he fools with the car. What more could he want?"

"It's all his mother's fault," she said. "If she told him to go out and get to work he would have to do something."

She brought her legs up under her body, and they bulged slightly, showing the muscles. I wondered if they were half as strong as they looked.

"How'd you get along before?"

"She sent him money."

"Did she?"

"She wrote every week and every time she sent a letter she sent a check. I blame her for his not growing up." She paused. "We were lucky to get along," she said. "We lived in cheap rooms and ate soup and it was hell. I even had a good watch that he pawned and I never got it back."

I felt sorry for her. She was a good kid, all woman, and she deserved something better than she had gotten.

"You should have known all that when you married him," I said.

"I should have known those things? A guy puts on an act when he's running after a girl and as soon as the knot is tied he becomes a bum. He worked for my father and my father said he was a bum but I didn't believe my father."

"Your father have a garage?"

"A big one."

"How come Frank didn't stay there?"

"His drinking. He would go out for lunch and not come back until four o'clock. You can't get away with that in any business. And you can't drink on the job. You drink on the job and half of the things you do aren't right. He ruined a new Buick, putting in pistons or something, and that was the end."

"Funny you stuck with him."

"What else could I do?"

"There's always something else you can do."

"Well, I didn't do it."

We were there for about an hour, talking, and the front of the suit got lower and lower. She hitched it a couple of times but then she gave up on the thing. She stretched out her legs and lay flat on her back, covering her eyes with one arm. The sweat stood out all over me. Any man who had this kind of merchandise in front of him and didn't know what to do with it was out of his mind.

"The window won't go up in our cabin," she said.

"It won't?"

"No, it's stuck or something."

"Why doesn't Frank fix it?"

"Don't make me laugh. The only thing Frank is interested in is that old car."

"The only thing?"

She uncovered her eyes and looked up into my face. "The only thing," she said.

I lit a couple of cigarettes and gave her one. We were still smoking when her husband came around the corner of the building.

"It's all together," he said. He didn't seem to mind that I was there with his wife or that the suit she wore didn't hide much of what she owned. "Now to try it out."

"That's good," I said.

Linda didn't say anything.

"You have any money?" he asked her.

"Not me."

"Guess I'll have to tap the old lady for some more."

"I guess you will."

He had washed his hands and arms in gasoline and the fumes were all around him.

"You coming with me?"

She shook her head. "Not in that car I won't, Frank. You've been drinking and something is bound to happen."

"Nothing's going to happen."

"Just the same."

He turned and walked away but he wasn't walking very straight. He was in no condition to drive, but that was none of my business. If he wanted to break his neck, it would be his neck he'd be breaking.

"I could fix that window for you," I said to Linda.

"Would you?"

"Why not?"

She didn't have to go with me, but she did. She walked ahead of me, her hips rolling, the bathing suit up high and snug on her thighs.

"I'm a nuisance," she said.

"No, you're not."

"First your cigarettes and now the window."

It was hot inside the cabin, blistering hot, and I wondered how she had managed to sleep there the night before.

"We left the door open all last night," she said in answer to my unasked question.

There was a bee making a racket against the window, and I killed that with an old newspaper. Her things were on the bed where she had left them and a garter belt and a bra hung over the back of one chair. I didn't see any panties and I speculated about whether or not she ever wore them. Then I remembered the wash she had been hanging out and I realized that she did.

"It's just stuck with some old paint," I said, working on the window. "I couldn't budge it."

The window came up hard, scraping, but I got it all the way to the top. I put it down and up a few times and after a while it began to work more easily.

A car started up, its motor racing, and I knew it was the Ford.

"Frank must have gotten what he wanted," I said.

"He always does."

I looked at the way she leaned against the door casing, watching me. "Always?"

"Just about."

"He's lucky," I said. "And he doesn't have sense enough to know it."

I should have gotten out of there, should have left her alone, and I had every intention of doing that. Most of what happened was due to her standing where I had to brush up against her to get by.

I never did get by.

"You're hurting me," she said.

I knew I was hurting her. I had her by the arms and I was pulling her in close to me. The need for her was overpowering and I couldn't stop myself.

"You know why I took this stinking job," I breathed.

She didn't try to avoid my mouth and her lips were hot and wet.

"Maybe I do," she whispered.

"And I know why you wanted me to."

"Maybe you do."

I carried her inside the cabin and kicked the door shut.

"I'm a married woman," she said.

"Does it matter?"

"It would if I was in love with him."

"But you're not?"

"You know better than to ask that," she said, kissing me. "You've seen him and you know."

A man can endure just so much.

I didn't keep her waiting long.

We both had our share of the flesh that afternoon.

4

That night after dinner Linda brought the dishes from the tables to the kitchen. The old lady was out front, talking with some of the men, and this left us alone by the sink.

Every time she came out with a plate I grabbed her and kissed her.

"You're crazy," she laughed.

"I'm nuts about you."

"And I'm a married woman."

"What difference does that make?"

"I've got a husband and that's a difference."

"A husband you don't love."

"Who says so?"

"I say so."

"And who are you?"

"The guy who just pleased you, that's who I am."

It was wrong, all wrong, but when you've got a yen you don't stop to think about that. All I could think of was how she had been, how she would be again, and how much I wanted her. Even with Mary it hadn't been as bad. Mary had been a little cool, distant, and it hadn't been until she was in bed and the lights were out that she fully came alive. This girl, this Linda, was alive all the time. I looked at her and I didn't care whether I did the dishes or anything else. I looked at her and there was just one thing that I wanted to do.

The old lady had found a uniform for her, something that another girl had left behind, and it was pink and tight. It made me a little angry to know that the other men out there were sizing her up, seeing as much as I could see. There wasn't one of them, unless it was Sparks, who wouldn't give a right arm to get what I had gotten from her. And it made me sore, wondering if she would let somebody else do the same thing as I had done.

There had been pork for dinner that night and the plates were particularly greasy. I had to change the water in the sink three times and when Linda started to dry she said some of the stuff wasn't too clean.

"The hell with it," I said. "This isn't the Astor."

I finished washing the silverware and then I helped her dry. She was close to me and she smelled good and she didn't move away when I kissed her on the cheek.

"We'd better be careful," she said.

"Why?"

"His mother will come around that corner and if she sees you doing that it'll be the end of your job."

"Small loss."

It was her turn to pull my head down and kiss me.

"But I want you here," she said. "I want you near me all the time." Her mouth moved against my lips. "Whether you know it or not, you do things to me."

We cut it out. It was a good thing we did because the old lady came out a couple of seconds later. She had one hand up to her forehead and she squinted against the bright light over the sink.

"I'm going to bed," she said. "I feel something terrible."

I figured she was paying me and that I ought to be interested in her troubles.

"What's the matter?"

"I've got a splitting headache."

"It's stuffy in here," I said. "If you had an exhaust fan put in over the stove it wouldn't be so bad."

"They cost money."

"Well, I haven't seen anybody giving them away."

"A lot of money. Even from Sears they cost too much."

She was a lost cause and I gave up.

"I'd like to use the car," I said.

"For what?"

"Maybe ride into town."

"That didn't go with the job," she said. "I didn't promise you could use the car or anything."

"So forget about it."

"You'd be better off getting your sleep than rambling around."

"Okay, okay."

She picked up a glass, put in a teaspoon of bicarb and ran the glass half full of water. She drank the mixture and made a face.

"It always helps me," she explained.

I didn't say anything.

"You can use the car," she said, turning away. "But put gas in it and pay for the gas yourself."

I glanced at Linda.

"Thanks," I said.

She limped toward the door that led upstairs.

"Don't ask me more than once a week or you won't get it," she said.

"I won't," I answered.

She went up the stairs, making a considerable amount of noise, and I threw the dish towel aside.

"We can get out of here for a little while," I said to Linda.

"You can but I can't."

"Why not?"

"You're forgetting about Frank. He'll be home pretty soon, drunk and nasty, and I'd better be around."

"What if you aren't?"

"You don't know Frank. He'd wait up for me and beat the devil out of me."

"Not with me backing you up."

"With you backing me up it would be even worse. You'd get into trouble with him and his mother. Then I wouldn't be able to see you at all."

It was disappointing. I had hoped we could go into town, have a few drinks and live it up. But she was right, of course. You fool with dynamite and it can go off in your hands.

"All right," I said.

I pulled the stopper on the sink and the water went out slowly. One of these days the drain would plug up completely and I would have a real mess on my hands.

"Kiss me, you big bum."

I kissed her and she clung to me, moving her head from side to side, burning the kiss in. I brought my hands to the front, lifting against her, and she began to shudder. I pushed her to the sink and bent her back. She began to tell me not to, not there, that we shouldn't.

"Hell," I said as the front door opened and closed.

I let go of her and she straightened up, tossing her head and fluffing out her hair.

"Boy," she whispered. "Boy, you certainly can't wait."

"Did you want to?"

She smiled. "No," she said. "I didn't want to."

Somebody came around the counter and approached the kitchen door.

"You back there, Mrs. Sprague?"

I thought it was one of the men from the job.

"Mrs. Sprague has gone to bed," I said.

"Oh, hell."

The man who came into the kitchen wasn't one of the men from the job. He was middle-aged, wore a dark blue suit and was carrying a briefcase.

"Gone to bed? Isn't it a little early?"

"She didn't feel well."

He took out a cigar but he didn't light it.

"That's too bad," he said. "I wanted to see her."

"Anything I can do?"

"No. It's personal. You just work here, don't you?"

"Yeah, I just work here."

"I'm her daughter-in-law," Linda said. "If there's any message I'll take it."

"Will you?"

"Of course."

The man was looking at her the way I suspected the men had looked at her during dinner. The pink uniform was so close to her skin that it made her look almost naked. Her breasts were full and round and the way the material pressed up to her thighs didn't leave much to the imagination.

"I'm from the oil company," the man said.

"Oh, yes."

"You know we've been talking to Mrs. Sprague about her property?"

"She wrote Frank and told him about it. Frank is my husband."

The man didn't seem to notice that I was there at all.

"We want to put up a gasoline station and snack bar. With this new highway going up through the mountains this is the best location for miles."

He was right about that. To the north there was nothing but rocks and trees and to the south most of the land was inclined to be swampy. Mrs. Sprague had the only desirable spot for miles.

"We offered her thirty-five thousand," the man said, "but she turned us down. We've been over it again, trying to be fair, and we're willing to go as much as fifty thousand."

"I see," Linda breathed.

The man patted his briefcase.

"You tell her that, will you? Tell her that fifty thousand is our top and final offer?"

"I'll tell her."

"Why she's stubborn about it is beyond me. Sure, she's been here for many years and it's part of her life and all that, but with that kind of money at her age she could retire and take it easy." He returned the cigar to his pocket. "I wish somebody would offer me the same kind of money for the place I own. I'd sign the papers so fast they wouldn't be able to read my signature."

"I'll tell her," Linda said again.

The man nodded. "See what you can do with her, will you? Maybe she needs a little prodding."

"Maybe."

"It's a young fortune, that's what it is."

The man gave Linda his card and left. After he was gone I lit a cigarette, blew out the match and dropped the match into the garbage.

"I get it now," I said. "I see why both of you came back here. The old lady is going to fall into a bundle of change."

"If she sells."

"Why wouldn't she?"

Linda shrugged her shoulders—and when that woman shrugged her shoulders she shrugged all over.

"She says it's all she's ever done and she wouldn't know what to do with herself if she did."

"That's not reasonable."

"It is to her. She's worked here ever since Frank's father died and she wants to go on working."

"If she feels that way you're both wasting your time."

"She's getting older."

"What do you mean by that?"

"She could die."

"She looks pretty healthy to me."

"Those steps down to the cellar are pretty steep. She goes up and down them half a dozen times a day. She could take a header and that would be that."

"Yeah, that's right."

"It's happened to other people before."

I saw it then or I thought I saw it. Frank was hanging on to his mother because she might be worth some money someday; and Linda was hanging onto Frank for the same reason.

"Where does that leave the two us?" I wanted to know.

"Right where we are."

"Nothing else?"

She came into my arms and tried to kiss away what was in my mind. But it didn't work.

"We've got each other," she said.

"Having each other this way isn't enough."

"What would be enough?"

"Getting married."

"I'm already married."

"You could get a divorce. You don't love him, do you?"

"I stopped loving him a long time ago."

"So?"

"But if he's got anything coming to him I want part of it. I've earned part of it."

"Money isn't everything."

"It's a lot with me."

"I thought your father owned a big garage."

She put her head against my chest and began to cry. "I lied to you," she said. "We never had anything. Daddy was just the shop foreman and nothing else. He made good money, nice money, but he never got home with any of it. He drank and ran with women. My mother had to take a job in a factory to keep us going. I was working in the same factory when I met Frank. I thought he was different, decent, and I married him. He turned out to be my father all over again. Only instead of women—though there have been some of them—his craze was cars."

She kept talking, almost blubbering, and I didn't know what to say. We were of the same cloth, both of us small people, and this money had become the biggest thing in her life. I could understand it—and at the same time I couldn't. You have to have money to buy the things you need, but money doesn't assure happiness. She was living with a man she didn't love, staying up with him, probably going to bed with him, and it made about as much sense as buying a new hat and stomping on it.

"Cut it out," I said finally. "Cut it out!"

"I'm—I'm sorry."

"That's okay. This won't get you any place. Neither you nor Frank can touch a thing she's got—not a thing—and you've got to realize that. And what if he did get the money? It would only go into cars or some other junk. You wouldn't see a dime of it."

"Yes, I would. I'd make him."

"How?"

"I just would."

It didn't make sense, any of it, so I stopped arguing with her. I started kissing her, shoving her body back over the sink again, tasting her tears; but she didn't respond. She was like a corpse lying there in my arms.

"We mustn't," she said.

"Why not?"

"She sleeps right over this room. She'll hear us."

"Not if she's asleep."

"She wouldn't be asleep with a headache."

"There's always my cabin."

She shook her head.

"Not tonight. What if Frank comes back?"

"He won't. He's on the town."

"No, he's just trying out the car."

I tried to get her to go to the cabin with me but she wouldn't. In a way, even though I wanted her, I was glad. I had to get away by myself and think this over. There was something big here, big as the mountains around the valley, but I wasn't sure what it was. She had come back here with Frank and, one way or another, it was obvious they were going to try and get what Mrs. Sprague had. The old lady wasn't terribly old and she wasn't sick; but those steps down to the cellar were steep and if she ever slipped …

"Let's go away together," I said. "Let's go tonight."

She looked deep into my eyes.

"Are you insane? Where would we go?"

"I don't know."

"What would we do?"

"What does anybody do? I'd get a job."

"You're forgetting Frank."

"No, I'm not. Divorce him. Marry me. You wouldn't be sorry."

Her lips crept up to my mouth.

"I love you," she sobbed. "I love you terribly but don't change me or try to change me. I have to do this my way or not at all. You have to understand, Jerry. You have to!"

"Okay. I'll try."

I buried my mouth in her lips and brought her body to me. She was alive and moving this time and when I tore her uniform, she didn't tell me to stop.

"Let's go to your cabin," she whispered.

"Weakening?"

"I'm weak, honey."

The car was closer than the cabin, and we didn't feel like walking very far.

5

For a long time after Linda left I sat brooding in the car. Marriage to Mary had been a luxury of living; soft, warm, and carefully regulated so there would be no danger of children. This with Linda was raw and violent, sex at its fullest. She gave of herself until there was nothing more to give, demanded until there was nothing more to demand. It was a rare experience to know such a woman, to have such a woman love me. The others who had said they loved me hadn't loved me. That had been sex, too, but nothing like this. This was beyond all reason, all thought.

But where did I go from here? What did I do? She was married and she couldn't be mine completely as long as she were married to that idiot hot rodder Frank. Of course, if it weren't for the money—but there was the money. Fifty thousand, perhaps more. It was a lot and the stakes were high. I wondered what I would do, how I would react, if I were as close to that much money myself. I didn't know. No one could know. You had to have it staring you in the face before you could possibly know.

Fifty grand. Maybe more.

I started the car and switched on the lights.

Fifty grand.

Fifty grand and whoever got it wouldn't have to worry.

I backed up, swung the car and started around the building. The lights probed the darkness of the night.

I was almost to the road when I saw her. She was standing there, her face white in the glare of the lights. I saw the suitcases on the ground beside her.

When I got to her I stopped the car.

"Hello, Norma." The window still wouldn't go down and I had to open the door to speak to her. "What's up?"

"I'm leaving."

"So I see."

"The cab was supposed to be here a long time ago."

The engine of the Plymouth began to miss and I pulled out the hand choke until it idled evenly.

"You won't get a cab out here," I said.

"But they promised."

"The promise of a cab driver in Sayville is about as good as the promise of a dead man. Once they find out that they've got to come over the construction, they write it off."

"What am I going to do?"

"You can ride in with me."

"Could I?"

"Well, naturally."

"Oh, thank you!"

She came around the front of the car carrying the bags and crossing the lights. She was all figure, all girl.

"You're a life saver," she said.

I boosted the bags up over the seat and put them in back. She got in and slammed the door shut. The dash light was on and I got a good glance at her legs. Linda had fine legs but nothing like these; these legs were as long and as brown as a shock of wheat.

"Short stay," I said, putting the car in gear.

"Yes, it was."

"Shortest couple of weeks on record."

She remained silent and I guessed that she didn't want to talk about it. We rode along, bumping over the holes and when I offered her a cigarette she accepted.

"You'll hear about it anyway," she said.

"About what?"

"About me."

"You do something wrong?"

"According to my father I did. According to my father, I'm the biggest slut in the county."

"Your father isn't always right."

"He isn't this time." She smoked thoughtfully for a moment. "Do you take any of the men's magazines?"

"No. I don't take any magazines at all. The last time I bought a magazine was so long ago I can't remember."

"You know the kind I mean? The ones with pictures of pretty girls and risqué stories?"

"I've seen them around but I don't read them."

"A lot of places ban them."

"I suppose they do."

"There isn't anything wrong with them, not really. The stories aren't exactly dirty and there are lots of movie posters around of girls with less clothes on."

"I wouldn't know."

"Am I boring you?"

"No, you're not boring me."

"I feel as though I have to talk to somebody."

"Go ahead and talk."

That perfume of hers filled the car and when I looked down the dash light showed me some more of her legs.

"I told you I was a model, didn't I?"

"That's what you said."

"I work for several artists. Sometimes they paint me with my clothes on and sometimes my clothes are off. Does that surprise you?"

"Not much."

"The greatest paintings of all times are of nudes."

"Are they?"

"Yes, they are, but you can't tell my father that. I tried to explain it to him but he got so mad and called me a slut." She laughed shortly. "You did an awful job on his eye. He can hardly see out of it tonight."

"Is that so?"

"For me it was too bad that he could see out of either one of them. One of the men had bought one of these magazines and he was passing it around and there I was as big as life—and just as naked."

"Tough."

"I didn't even know it was going to be in there. Once an artist pays you he can do what he wants to with the picture."

"So he sold it?"

"What else was he supposed to do with it?"

"I don't know."

We cleared the construction, got on the concrete and I coaxed the Plymouth up to forty.

"He was certainly angry," she said.

"I can bet."

"He said I had disgraced him, but I don't think I did. There's nothing wrong with having a beautiful body."

I made a mental note to get hold of that magazine and see what she looked like.

"So he kicked you out?"

"He said I could go back to the city."

"Are you?"

"No, I'm not. I'm staying right in Sayville. I'll stay there until he sees things my way. I won't go off with him feeling the way he does."

"I don't know if there are any artists in Sayville."

"I don't care. I've worked in diners and stores before, waiting on people, and I can do it again."

I felt two things for her: pity and admiration. She had plenty of guts and her old man had no business feeling the way he did. What was wrong with her posing in the nude? A lot of girls did it, even famous ones. Again I thought of that magazine and wished that I had a copy. She must be something, all right.

We approached Sayville along the straight stretch that bordered the river, and the lights of the town reflected against the night sky.

"You going to a hotel?"

"Is there a good one?"

"I don't know if they're any good or not but there are a couple. And three or four motels."

"Make it one of the hotels."

"Okay."

After we got to town we cruised around for a while and she eventually settled on The Benson House. The Benson House wasn't the newest of the hotels but it had a clean appearance. And there was a bar. The room was only five bucks a night, with bath, and the woman at the desk said she could have it cheaper if she stayed by the week.

"For four," the woman said.

"I'll take it."

She paid a week in advance and the woman said she was sorry there wasn't a bellhop around to carry up the suitcases. I had an idea they didn't have a bellhop and that they had never so much as seen one.

"It's okay," I said. "I'll carry them up."

The woman's look was unhappy.

"Don't you stay. I don't allow—"

"I won't."

The room was on the second floor, a single with a narrow bed and old furniture, but it seemed clean. I put the suitcases on the luggage rack and Norma thanked me.

"You've been most kind," she said.

"Forget it."

"I'd still be out there waiting for that cab."

"That's for sure."

I didn't have anything to do, I wanted a drink, and the bar was just downstairs.

"Buy you a drink?" I inquired.

She thought about it for a moment.

"I guess I could use one. That business with my father left me up in the air." She looked at herself in the mirror. "Do you think I should change?"

"You look fine."

"Do I?"

"Yeah, fine."

"I'm putting you to a lot of trouble," she said.

"Not me."

"First I almost cry on your shoulder and now I sponge on you for drinks."

"Would I ask you if I felt that way?"

Her gaze was direct.

"You might," she said. "I think you're that kind."

"What kind?"

"The kind who doesn't know what he wants."

I laughed. "You've got a fifty-fifty chance of being right."

The bar downstairs was a horseshoe-shaped thing and there were only two men sitting at one end of it. They were talking about bass fishing and the right lures to use and they were far from being in complete agreement.

"Double rye," I told the bartender.

"Make mine the same," Norma said.

We drank and listened to the fishermen for a while and then she started to talk about herself. She had wanted to be a model ever since she was in her teens—not an actress or a television star, just a model—but she had found New York a tough place. For high fashion modeling a girl had to be as skinny as a dollar bill in a clip joint; what she had didn't fit that description at all.

"I'm built too large for that," she said.

She had worked in a lingerie house for a while but the place had closed and she found herself out of work. An offer had come from an artist and she had taken him up on it.

"At first it wasn't nudes," she said. "They wanted me to do them but I wouldn't. And then I just drifted into it. I found myself wearing less and less and after a while not wearing anything at all didn't bother me. I could strip in front of an artist and not even blush. Anyway, it's business with them. They look upon a model as a butcher does his meat."

"Some meat."

"Don't get sarcastic."

"I didn't mean to be."

We had five or six drinks, all doubles, and we were both feeling them. We sat close at the bar, our thighs touching every once in a while. The fishermen were still arguing and they didn't pay any attention when I tried to kiss her on the cheek. She wouldn't let me.

"Don't do that," she said.

"Why not?"

"You know why not."

"I wish I did."

Her eyes locked with mine.

"Do you want me to tell you?"

"If you would."

She polished off the drink and the bartender came over and poured another one.

"You didn't see me tonight, but I saw you," she said.

"When?"

"Can't you guess?"

"No."

"When you took that girl to the car." Her gaze never wavered. "She seemed very willing and so were you."

"I see."

"I doubt if you do. She's married, Jerry, and nothing good can ever come of it."

I was annoyed. "So one of your pastimes is peeking?"

"I wasn't peeking. I was carrying my stuff out to the road and I saw you." Her voice became softer. "I didn't mean it that way, Jerry. Honest I didn't. Only you seem like a nice guy and I don't think you should be caught in the middle of a mess."

"Let me worry about that."

"It is your worry."

We didn't last long after that. The fishermen left, we had stopped drinking and the bartender said he wanted to close.

"There's a place down the street," he said.

But we didn't go to the place down the street. I walked her up to her room, unlocked the door and she took the key from my hand.

"Don't come in," she said. "I couldn't trust myself tonight."

Again I tried to kiss her and again she rebuffed me.

"Why not?" I demanded.

She patted my arm and blew me a kiss.

"Because I'm lonely," she said. "And so are you. Only you don't know it," she added. "You're the loneliest man in Sayville."

I was drunk and I was angry at her.

"To hell with you," I said, turning away.

"You don't mean it," she told me softly. "You don't mean it at all. Tomorrow you'll know you don't mean it."

I didn't find any gasoline stations open in Sayville so I couldn't get any gasoline. As a matter of fact, I didn't look very hard. The old lady could afford it and I couldn't. Liquor costs money.

A mile outside of town I saw the red lights of a police car and a lot of cars pulled over to the side of the road. I pulled up and stopped.

"Must have been going a hundred," somebody said as I got out of the car.

"Drunk," somebody else said. "Drunk and driving a souped-up pile of junk."

I walked forward until I came to the mess. The Ford had plunged into a large oak tree, rebounded across the highway, gone through a guard rail and down a low bank. They were just taking him out of the wreckage when I got there. No one had to tell me that Frank Sprague was dead.

I turned and made my way back to the Plymouth. Frank was dead and Linda was a widow. There was no reason now why she couldn't belong to me. No reason at all.

I drove past the scene of the accident and on down the highway. When I got to the construction I slowed the car and then, just as I thought of something, I almost stopped.

The Dell was worth fifty thousand dollars.

And Linda was the only relative Mrs. Sprague had now.

PART TWO

6

The ice in the tub had long since melted but I found six cans of beer in the water and I carried these into the kitchen. I opened one, sat down at the table and made a face as I took a long drink. Pretty soon the cops would be coming out and the death of her son would hit old lady Sprague right between the eyes. I wondered what she would think of his hot rodding now.

I was on the third can of beer when a car pulled up into the driveway. I finished off the open can and threw the empties into the garbage. Then I walked to the back door and flipped on the light.

A trooper came up onto the porch.

"Mrs. Sprague here?" he inquired.

"Yeah, but she's in bed."

He entered the kitchen.

"Know where she sleeps?"

"Upstairs."

"Her son was just killed in an accident down the road."

"I know. I saw it."

"The accident?"

"No. What was left of the car."

"There wasn't much."

"You can say that again."

"How come you didn't tell Mrs. Sprague?"

"I mind my own business."

The trooper noticed the three cans of beer on the table and frowned.

"Go up and call her, fellow."

"Okay; sure."

I left him there and walked to the stairs. The stairs were almost as steep as the ones going down cellar. There was a rope along one side and I supposed she used that to help her.

I didn't know which room she slept in so I tried all of the doors. On the third one I had luck.

"Who is it?"

"Jerry."

She groaned.

"Oh, good heavens! What do you want at this time of the night? Don't you know I've got a headache?"

She'd have more than that before she was through.

"Sorry, but there's a trooper downstairs who wants to see you."

"Me?"

"About Frank?"

"What's Frank done now?"

"Better ask the trooper. He said for me to get you."

I heard the springs squeak, followed by the sounds of slippers shuffling across the floor.

"They're always bothering him," she complained. "They did it before when he was home. A boy works on his car and where can he run it except on the road?"

I hung around to wait for her, but she told me not to, to go ahead.

"You tell that trooper I'll be right down," she said. "These cops have to stop bothering Frank."

I shrugged and walked away. The cops wouldn't bother Frank again; the undertaker would.

I descended the stairs, and told the trooper that she would be along in a few minutes.

The trooper sat down at the table and regarded the beer as though he were willing to have a can. I didn't offer him one.

"Crazy driving," the trooper said. "The speedometer needle was lying right in the bottom of the glass."

"He had it souped-up. He said it would do ninety in second."

"Well, it won't do it again."

I considered having a beer but rejected the idea. I had had enough to drink.

The old woman came down, wearing a faded red robe, and her hair was a mess. She didn't give the trooper a chance to say a word.

"You've got some nerve waking me up at this time of the night," she began angrily. "What's it this time? The mufflers on Frank's car too loud? Mister, you should have heard some of those trucks that used to go by here, bellowing and blasting. Why don't you give those fellows tickets? Why do you pick on Frank? You picked on him when he was living home and now I suppose you're up to it again. Aren't you proud of yourself?"

"Look," the trooper said.

"No. You look. If there's a fine I'll pay the fine but I think it's a rotten shame. What's this country coming to, anyway? If it isn't right to have that hot rod stuff why do they sell it?"

She kept tearing into the trooper, telling him that she would get a lawyer, and he just stood there and waited. A couple of times he tried to say something but she was too much for him. Finally, however, she ran out wind and he got his chance.

"Your son is dead," he said gently. "His car hit a tree and he was killed instantly."

Her face fell apart in a thousand pieces. First her chin trembled and then her eyes clouded. She reached for a chair, almost missed it, and sat down.

"Oh, Lord," she breathed. "Oh, Lord!"

I wanted to say something to her to console her, but I'm not much good at that sort of thing. Death reaches all of us at one time or another. There just isn't much you can say. A few hours earlier he had been alive and drinking and now he was dead. The law of averages sometimes runs out.

"Where is he?" she wanted to know, trying to control herself.

"In the ambulance. We didn't know where you'd want him taken."

She thought about that for a little while.

"Mr. Cole was always a friend of the family," she said. "He buried my husband and I guess it's only right that he take care of—Frank." Tears were streaming down her face. "I can't believe it. I can't. He was so pleased with what he had done to the car and he said he was going to get a job. He was going to Sayville in the morning to see about work."

My guess was that Frank had fed her a line, that a job had been the furthest thing from his mind. But that mattered little. What was done was done and nothing could change it.

The trooper stood up.

"I'll see that Mr. Cole is notified."

"Thank you."

"And—I'm sorry."

The trooper departed and she sat there crying. I got the opener, punched a couple of holes in a can of beer and drank it. She was having it rough, real rough.

"Somebody had better tell Linda," she said after a while.

"Yes."

She dried her eyes on one sleeve of the robe.

"Would you, Jerry?"

"Okay."

"He thought a lot of her, Frank did. I didn't like her first but now she's all I've got. All I've got," she added. "Isn't that terrible?"

"Rotten," I agreed.

"He was a good boy but I guess he was a little wild. He got that from his father. His father would do some of the strangest things."

There was no hurry about telling Linda so I had another beer. The old lady seemed not to notice.

"I want you to call Reverend Stark in Sayville. He's listed in the book. I want him to come out here and see me. I have to talk to somebody."

Of course I was somebody, but I wasn't very much help.

"What should I do first?" I asked her.

"Call Reverend Stark. He'll come. I know he will."

I left her in the kitchen and walked out front. It required only a few seconds to look up the number and I put in the call. The phone rang quite a while and just as I was about to give up a man answered. I told him what the situation was. Yes, he would come out. He would come right away.

"He'll be here," I said when I returned to the kitchen. "As soon as he can."

"Thank you, Jerry."

"What church is it?"

She rubbed at her eyes again.

"It isn't a church, not a real church. It's just a meeting hall where some of us go."

"Sort of independent?"

"You could call it that, yes. We only have about fifty members and sometimes I wonder how he sticks it out. When my husband was alive I used to go every Sunday but after the work started on the road I got so busy I couldn't." She hesitated, her chin trembling again. "Maybe this is payment for it. Maybe this is payment for me putting everything ahead of being a good church member."

"Don't think of it that way."

"I can't help it."

I took the last can of beer and lit a cigarette.

"I'll go tell Linda," I said, starting for the door.

"You'd better. And—Jerry?"

"Yeah?"

"Can you cook?"

"Don't tell me you want me to do that, too."

"I just asked you."

"I can cook out of a can but that's all. Give me a can of stew and I can do a bang-up job on it."

"You must know how to fix eggs."

"You fry them, boil them or eat them raw."

She ignored the remark.

"You may have to help with the cooking tomorrow," she said. "I may not be up to it. This has hit me very hard, Jerry."

I walked out to the porch and closed the screen door after me. I would make some cook. I would be a dandy. What did she want for forty a week—a guy with four legs and six arms?

Her cabin was dark and the door was open. I knocked a couple of times, received no answer and stepped inside. After fumbling for the light switch I found it and snapped it on.

She was on the bed, her eyes closed.

She wasn't wearing a damned thing.

"Linda?"

She opened her eyes and smiled.

"I'm not asleep. I thought you would be coming."

It wasn't quite the moment to admire her but I couldn't help doing so.

"Turn out the light," she said. "And come here."

"No."

"You don't have to worry. He won't be coming back."

"I know he won't be coming back."

"He got some money from his mother and he probably found another girl. He won't be back until the money is gone or until the girl kicks him out."

I gave it to her straight.

"He's dead," I said. "He rammed a tree with that car."

She didn't seem to understand me at first.

"Dead?"

"Dead as they come. His mother wants you up at the place. She sent me down here for you."

Linda sat up and the deep breath she took didn't do her shape any harm.

"Dead," she repeated. "I can't believe it."

"The trooper just left."

She swung her legs over the side of the bed.

"How did it happen?"

"Who can say? The tree was there and so was he. He must have been going like the hammers of hell."

"That supercharger, or whatever it was?"

"I would guess."

She got to her feet and walked to the foot of the bed.

"Wait for me," she said.

I waited for her.

When she slid into the dress and I had to help her with the zipper on that. A couple of times my fingers touched her warm flesh and I wanted to crush her in my arms.

"Don't," she said as I tried to kiss her on the neck.

"Why not?"

"I didn't love him but this isn't easy. He was a human being. Everybody is entitled to live."

"Yeah."

She put on her shoes and we walked outside. I took her arm, and she didn't resist me.

"I don't know what to say to his mother," she said once.

"Don't say anything."

But she knew what to say. As soon as we were in the kitchen she exploded in a fit of tears and put her arms around the old woman. I had a feeling that she didn't mean it, that it was all front; it made me a little sick.

"I asked him not to," she said over and over again. "I asked him to leave that car alone but he wouldn't."

"I know you did."

"If only I could have made him see! If only—"

"It isn't your fault," Mrs. Sprague said. "It's more mine than yours. I gave him the money and I encouraged him. If I just hadn't given him money, made him get a job—well, what's the use? We have both lost someone we loved and it is too late to wipe that out."

They clung together, patting each other on the back.

"I loved him," Linda said.

Now you know why I was almost sick right there in the kitchen.

"I know you did, dear. I wondered if you did at first, but now I know differently. You're sweet and young and both of you had so much to live for. I'm sorry if I was mean to you, if I ever said anything sharp or wrong."

"That's all right."

"He was my life, all of my life, and now you have to take his place with me."

"I will!"

I gagged.

"We'll make out all right, Linda. You help me here with the restaurant and the cabins and you won't have any cause to worry."

"Oh, Mom, I'll help you."

The old lady broke down again.

"I'm glad you called me Mom. It's so good to hear. That's what he used to call me. Mom, he used to say. Mom this and Mom that. Oh, why did it have to happen?"

I couldn't stand any more so I left. But I didn't really blame Linda for the way she had acted. If anything should happen to the old lady she was the only living relative and the place was worth fifty thousand dollars. Anybody would have been interested.

Including me.

7

It was a terrible breakfast, one of the world's worst. Mrs. Sprague was still torn apart by her son's death and Linda didn't know which side of an egg you fried. Neither did I. The scrambled eggs stuck to the pan and those that were supposed to be sunnyside up somehow got turned over. You could call it a mess six times in a row and be right every time.

"As a cook you make a good shovel operator," Sparks told me in the dining room.

"You didn't think so yesterday."

"That was yesterday."

"And today is an exception to the rule?"

He pushed the eggs aside and chewed on the toast. I imagined that it was painful. His black eye was almost shut and the swelling extended all the way down to his mouth.

"Come back to work," he said. "And dig the way you want to dig."

"Thanks for nothing."

He was mad. "I'm giving you a break. What have you got here?"

I picked up his plate of eggs.

"You'd be surprised at what I've got here."

Back in the kitchen Mrs. Sprague was drinking coffee and staring out of the window. I got the impression that she was seeing nothing.

"You're trying," she said, "I can't ask more than that."

"It's a poor try."

"Even so."

Linda wasn't much help. She let the hot water run until it was all gone and then we had to stack the plates near the sink. I knew what would happen. The eggs would stick to the plates and we would need a crowbar to pry the stuff loose.

"I'll look at the sump pump," the old lady said.

"Let me do it for you."

She turned away from the window.

"No, you don't know how the floats work. Clean up the dining room and by that time the water will be hot again."

Sparks had left but a couple of fellows were still sitting at a table. They had a magazine.

"I knew it was her," one of them said. "I saw her face and I knew it was her. Look at that, boy!"

I pushed the broom across the floor and looked down at the picture spread before them.

"You like?" one of the guys wanted to know, glancing up.

"Not bad."

"Bad? Hell, I could go for that at high noon in the town square." He snickered. "With a crowd to watch me, even."

It was Norma Sparks, all right, and she certainly had a body.

"Can you imagine what the guy got who took this picture?" the other fellow wanted to know. "He got it good, either before or after he took the photo. No man in his right mind would let that get away from him. No wonder her old man was sore. He knew what the guy got."

"He got it," the other fellow agreed.

"And got it good."

I don't know why I did what I did but I did it. I flung the magazine from the table, sending it as far as the counter, and I hit the first man who got up. I hit him hard, cutting his upper lip and driving him the whole length of the dining room. He came away from the wall with blood streaming down his face and he plunged for the door, cursing me. The other guy didn't get up; he just sat there.

"You stinking crumbs," I told them. "You take a nice girl and rip her apart. What's the matter with you?"

When I went out to the kitchen Mrs. Sprague jumped on me.

"What was the fighting about?"

"Nothing. Just two guys getting out of line."

"I don't pay you to fight."

"I don't have to get paid to fight."

The water was lukewarm but we did the dishes. About nine o'clock a car came out from town to take Mrs. Sprague to the undertaker. She said for us to manage lunch the best we could and that she might not be back.

"The hell with her," Linda said after she was gone.

I hung the dish towels on the rack over the sink.

"You didn't talk that way last night."

Her eyes flashed. "How did you expect me to act?"

"'Act' is right. My poor eyes were dripping tears when I woke up this morning."

"Don't be wise."

"Who's wise? Not me. You hated his guts and you know it. You stayed with him for one reason and now you're hanging on to her for the same reason."

"I wasn't brought up in hell for nothing," she said. "I didn't see my mother kicked around and my father drunk and not learn from it. I learned plenty, Jerry. I learned that you take from life all that you can get."

Who was to say she was wrong? She had been his wife and if anybody had a right to what the old woman got she did.

"Who says you're going to get anything?" I wanted to know.

"Someday I will."

"When is someday?"

"Tomorrow." She shrugged. "Next week. Next month. I'm young. I can wait."

"How long?"

"You'd be surprised. Why do you think I stayed with him as long as I did? For love? Don't make me laugh. There was love at the start but when I found out what he was, the love died." Her voice rose slightly. "Died— you hear me? The way a chicken does when you chop off its head."

She had a hell of a way of putting it but I thought I knew what she meant. In the beginning there had been love and roses and all that goes with new love, but his foolishness had ended it. Now it was over, finished. All she had left was what she could get from old lady Sprague. And that was a lot. Fifty grand. Fifty grand the oil company would pay for the property. It would buy a spot on a beach in Florida and it would buy clothes and drinks. What more could a sane person want?

"What's for lunch?" I asked her. "My guess is the old lady does the weeps in town and won't be back for hours."

She shrugged again and let me tell you when she shrugged all of her moved.

"You're the cook," she said. "You tell me."

I checked the storeroom and came up with six cans of hash. The hash wouldn't go over very big with the men, but what else was I to do?

"They'll love you for that garbage," she said.

"The hell with them. You know of something better?"

"Not me."

It was about ten; most of the work was done and it wouldn't take much time to fix the hash. Maybe I would have to throw a couple of cans of peas on the stove but that would take even less time.

"Don't," she said as I went to her.

"Why not?"

"Because I don't want you to."

"It was all right before."

"That was before. What would she think of me if I got caught with you?"

"How do you mean that?"

"Any way you want to take it."

I had a desire to bruise her lips, to crush her body to me, to take her with such a savage storm that nothing else in the world would exist for her. There was no reason to be afraid, no reason to put it off, but if that were the way she felt then that was the way she felt.

"Okay," I said.

"That's being sensible."

I got a broom from the corner behind the stove and began to sweep up.

"Wear something different to hop tables in," I told her. "You go out there in that rig and somebody'll rape you."

"What about you?"

"I take only what's given to me."

"One way or the other?"

"One way or the other."

She said she was going down to the cabin for a while and I did a good job of sweeping up the floor. After I finished the kitchen I moved out to the dining room. I didn't get any further than that magazine.

She was ripe. Stacked. Wild. She had twice what most women had and she had it all over. She was posed with her arms over her head, leaning back, and she was even better than I had thought she would be. Anybody who looked at that picture could go out of his mind without half trying.

A car pulled into the driveway and I hid the magazine under the counter, behind the extra salt and pepper shakers.

The man who came in was short and he had gray hair.

"Mrs. Sprague?"

"She isn't here. She's in town, seeing about her son's funeral."

"I guess I should have known that. I was out here last night and I merely wondered if there were anything I could do."

"You must be the minister?"

"Yes, sir, I am." He hesitated. "Are you a church-goer?"

"Sorry to say but I'm not."

"You should be. Everybody should be." He reached into his pocket and took out a card. "If you are ever in Sayville and you wish to join us you will be most welcome."

"Thanks."

"It isn't a church, just a meeting hall, but we find the way of God."

"I'm sure you do."

"Tell Mrs. Sprague I will come back again."

"Okay."

As soon as he was gone I went back to that magazine. She had it, that girl; and I couldn't blame her old man for getting sore at her. A girl with a shape like that was meant for a bedroom.

Lunch didn't go over very well and the men complained about the hash. I told them they could eat it or starve; they ate it.

"That offer is still good," Sparks told me.

"I'll remember."

"I'd jack you up to four bucks an hour."

"Let me think about it."

Linda was wearing some tight-fitting black thing and all of the men looked at her. The fellow with the cut lip patted her on the fanny whenever she went past his table and after the third time she slapped him.

When lunch was over I helped her clear the tables and we did the dishes.

"Just stack them up and let them drain," I said.

"She won't like that."

"So who's doing the dishes—me or her?"

"You and me."

"Okay. Stack 'em."

Mrs. Sprague returned at two o'clock and asked me to stick around.

"I've got to get some rest," she said. "If I can."

"Go ahead."

"You can use the car tonight if you want to."

"Breaking down?"

"Trying to make up to you for what you're doing. It isn't every young man who would pitch in the way you have."

Nothing came up that afternoon and I sat in the kitchen drinking one cup of coffee after another. The offer from Sparks had me thinking. At four dollars an hour, with overtime, I could knock out two hundred a week. I had earned more on other jobs but that wasn't bad. It wasn't as bad as forty with room and board.

"Hello, Jerry."

Linda had come in and I hadn't heard her. She was wearing shorts and a halter and she had some kind of sun tan oil all over her skin.

"The grieving widow."

"Shut up."

She poured a cup of coffee and sat down opposite me. The halter was one of those things that tied in the back, no strap around the neck, and she hadn't tied it too tightly.

"Take a good look," she said.

"I am."

She stirred her coffee.

"Where's the old lady?"

"Still upstairs."

"You going to fix supper?"

"Not me. You're the woman around here."

She drank some of the coffee and pushed the cup aside.

"A lot I know about it," she said. "The only place I could get a meal is in a restaurant."

"This is a restaurant."

"Oh, stop it."

"You stop it."

She got to her feet.

"The hell with this," she said. "I'm going to get some sun."

"Get it all over."

"Fresh."

The old lady came down at four and I helped her cut up the pork chops for supper. As soon as that was done she put me to work peeling potatoes.

"I ought to pay you a little more money," she said.

"I'm not stopping you."

"You're worth fifty a week."

"I'm glad you think so."

"It isn't as much as you can make on the road."

"I'm not crying."

The money had nothing to do with it and I knew it. There was something big here, something so big that I didn't understand it, and it wasn't only Linda. Oh, I was hot for her, sure, but it was more than that. If it were only the physical urge I could have satisfied that in almost any bar. I just had no idea what was keeping me.

Supper went off that night without a hitch and I had the dishes done by seven.

"Dry them," Mrs. Sprague said.

We dried them.

Linda was wearing the uniform the old lady had given her and she got it all wet down the front. The uniform stuck to her skin and it wasn't any trick to see that she wasn't wearing underwear. While the old lady was out talking to some of the men, telling them about Frank, I tried to touch her. She told me to cut it out and I cut it out.

"You'd think you were sweet sixteen," I said.

"I don't like that."

"And I don't like you being so high and mighty."

She gathered up the dish towels.

"The other was a mistake," she said.

"Was it?"

"Let's forget it, Jerry. You found me at a moment when I was so lonely and disgusted that I didn't know what to do."

"You knew what to do, all right."

"There you go again."

"On what?"

"Sex."

I helped her hang up the towels and when I rubbed up against her she moved away from me.

"I told you not to."

"Cripes."

The old lady came back from the dining room and she said she had another headache.

"As soon as I look at that sump pump I'm going to bed."

"I'll look at it for you," I offered.

"No. You don't know the first thing about it. It's tricky and the floats have to be just right."

She left for the cellar.

"Some night she's going to take a header down those stairs," Linda said.

"And you'll fall into a piece of property worth fifty grand."

"I won't fall into it. I worked my way into it."

"Have it your way."

When the old lady returned she said the pump was running all right. She fixed some baking soda and water and gulped it down.

"Come upstairs with me," she said to Linda. "I want somebody to talk to."

"Yes, Mother."

Mother? Oh, cripes.

I changed clothes in the cabin, wished I had that copy of the magazine, and walked out to the Plymouth. There wasn't much gas in the car but enough to get into town and back. That was all I cared about.

A quarter of a mile down the road it started to rain and I turned on the windshield wipers. They didn't work. The wipers were like the rest of the car—junk. Even on fifty a week a guy could afford something better.

There was a guy stuck in the ditch and I stopped to help him out. He was drunk and I told him to let me get behind the wheel. It took only a couple of minutes to get him on solid ground and then I drove on.

No one was at the desk in the Benson House and I walked up to her room. She didn't answer my knock right away.

"Who is it?"

"The fellow who brought you here last night."

"Oh. Just a minute."

It was longer than a minute and while I was waiting I made up my mind that fooling around with her was stupid. My time might better be spent in a bar. In a bar you get drunk or you get a woman or sometimes you get both. Either one, if you feel the way I felt, is fine.

She opened the door.

"Hello," she said, smiling.

She was wearing a blue robe and it wasn't one of those loose things, believe me.

"Well, don't just stand there. Come on in."

I walked in and closed the door. I could smell her perfume and something else, something that was all woman.

"I expected you," she said.

"Did you?"

"Yes. I don't know why. I just did."

She sat down on the edge of the bed and I sat in a chair that had a spring coming up through the bottom. But I didn't pay any attention to the spring; I was too interested in what I could see of her legs.

"Get a job?" I asked her.

"This morning. Just like that."

"Fine."

"In the diner."

There was only one diner in Sayville. "Well, that's something."

She crossed one leg over the other and she was careful about how much she let me see. I saw enough, though, to remember that picture and to start sweating.

"I was working on a puzzle," she said. "Do you ever fool around with puzzles?"

My whole life since Mary's death had been a puzzle. I was still trying to figure it out.

"Seldom," I said.

She tossed something toward me and I caught it.

"Maybe you can do better than I did."

The puzzle wasn't much, just a square piece of plastic with sixteen spaces in it. There were fifteen numbers and the trick was to get the numbers in their correct order.

"You ought to be able to find something better to do than this."

"In Sayville?"

"There's the movies."

"I already saw the picture."

"You bowl?"

"Never."

I started working on the puzzle and it only took me a couple of minutes to get the numbers in the correct order.

"There you are."

"Smart."

"Not so smart. Lucky."

She got a cigarette from the night stand and lit it.

"Did you see my father today?"

"He offered me my old job back. At a raise."

"Why don't you take it?"

"I don't know."

She uncrossed and recrossed her legs and I got a better look.

"I don't know what to do about him," she said. "I hate to stay here wasting my time and I hate to go and leave him feeling the way he does."

"I saw your picture."

"Did you? What did you think of it?"

"Nice."

"It isn't the best one."

"Maybe not, but it'll do."

I had a feeling that she knew I was mentally undressing her. I doubted if I were the only one who had ever done it. Looking at her, I didn't see that robe. I saw those breasts, rich and alive, and I saw the rest of her body. I knew then why I had driven in to see her. I wanted some of that.

How do you separate feelings? What I felt for Linda Sprague was sex but it was also more than that. What I felt for this girl was sex alone. Nothing else—only raw sex. Sex that was powerful and terrible and beautiful.

"Buy you a drink," I said.

"I thought you would say that."

"And what did you think you might say if I said it?"

She smiled. "Why, I thought I might accept."

"Wait for you in the lobby?"

"You will if I get dressed."

That picture came back to me again. What could she possibly show me that I hadn't seen before?

"Okay," I said, getting up. "Five minutes?"

"Give me ten."

"Hell, you're like all women."

"Why?"

"You take twice as long as you should."

"A woman has more clothes to put on than a man."

"Does she?"

"Yes. She has—well, you know."

"How would I know?"

Our eyes met.

"A man like you would."

Down in the lobby, sitting on one of the leather chairs, I tried to get interested in the *Sayville Gazette*. I couldn't. I didn't know any of the people they wrote about and I cared less. On the back page there was a photo of a movie starlet. The caption said she would swim nude in her next picture, something to be made in France for the European market. I looked at the photo and thought of Norma Sparks upstairs. This girl only had part of what Norma had and what she had wasn't nearly as good. Not eighty percent as good.

Norma Sparks was a woman worth waiting for.

She came toward me across the lobby wearing a green sheath dress. If that dress had been pressed onto her with a hot iron it couldn't have been a better fit. It was low, clinging to her breasts, flat across the belly where it should be flat, and what her hips did to the bottom part of it was something to see.

"Well," I said, standing up.

"You like?"

"The way a thirsty man goes for a glass of water." The bar we had visited the day of her arrival in Sayville wasn't very far and we walked. More than one man stopped to stare at her. I felt like a guy who has a million dollars' worth of merchandise at a Saturday night auction. She could have anybody she wanted, anybody, and she didn't need the nude picture of her to do it.

"You wear that dress to the diner," I said, "and somebody is bound to attack you."

She didn't like that at all.

"Must you be so crude?"

"Sorry."

At the corner we had to wait for some cars to pass.

"It's my turn to be sorry," she said. "Maybe you're right. The dress is a little tight."

"A little?"

"It was a choice between this and a sack."

"I'll stick with this."

The bartender remembered us and he set up a double rye for me. Norma ordered a rum collins and while the guy was making it she asked for a cigarette. I held the light for her and she kept looking into my face in a curious sort of way.

"You're a funny one," she said.

"Am I?"

"You're rough and you're not. You try to act the tough guy, say things that most men wouldn't say. But I don't think that is the real you at all. I think it's a shell."

"Go on."

She tasted the rum collins and told the bartender that it was good.

"Have you ever been married, Jerry?"

"Didn't I tell you I had been?"

"You may have. I don't remember."

"She was killed in an auto accident."

"How awful!"

The double rye went down easily.

"She was a good kid," I said.

"Pretty?"

"Reasonably so."

"Not beautiful?"

"Not the way you are."

The bartender was busy and we had to wait a while for our second round. Finally he took care of us.

"What did you think of my picture in the magazine?" she wanted to know.

"Neat."

"My father didn't think so. Why couldn't he understand? Lots of girls pose for nudes and people don't think anything about it."

"But not his own little girl."

"That must have been it."

She had told me before how she had gotten into the field but she told me again. I listened to her and watched her. Hers was a beauty different from Linda's, far different. With this girl it was just sex, but with Linda it was something else, far deeper. What I wanted to do with this girl was get her drunk and make love to her. Why not be honest about it? That magazine picture returned time and time again and I wanted my hands on her, touching her skin. She put on a good front but that's all it was. She hadn't posed in the nude and not had some guy take her. It wasn't possible. Even an artist, accustomed to seeing female flesh, could stand only just so much. Put her in a room, any room, and the male had to assert itself.

"I'm doing all the talking," she said.

"I don't mind."

"Most men want to talk about themselves."

Anything I could tell her about myself wasn't good. The only good part had been my marriage with Mary and you don't talk about those things to another girl. You try to forget, just as I had been trying to forget, because out of the past you get nothing but memories. If they are pleasant memories they hurt and if they aren't pleasant, like the accident, they hurt, too. You have to kick the past aside and grab for the future. You have to take what you can get where you can get it and no matter how it comes to you.

"I'm feeling those drinks," she said.

"Have another."

"I shouldn't."

"But you will?"

Her gaze was level.

"But I will."

I started thinking about the Benson House and how I could get past the desk again and up to her room. They had said they didn't go in for that sort of a thing but that was a lot of garbage. Every hotel does. You pay a few bucks, get a room, and what you do inside the room is your own business. And there was just one thing I wanted to do inside of her room. Just one.

"You could talk to my father," she said.

"About what?"

"About me."

"What would I say?"

"Say you know lots of girls who do the same thing and that there isn't anything wrong with them. Try to get him to see my side of it."

"I'll do what I can."

When you want something badly enough you'll promise anything, anything at all. I felt I might as well talk to the bartender as her father but at this point anything she said was all right. I remembered that picture and how she had met me at the door in that robe and the next time I didn't want any robe. I didn't want her wearing anything at all. I wanted her alive and wildly willing, and I wanted to stay with her for so many hours that we would both lose count. You can call it sex if you want to; that's exactly what it was. She had been had before and she could be had again. I didn't intend to let somebody else beat me to the job.

"No more," she said.

"Why not?"

"I have to go to work at eight in the morning."

"And I have to go before that."

"Then you ought to be ready, too."

I coaxed her but she was firm. She said she didn't often drink and when she did it never was much. I didn't believe her. When you got right down to it, I didn't believe anything about her. She had a clever act, but that's all it was—an act.

"Talk to my father if you can."

"Okay."

"Maybe an outsider can make him see." She got down from the stool and waited for me. "I wish I had never posed for nudes."

"It's too late for that now."

"Yes, it's too late. I was doing all right the other way, doing fine, but we were saving for a house, for his retirement in a few years, and the extra money came in handy. I put it in the bank, every cent of it."

"The girl with the bundle."

"There you go, trying to be hard again. No, it isn't a bundle. It's only four thousand and part of it belongs to him."

"Not bad."

We left the bar and walked toward the hotel. When we passed a liquor store I hopefully suggested getting a bottle but she said no.

"I can use it myself."

"You've had enough."

"It gets pretty dry out at The Dell."

She waited for me while I went in and got a quart of Old Grand-Dad. When I came out she took my arm and we continued along the street.

"I like you," she said suddenly.

"That the rum collins?"

"No, I know what I'm saying. It's me."

"And I like you."

I didn't know whether I did or not. I was after her for just one thing. She was a dolly who showed herself off to thousands of guys and if she was half as lily-white as she pretended she wouldn't have done it. I could just imagine what Linda would do if somebody asked her to do the same thing. She would scratch his eyes out and kick him blind.

"We could have a ball," I told her as we approached the hotel.

"Doing what?"

"With this jug."

She let go of my arm.

"You've got me all wrong," she said.

"Have I?"

"I saw you with that girl, remember? But I'm not that kind, Jerry. I hoped that you wouldn't think I was."

I felt like calling her a slut and a teaser, but I didn't. This wasn't the only night in my life. There would be other ones. Some night I would take her out in the car, get her stinko, and then I'd show her what I thought of her. I'd park on a lonely country road and I'd take from her what I wanted to take.

"Don't come in with me," she said when we reached the front of the hotel.

"Why not?"

"You know what they said."

"The hell with them."

She stopped and turned to me. Her head was tilted back and her blonde hair was down over her shoulders. I had an urge to drive my hands into that hair, force her into an alley and make her want me as much as I wanted her.

"I meant what I said before," she told me. "I said I liked you and I do."

"Thanks."

"I haven't said that to a man in over two years."

"Thanks again."

Her chin moved as though she were going to cry and she blinked her eyes.

"I was wrong two years ago, Jerry."

"Were you?"

"He worked for an advertising agency and I didn't know he was married. He had two children and a wife he didn't support and it took me a while to get over it."

"A skunk," I said.

"Don't make me regret what I just said, Jerry."

She was playing this serious, and that was all right with me. Some girls have to feel that you love them, whether you do or not, before they come across with the one thing that they think you can't get anywhere else.

"I won't," I said.

A salesman entered the hotel, carrying some heavy sample bags. He was breathing heavily and when he got to the top of the steps he put the sample cases down and stared at us. Or he stared at Norma. I gave him a dirty look.

"You can see me tomorrow night, Jerry."

"Okay."

"If you want to. Maybe I'm taking a lot for granted."

"You're not taking anything for granted."

"I get finished at five."

"I'll be later than that. The old lady's son got killed and it's fouled everything up."

"I read it in the paper."

"She's trying to make a cook out of me."

"You could get around that by going back to work for my father."

"I'm thinking of it."

We stood there, saying nothing, and the salesman picked up his bags when I gave him another dirty look.

"And talk to him, Jerry."

"Sure."

I didn't see her in that green sheath; I saw her as I had seen her in the magazine. The room was so close and yet so far away. It was enough to make me uncork the bottle right there.

"Good night," she said.

"Good night, Norma."

"I'll be waiting for you in the lobby."

"Make it about nine."

"Nine it is."

She walked up the steps and my glance followed her. At the top step she turned and waved at me. I waved back.

Walking toward the car I made up my mind about one thing—some night I was going to have me a hunk of that. I was going to find out if she was half as good as her picture looked.

It had long since stopped raining but I had left the windshield wipers turned on. They worked like crazy on the dry glass. Well, wasn't that just like a piece of junk? When you wanted something to work it wouldn't work and when you didn't care it worked fine.

I took it easy driving back to The Dell, splashing through the mud and water on the detour. Everything was dark when I arrived, even the cabin where they held the crap games.

I didn't go directly to my own cabin.

I went to Linda's.

I had to have something that night.

8

She wasn't happy to see me. She sat up, after I turned the light on, and rubbed her eyes.

"What the hell do you want?" she demanded.

I leered at her. "What do you think I want?"

She was wearing panties and a thin bra. I wondered why she had been sleeping like that.

"You're drunk," she said.

"A little."

She sat with her legs over the side of the bed. Her legs were creamy and desirable.

"You shouldn't be here, Jerry. You know I have to be careful."

"I'll be careful."

"You know what I mean. If Mrs. Sprague suspected anything between us she'd throw me out on my can. And I'm not throwing this up for you or anybody else."

I tore the bottle open and held it toward her.

"Have a belt."

"No."

"It'll do you good."

Her stare was frank.

"Or it'll do you some good?"

I gave up and had a drink myself. The liquor was warm and it burned going down.

"Who are you kidding?" I asked her.

"Nobody."

"Except yourself and the old lady."

"I feel sorry for her."

"Come again?"

"She was wrapped up in Frank and now that he's dead she's lost. You should have heard her crying up in her room tonight. You'd think her whole world had stopped running."

I had done the same thing after Mary's death. I had locked myself in a room, all alone, and I had cried so hard that I thought I would never stop. It wasn't easy to lose somebody you loved, not easy at all.

"Have a drink," I said.

She demurred, staring at the bottle.

"I shouldn't."

"It won't be the first thing you shouldn't have done."

She got up.

"But not out of the bottle. Out of a glass."

"Please yourself."

She found a glass and I poured her a stiff one.

"You think you can run all over me," she said. "You think just because it happened once it can happen again."

"Give me a better reason."

She sat down on the bed again, holding the glass in one hand, and when she crossed her legs my head began to pound. She was rich in everything that a woman should have.

"I told you I lost my head before. I told you that, Jerry. The same thing happens to plenty of girls. There is always a moment in your life that's empty and you have to do something to fill it up. If it hadn't been you it would have been somebody else."

"That's a compliment if I ever heard one."

She drank some of the whiskey and coughed. I liked it when she coughed. There wasn't anything about her that was fastened down so that it couldn't move.

"It isn't any compliment," she said. "A girl wants certain things and she expects them. With Frank there was very little of that. He was always fooling around with the car. When he wasn't doing that he went out and paid for it."

"With you around?"

"With me around."

"No wonder he killed himself. He was too stupid to live."

She finished the drink and said she would take another. She also told me to turn out the light. I turned out the light.

"My view is all shot to hell," I said.

Her voice came from the darkness.

"You saw me the other way."

"And I'm not forgetting it."

"If she saw a light down here she might get curious and that wouldn't be good."

"She won't know if I stay here tonight," I said.

"No."

"What do you mean by that?"

"I just mean no. You have your cabin and I have mine. You stay in yours and I stay where I am."

I had another drink.

"You must be getting fussy."

"It isn't that."

"What is it?"

"My husband is dead, don't forget that. Maybe I didn't love him the way I should have, but he's gone and I can't help feeling empty."

I couldn't see her in the dark but I could hear her breathing.

"Oh, dammit," I said.

"You don't have to say that."

I put the bottle down on the floor. I couldn't see her but I found the bed and then I was sitting beside her. She tried to move but the mattress sagged in the middle and every time she moved she slid back against me.

"I know what I want," I told her bluntly.

"So do I."

"You're all I want."

"Am I?"

My arm went around her, and I felt her bare skin. "I wanted you the moment I saw you hanging up those clothes. I said to myself that this was what I had to have, what I had always been looking for."

"You're crazy."

"Sure, it's crazy. Everything is crazy. You go days and weeks and you never touch a woman and then you see somebody you have to have."

I put my lips on her neck.

"Don't," she said.

"Why not?"

"You're a hard one to convince! A girl goes for you once and you think she has to go for you whenever you get the urge. I'm not built that way, Jerry. What I feel I feel and what I don't feel I don't."

"I know what I feel."

"Yes, but you're only interested in yourself."

"Baby!"

"I said go away from me. Here I am thinking about my husband and his mother and all you want to do is go to bed."

"Have another drink."

"I don't want another drink."

"Do I have to finish this jug by myself?"

"You do if you finish it."

"You aren't the only one," I said, getting up from the bed. I was furious at her and disgusted. "There are others."

"Find one."

I took my bottle and I left. I didn't say anything. There wasn't anything to say. She was playing this string all the way out and I was only a knot in the middle of it.

I met Sparks outside. He was sitting in front of his cabin, smoking a cigar.

"Sit down," he said.

There was room on the step beside him and I sat down. I had the jug in one hand and I asked him if he wanted a drink.

"A short one," he said. "A short one never hurt anybody."

We both drank from the bottle.

"You think any more about coming back to work, Rebner?"

"Not a great deal."

"I'll have to get somebody else if you don't. That shovel can't stand up there in the woods and do nothing." He had offered me a pretty good deal but I wasn't interested in the money. I was interested in something else, something with a beautiful pair of legs.

"You'd better get another guy," I told him. "There would be overtime."

"I know."

"And you can run the shovel the way you want. I won't stick my nose into what you're doing again."

"Thanks."

He laughed a little. "I don't want another black eye."

His short drink turned out to be three or four rather long ones, and I began to wonder if there would be anything left in the bottle for me. Finally, he returned the bottle and rubbed the back of one hand across his mouth.

"I can hardly see out of this damned eye," he said.

"It won't last."

"But I can see well enough to see where you just came from." He paused. "You're a fool if you mess around with that, Rebner. She's as dangerous as they come."

"How do you know?"

"I can tell. You can see it in her smile, the way her eyes light up when she looks at a man. I've seen her kind before. There isn't anything she wouldn't do."

He was wrong about that. There was one thing she wouldn't do—not a second time.

"I was in town tonight," I said.

"It figures. You wouldn't have the bottle otherwise."

"I saw your daughter."

He didn't say anything but he reached for the bottle again.

"She feels pretty bad, Sparks. She thinks you've judged her unfairly."

He took a long belt of the whiskey.

"She's a slut, Rebner."

"That's a hell of a thing to say."

"A slut or she wouldn't have her body plastered all over that magazine. And that's only one magazine. What about the others? How many other things has she done like that?"

"You'd have to ask her."

He had another drink.

"All the time I thought she was being a model and living decently. We had so much planned together. A couple of more years and I was going to retire. We were going to get a place in the country, settle down, and maybe I'd raise a few chickens. Around here would be all right. Sayville is a nice town and a fellow could work up an egg route. I wouldn't get rich, but who gets rich? A poor man breaks his back for the rich and if he's going to do that he might as well be happy and his own boss. Don't you think?"

"Sure."

"She was saving and I was saving. I wondered how she could put so much money away. Now I know. She took off her clothes and sold herself the way a prostitute sells herself."

"You're looking at it all wrong."

"It isn't any of your business."

"I suppose not. It's just that I was talking to her and I know how badly she feels."

He had another drink and I was pretty sure I had seen the last of that bottle. It didn't matter much. It was still quite early; there was some gas in the car and I could go into town and get another one. Another one? Hell, I'd get two. I'd get two and I'd get stinko.

"What's she doing in Sayville?" he wanted to know.

"Working in a diner."

"That's better than showing herself off to a million men."

"What's so wrong about what she did?"

"What's so wrong?" he demanded. "Wouldn't you feel ashamed if somebody you loved did a thing like that?"

"The movie stars do. Some of them got started that way. And a lot of them keep it up after they're on the top."

"That's different."

"Why is it different?"

"Because she's my daughter. What do I care what the movie stars do? I care what she does." He emptied the bottle. "It's a good thing her mother didn't live to see this. Her mother was a good woman, a clean woman. If she weren't dead already a thing like this would kill her."

It was impossible to talk to him; it was a waste of time. He was convinced that she was no good, and it was senseless to attempt to sway him from that feeling. In his book, daughter or not, she was a tramp.

"I think you're wrong," I said.

"Who asked your opinion?"

"Nobody."

"Then keep it to yourself."

He was feeling the booze and he was getting nasty. I didn't want to fight with him. I had done what I had promised her I would do and had flopped. She would have to take it from there by herself.

"So long," I said, getting up.

"Remember what I said about the girl, Rebner."

"Sure."

"She's on the make and any guy who gets in her way will be cut down. You press your luck and you'll find out that I'm right."

"Thanks for the advice."

"You're welcome. There's no charge."

I didn't go into my own cabin but walked on out to the car. It made a hell of a noise when it started up, as though the head pipe were loose from the block and the exhaust weren't going through the muffler at all. Probably I had bottomed out on one of the holes and torn the thing loose. It sounded like somebody was shooting off a cannon when I pulled out of the drive.

I took my time going to town. Sparks was right and I knew he was right. She was dangerous, the way a rattler is dangerous when it's shedding its skin. But, like the rattler, there was a fresh beauty about her, a beauty that drew me close to her. I wanted her more than I had ever wanted any other woman, wanted her so badly that I would do anything to get her.

Mary, I thought; Mary, help me. Make me see what's wrong here. Make me have some sense and give me the strength to push this aside before something terrible happens.

Mary ...

Mary had been a good girl, sweet, generous, loving. But Mary was dead, killed in that accident, and I was alone. I was alone, a little lost, and I didn't know what to do.

Run, I told myself; run, you crazy bastard, run. Run so far and so fast that you never see her again, that you never think of her again. Find a woman, any woman, and take it out on her. Get it out of your system. She isn't the only one with pretty legs and a big bosom. There are others you can buy or borrow for the night. There are those who cry for it. Why waste your time? Why take a chance? Get a loose jane and park with her in the car. Take her in the back seat and have your fun. Have it once or a dozen times but have it. Forget about her. She's playing for the jackpot and there's only one way she's going to get it. Only one way. The old lady won't die, she's too healthy for that, and she won't tumble down those cellar steps. She's been up and down those cellar steps so many times that she could do it in the dark. There's a railing and she hangs on all the way down. She knows the steps are steep and she's careful. There's only one way she could fall. Only one.

I was sweating when I reached Sayville, sweating so heavily that my shirt was soaked. I thought of going to the hotel and getting Norma out of bed, but I knew that wouldn't be right. She wouldn't let me into her room, there would be a scene and I would lose every chance I had with her. And I wanted that chance. I wanted it so much that my jaws ached when I thought about it.

I found a bar near the railroad. There were a lot of drunks at the bar and four or five girls. The drunks were talking about the railroad, switching cars all over the bar, and a couple of the girls sat together, not saying much of anything. The one girl was dark and the other was blonde. I ordered a double rye and smiled at the blonde. She smiled in return.

Two drinks later she came over to where I sat.

"Hello," she said. "Don't I know you?"

"I don't think so."

She sat down on the stool next to me.

"Well, it's a good gag, isn't it?"

"An old one. Have a drink?"

She drank beer, the small bottles, and it was only fifteen cents a trick. That was cheap but she drank fast and pretty soon she was ahead of me.

"You a railroader?" she asked me.

"No."

"I hate the railroad."

"How come?"

"My husband works on it and it's all he talks about." This surprised me. I hadn't noticed a ring on her finger and I mentioned the fact.

"I take it off," she said, smiling. "When I go out."

"Kids?"

"Two."

"Boys or girls?'

"Both."

She wasn't awfully pretty but she wasn't ugly either. She had a pleasant smile, deep brown eyes, and the blouse she wore, a red and white thing, showed off her breasts. Down below she wore a red skirt, rather tight, revealing her full, solid thighs.

"Who stays with your kids when you're out?"

"My sister."

"And if you don't get home before your husband does?"

"He takes her to bed," she said frankly.

"Some arrangement."

"It will be until he gets her pregnant. After that it's anybody's guess."

A guy down the bar fell off his stool, got up and staggered on outside. The girl who had been with him laughed and turned to the man next to her. This was quite a dump, all right.

We continued to drink and she talked about herself. She had been married three years to a fellow named Bill and Bill had gone with her sister before that.

"And he jumped the fence," I said.

"Because I was carrying his kid."

"You sure it was his?"

She wasn't sore. "I never tried to figure it out. He had a good job and he was there when I needed him. I wasn't going to have a baby and not have a father for it."

I wondered if this Bill were the daddy of the second one but I didn't press my luck by asking her. It was my guess that she couldn't have told me for certain, anyway.

"You got a car?" she asked after a white.

"I've got a car."

"Let's get out of here."

"Why?'

"If you don't know why I won't tell you."

She wanted to ride by her house and we rode past her house. There was a light in one room.

"He isn't home yet," she said.

"Maybe they don't turn out the lights."

"With Helen he would. She won't let a man do anything to her unless it's dark."

I didn't know where to take her but she knew of a place and we drove out there. She said it was the town park, a memorial to the men who had died in the service. There were lots of cars parked along the road but we eventually found a spot under some trees.

"The cops stay out of here," she said as I shut off the motor.

"That's good."

"Once in a while some kids run around with flashlights and peek in the cars. I was here one night with a fellow and they did that to us."

"What did you do?"

"We kept on doing what we were doing."

"They must have gotten a show."

"Who cares? They have to learn about it someday."

"Doesn't everybody?"

"I didn't, not until I was sixteen. When I was sixteen I still thought babies came from nowhere."

"That's not unusual."

"But a boy at a school dance straightened me out. He straightened me out for good. It was four o'clock when I got home and my old man beat the hell out of me."

It wasn't very long before she showed me just how much and how well she had learned. Good teacher, that guy.

Later, her passion gone, she dressed herself, even putting on what I had torn.

"Take me home," she said.

We didn't speak all the way into town.

The light in the room was out.

"We could go back to the park," she suggested.

But I didn't want to go back to the park. I didn't want to go anywhere with her. All I wanted to do was to get out to The Dell and get some sleep.

She was crying when she got out of the car.

She said she wouldn't be able to go into the house until the light was turned on again.

There was a bar down the street and I had an idea what she would do with her time.

9

The old lady prepared breakfast the next morning, but she looked as though she hadn't slept at all. There were dark circles under her eyes and she couldn't stop yawning.

"Tomorrow is the day," she said, barely able to hold back the tears.

"Tomorrow they bury Frank and then he's gone for good."

I was drying dishes and I glanced at Linda. I got the impression she was trying to work up some tears but they wouldn't come.

"Poor Frank," she managed to say.

Mrs. Sprague nodded. "It isn't right to have death so young. For somebody my age it isn't so bad. Death to the old is sometimes a salvation."

Linda glanced at me and then away.

"It should have been me and not him," Mrs. Sprague said "He had so much to live for." She smiled at Linda. "So much that was pretty to live for."

"Thank you, Mother."

"If there had been a baby it wouldn't be so hard on you. You would have some of him left."

"Frank didn't want children."

I suspected it had been the other way around but I didn't get into the discussion. This was something private and I didn't belong.

She fixed dinner, breaded pork chops because she said it was quick and she put a roast of beef in the oven.

"I won't be here for supper," she said. "The meat will be ready and all you'll have to get is the potatoes and vegetable." She was looking at me. "Linda ought to be there, too."

"I've got two hands," I reminded her.

"I'll pay you extra, Jerry."

"How much extra?"

"All I can afford is ten dollars."

"Okay."

Linda hung up the towels and smoothed the uniform down over her hips.

"You can't leave Jerry here all alone," she said. "You know how it is to work in the kitchen and wait on table."

"Don't you want to go in with me?"

"It isn't that. You have to be fair and Jerry has been decent about things."

"Yes, he has."

"You could go in with the undertaker's car this afternoon and Jerry could drive me in after supper. We can tell the men they have to eat early and I'll get there in plenty of time."

"Well, all right."

I didn't know what her reasons were but they were fine with me. I could just imagine how I would be, cutting up the meat, dishing up the potatoes and vegetable and running my butt into the ground just to feed pack of hungry men. Not only that, but there were the dishes to be done; if I had to do everything by myself I'd never get to Sayville by nine o'clock.

I peeled the potatoes and thought about the night before. I had been out of my mind drunk, and it hadn't proven a thing—except that you can usually get what you want if you try hard enough. On the way back I had picked up a bottle but I hadn't opened it. I went to sleep with my clothes on and I felt terrible when I woke up.

Twice that morning Mrs. Sprague went down the cellar to look at that sump pump. Linda had changed into shorts and halter and she stayed around the kitchen, drinking coffee and smoking cigarettes.

"Some day she'll hit bottom," Linda said.

"Will she?"

"Those steps are rugged."

"Well, she won't let anybody else do it."

"Who wants to do it?"

Lunch didn't take long and there weren't many dishes. Linda waited on table, dressed just as she was, and the fellow with the split lip made a pass at her. She slapped him for his trouble and after that he left her alone. On the way out Sparks pulled the fellow aside and told him where the bear crossed the buckwheat patch.

"Leave her alone," Sparks said.

"How comes she dresses that way?"

"The way she dresses is her own affair."

"I wish she didn't dress at all."

"Shut up!"

"Who are you to talk? Your own daughter showed everybody what she's got."

I thought there was going to be a fight but there wasn't. Sparks took it hard and choked up, but he left without saying another word.

"Where's that magazine?" one of the men asked.

"Somebody stole it," another man said. "It was right here and now it's gone."

"The hell!"

"I miss it, too. I could look at her all day and not get tired."

Mrs. Sprague went upstairs, dressed herself in black and came down to wait for the undertaker's car.

"No insurance," she said. "It makes things worse."

Linda poured a cup of coffee.

"He had his GI but it ran out because he wouldn't pay the premium."

"That's as much your fault as his."

"Is it? Where would I have gotten the money?"

"He must have given you money."

"When I begged him."

"Don't say things against the dead."

Linda drank her coffee quickly and rinsed out the cup. Her eyes flashed and her lips were tight.

At two o'clock the car came for Mrs. Sprague and she waved at us as she drove off.

"He was perfect," Linda said, "in her eyes."

"She has the eyes of a mother."

"And I have the eyes of a wife. Is that it?"

"Some wife."

"Don't be smart."

We walked back inside.

"I'm not smart. I'm stupid. If weren't stupid I wouldn't be here. I would be running a shovel and making myself a couple of hundred a week."

"Do you earn that much?"

"Usually."

"That isn't bad," she said. "It isn't bad at all."

"It's better than what I've got."

"Who's stopping you, for Pete's sake?"

I made no reply. I took the broom from the corner and walked out to the dining room. It took me only a few minutes to sweep up and then I looked at that magazine again. She was all right, that was for sure. She had them where they belonged and she had a good supply.

I had just put the magazine back under the counter when the minister came in.

"I keep just missing her," he complained. "I have to talk to her about Frank before I can preach a good service."

"She's at the undertaker's."

"What do you know about Frank?"

"Nothing, except that he's dead."

He seemed pained. "You should come to our meetings," he said. "We could help you."

"I doubt it."

"No one is beyond help. In our own minds we may think so, but if we will just let ourselves go we discover that the world is a wonderful place filled with golden opportunities."

There was only one opportunity I wanted just then and it was in the kitchen. Or it had been in the kitchen. Maybe by this time she was outside showing herself off to the sun.

"Right now I've got work to do," I said.

"Think about it, young man."

"Okay."

"You don't have to belong to a church. You don't have to join our movement. Just give us your heart and we'll do the rest."

Maybe it was a good idea and maybe it wasn't. I needed something.

"Oh, sure," I said.

He was unhappy with me and I could tell it when he left. Small wonder—I was no bargain.

No sooner had the minister gone than the man from the oil company showed up.

"She's in town," I told him. "Her son got killed."

"Oh, I see."

"Rammed his hot rod into a tree."

"These kids."

"You know it."

He had opened up his briefcase but now he closed it.

"What did she say to our latest offer?"

"Beats me."

"And it beats me why she wants to stay on here. Fifty thousand is a lot of money."

"Yes, it is."

"At her age she could retire."

"I could quit for a while myself."

"So could I."

He walked to the door.

"I'll tell her you were here," I said.

"You do that. And thanks."

"Don't mention it."

I spent the afternoon in the storeroom, sorting out cans and cleaning off shelves. I don't know why I did it. I didn't have to. The place wasn't dirty but I hoped the work would give me a chance to think. About Linda. It didn't. All I could think about was one thing and that didn't help. It only made things worse.

At four, after peeling the potatoes for supper, I gave up the battle with myself and walked outside. She was lying on the grass, all right, face down, and she had the halter untied so that she sun could get at her back.

"We've got to do something about supper," I said.

"You do it."

"Why me? You're supposed to help."

"And what do I get out of it?"

"A bundle—if she isn't around."

She lay there quiet for a moment.

"Tie me," she said.

I tied her. I didn't want to tie her. I wanted to rip that thing loose and take her right there. And I almost did. There was nobody around, just the two of us. She could have fought and screamed all she wanted to and nobody would have heard her or cared. But I didn't. I was crazy about her and I didn't want it to be that way for us. It either had to be right or not at all.

"Thanks," she said, sitting up.

"You're welcome."

I hadn't tied the halter very tight and it was loose in front. She noticed it and pulled it up into place.

"You fooled me," she said.

"Did I?"

"Yes."

"How?"

"You know how."

I thought of the jug in the cabin and I asked her if she wanted a drink.

"Yes, I want it. But I better not. She might smell it on my breath and that wouldn't be good."

"Not then. It'll be gone by then."

"Do you think so?"

"Naturally." I kicked my feet in the grass. "How about it?"

"You got any?"

"In the cabin."

She smiled. "I'm not going in there with you."

"I'm no cripple. I can go and get it."

She considered the suggestion for a moment.

"Go ahead," she said. "I'll meet you in the kitchen."

I got the bottle and we went to work on it right away. When it was nearly five I checked the meat in the oven and put the potatoes on to cook. She sat at the table, her legs crossed, smoking and watching me.

"Am I wrong?" she asked me once. "Am I?"

"Wrong in what?"

"Staying with her?"

"You can answer that better yourself."

"Somebody has to stay with her. She can't be left alone."

I threw some salt in with the potatoes—I didn't know and didn't care whether it was too much or too little—and brought the fire up high.

"Not with fifty grand in the poke, she can't be," I said.

"Do you think it's just that?"

"Have another drink. You're getting drunk if you think it's anything but."

"Maybe I like her."

"Maybe you do."

I opened six cans of peas and dumped them into a pot. I cut the fire under them low and put on the lid.

"I told you about myself, Jerry."

"Yeah."

"I haven't got anything to go home to. I'm as well off here as I would be anyplace."

"Better off if she sells."

"Still, on that?"

"On that."

The bottle had taken a beating from the two of us and I poured myself another drink. I didn't have to pour one for her; she poured her own.

"You'd do the same," she said. "I know you would."

"Why would I do the same?"

"Because you're that kind."

"Am I?"

"You're harder than you think. Life has done things to you, too, Jerry. Once it may have been good for you but it isn't that way any longer."

"Go on."

"You're chasing things that you don't understand."

I gave her a grin. "I know what I'm chasing."

"Do you?"

"At least, I think I do."

We emptied the bottle and both said we wished we had more. I also wished that we had more time. The liquor was pounding through my veins and the need for her was a powerful urge that didn't want to die. I thought of taking her there in the kitchen, of forcing her, but something told me that I shouldn't. She would come around again sooner or later and when she did I would be there. Oh, man, would I be there!

"You'd better change," I said.

"For what?"

"For waiting on tables. You keep wearing that rig and somebody's going to go after you."

"Would that somebody be you?"

"I've thought about it."

"And?"

"I'm not that high."

She turned at the door.

"Don't ever get that high, Jerry. You'd regret it the rest of your life if you did."

"Until I died."

"Until you died."

She stood there, waiting, and I walked over to her.

"I could do with a kiss," I said. "A kiss would make up for some of it."

"This isn't the time."

"When is the time?"

My mouth was close to her lips but I didn't press the point.

"You'll know," she said softly. "I won't have to tell you or write you a letter. You'll know it probably even before I do."

I knew it then and she didn't. What was she trying to prove? I knew what she was trying to prove. She was trying to prove who was the stronger of the two. And she was right. She was.

"I like you," she said.

"But not enough?"

"Enough is a big word."

"I know something bigger."

Her stare was frank. "So do I."

Supper was a miserable affair. The drinks had caught up with her and she dropped one of the plates between the kitchen and the dining room. Most of the guys yelled for gravy but I didn't know how to make any gravy and I told them to settle for butter. A lot of them said the potatoes were too salty, the peas burned and the meat dry. All in all, it was a mess.

We washed the dishes, let them drain, and again she was all wet down the front of her uniform. I didn't know how she managed to get so wet but she did. The wet made the uniform stick to her and it gave me ideas.

"Wow, I'm glad that's over with," I said.

"You and me, too."

"I'll never make a cook."

"Nor I."

"Cooking is for women and not for men."

"Some of the best chefs are men."

"You might be right, but you can't prove it by me."

"Hardly."

I went to the cabin, put on some clean clothes, and then I waited outside of Linda's cabin for her.

"Jerry?"

"What?"

"Can you come in and get this zipper for me?"

Her slip was stuck in the zipper and I had a hell of a time getting it loose. When I did I didn't let go of her right away. I kissed her on the neck, and I thought she sighed.

"Don't," she said.

"Why not?"

"Because we have to hurry."

"What I want to do wouldn't take long."

"Jerry!"

"Why not be honest about it? You know what you do to me."

"Not here, Jerry. Not now."

"Oh, hell."

She sat on the other side of the seat as we rode toward town. She was wearing a black dress and it looked nice on her. A couple of times she spoke about Frank but she didn't say very much. She had wanted a child and he hadn't. She had wanted a home and he hadn't. None of their wants had been alike.

"Just that car," she said. "He was married to that car. If he could have taken it to bed with him he would have done that."

"He took it to bed with him, all right."

"For the last time."

"For the last time."

We had a little difficulty finding the undertaker's but a cop told us where it was and after that we didn't have any trouble.

"Cry," I told her.

"I wish I could."

"Think of not getting fifty thousand bucks and it'll come easily."

After I left her I was sorry I had said what I had said. She might not have loved the guy but he had been her husband and she was bound to feel something.

It was still early, not yet eight-thirty, so I had a few drinks at a bar. Someday I would get her. Someday I would know her again. I wondered if I could wait.

Mary, what is happening to me? Mary, what am I doing?

Oh, God, Mary ...

Norma was waiting for me in the lobby of the hotel when I arrived.

"You're late," she said.

"Much?"

"Ten minutes."

I shrugged it off.

"Business," I said. "It comes before pleasure."

She was wearing a yellow dress, as tight as the one the night before, but with a high neck. I felt cheated because it had a high neck. A girl who had displayed her wares the way she had shouldn't be fussy about the neckline. She wasn't kidding me any. She had what she had and half of the world knew what it was. What was she hiding it for?

"Nothing to drink," she said. "Not tonight."

"Why not?"

"Tired. Dead on my feet. That diner is enough to kill a person."

"Keep you stepping?"

"In high gear."

There was only one movie house in Sayville and I asked her about that, but it was the same picture as before and she had already seen it.

"Maybe you're hungry," I said.

"Starved!"

"After working in the diner all day?"

"I wouldn't eat what they had. I want my food clean or I don't want it at all."

I hadn't eaten at The Dell—had forgotten about it, for that matter—and my stomach was empty.

"Let's find a place," I said.

"I'll go if it's dutch."

"How come?"

"You don't make much out there. I know you don't. I don't want you spending it on me."

Most girls take you for what they can get but this one was playing it cute.

"Okay."

I stopped for some gas on the way out of town; the guy said the muffler had a hole in it and why didn't I get it fixed? I told him it wasn't my car and that I wasn't paying to patch up somebody else's troubles.

We found a place about five miles out of Sayville that was clean and small. She had changed her mind about the drink and we had rye and ginger while we waited for our steaks.

"Did you see my father?"

"I saw him."

"What did he say?"

"Pretty much what he must have said to you. He's stubborn and no matter what you tell him, it doesn't do any good. I think it'll wear off, though. It was a shock to him and he has to get used to it."

"I hope so."

The steaks were good and we had more to drink. The waiter asked us if we wanted coffee but we stuck to the rye and that was all right with me. I had made up my mind that I wasn't taking her straight back to town. We were going to stop somewhere else first—one of the picnic groves I had seen on the way out. She wasn't Miss Innocence and I wasn't Mr. Good. You rub us two together and you know what you get.

Long after the waiter took our plates away we sat there drinking. I kept looking at that yellow dress and wishing that she looked as she did in the magazine photo.

"What are you thinking of, Jerry?"

"You."

"Be serious."

"I am."

Her eyes were half closed. "How serious?"

"Very."

"What about the other girl?"

"It was one of those things."

"A moment of hunger?"

"Something like that."

"She's all female."

"Yes."

"She could be a model."

"Maybe."

"For the kind of things they use in the magazines. You have to be big and she sure is."

"I guess so."

"What do you mean, you guess so?"

"I know so," I said, not lying. "But she isn't any better than you."

"Isn't she?"

"Not from what I see, but I don't see much."

She laughed. "Cheat you?"

"Some."

"Just—some?"

"A whole lot."

"You can always look at me back in your room. You've got that magazine, or you can get a copy of it, and you don't have to guess about much. It's all there for you to see."

I didn't know how we had gotten on this subject but it suited me fine. For a girl who hadn't wanted anything to drink she was doing pretty well with the liquor. I wasn't doing so badly myself, yet I didn't think I was feeling them.

"I don't want any more," she said all of a sudden.

"Why not?"

"I just don't."

"I've still got a few bucks left. If I don't spend it on you I'll spend it on somebody else."

"This was to be dutch."

"I've forgotten about that."

"Well, I haven't. You can't afford to buy whiskey and steaks and neither can I, really. That's what's so crazy about us being here."

"You have to eat."

"But not steak."

"And you have to drink."

"No, you don't. You just think you do. I'm no different. I face something that I don't want to face and it seems to be the easiest way to solve it. But it isn't. Liquor, to me, just makes the problem all the worse."

"And that's your father?"

"With me, it's my father. With you, it's something else. With everybody it's something different. We're weak, most of us. We're afraid to meet a challenge and resolve it."

"That must be something you learned in college."

"I learned it by myself. You know it as well as I do but you won't admit it. Why do you drink, Jerry?"

"It's something to do."

"No, it's more than that. It's a way of forgetting or of gearing yourself to do something that you know you shouldn't do."

I knew one thing I wanted to do and the booze didn't have anything to do with it. I had wanted to do it when I first saw her picture and I had wanted to do it the night before. Well, tonight would not be the same; tonight I would take it from her if I had to, take it, and she wouldn't be able to stop me. Who did she think she was, for Pete's sake? Untouchable? It was enough to make me laugh. You don't do what she did for a living and not have plenty of men. I was probably worse than some and better than others. But I had as much right to her as anybody else.

"Let's get out of here," I said.

"I pay half the check."

"No, I pay it all."

She was firm. "Don't argue with me, Jerry. That was our agreement. You wouldn't want me to think that you went back on your word, would you?"

There was no reason to fight with her about it. If she wanted to pay, she wanted to pay.

"Okay," I said.

"That's better."

"I'll leave the tip."

"Half of it."

The bill and the tip came to around fifteen bucks and we split it down the middle. I felt funny about her paying her own way. I hadn't gone dutch since high school and then I hadn't had the money.

"Gee, you're quiet," Norma said as we walked outside.

"I was thinking."

"What about?"

"Nothing much. Nothing at all."

"People don't think about nothing."

"There goes your college again. You're always one ahead of me."

We got into the car and I opened the vent so that the wind would blow in around our legs. The Plymouth still sounded like a stone-crusher when it was running but she didn't seem to mind. She lay back, her head against the cushion, and put her legs out straight.

"It's such a nice night," she said. "I wish this was a convertible and I could look up at the stars."

"You want me to rip the top off with my bare hands?"

She sighed. "Oh, you're so funny. Sometimes a joke dies before it's born, Jerry."

"That one did."

I rolled the Plymouth out to the highway and pushed it up to thirty. The noise of the exhaust made it impossible to talk but I was content to watch, in the glare of the dash light, how the wind lifted her skirt. A couple of times it came up above her knees and what I saw was a nice pair of legs and perfect knees.

Who was she? I asked myself. Who did she think she was? Hell, she was just another broad. She wasn't anybody special. She tried to act special but she wasn't. She knew what a boy did with a girl and she knew how. My guess was that she knew as much, or more, about the subject than I did.

"Where are we going?" she said when I didn't take the road toward town.

"Just riding."

"I don't want to ride."

"Well, I do."

She sat up and lit a cigarette, and when the wind lifted her skirt again she quickly put it down, folding the material under her legs so that it wouldn't do the same thing another time. It made me grin. She was a phony and it stuck out all over.

I didn't know where we were but I found a wood road and I pulled down that, cut the engine and dimmed the lights. She didn't say anything for a moment and in the silence I could hear her breathing there beside me. When she puffed on the cigarette I saw part of her face and her eyes. Her face was turned toward me, her eyes watching.

"Why did you stop here, Jerry?"

"To be with you."

"Yes, I know that. But why?"

"Does there have to be a why?"

She found the ash tray and put the cigarette out.

"I want to go," she said.

"In a minute."

"No, now. Jerry, you've got me all wrong. I don't park. I never have. I wasn't brought up that way."

More bull. Maybe she was kidding herself, but she wasn't kidding me. She was stuff.

"You're parked now," I said.

"Please, Jerry."

"What's wrong about it?"

"Nothing—yet."

She was playing hard to get. That was okay with me. I had all night to fool around with her.

"I like you," I said.

"And I like you. I told you that. I meant it. You've been good to me and good for me. Let's not spoil it."

She wasn't dumb; she was smart. She knew what set a blaze going in a man's blood.

"Baby," I said.

I reached for her in the darkness and tried to bring her toward me.

"Jerry, no."

"Oh, cut it out. You'd think I was poison."

"I don't think you're poison. I think you're nice. But we shouldn't have had so much to drink. It was foolish."

"You didn't refuse any."

"I know I didn't and that's my fault. If I hadn't drunk you wouldn't have either and we wouldn't be here."

She avoided my hand again.

"I like it here," I said. "I like it fine."

"Leave me alone, Jerry."

"I only want to kiss you."

"No, you don't. I know what you want to do."

"What of that?"

"I told you I'm not that kind. If it has to be that way with you, there's always that girl at The Dell." Her voice rose. "Jerry, don't touch me. Please don't touch me."

"Try and stop me."

"I can't stop you. You're stronger than I am. But Jerry, listen to me. I like you. I like you a lot. Isn't that enough? Can't you understand?"

I understood, all right. I was good enough for her to go out with but not good enough for her to have. The thought angered me. Where did she get off, putting on such a front?

"Jerry!"

My hands were on her now, on her shoulders, feeling the thin line of her bra strap beneath the dress.

"Let's stop horsing around."

"I'm not horsing around, Jerry. Believe me. All I've said I mean. Why can't you see that?"

I shoved my head in close.

"Give me a kiss."

"Jerry!"

"It won't be the first one for you, baby—and it won't be the last."

She twisted in my grip but I got to her mouth. I kissed her hard, jamming her head back against the cushion. She didn't respond. She just lay there.

"Kiss me back!" I yelled at her.

She started to cry; her lips moved beneath my mouth.

"I knew this would happen. I knew it! I knew I shouldn't have come with you." She pulled her head away from me. "Jerry—Jerry, listen to me. I know what you think of me. I don't blame you. Other men have thought the same thing, but—Jerry, the other men didn't count. You do count. Don't ruin it. Don't tear apart what we have. It's little enough, just the two of us, but it's something. Please, Jerry!"

She went on and on but I hardly listened to her. I had heard the same pitch before. The first time I made love to Mary she had said almost the same thing. But love had been real with Mary; with this girl it was a fraud. She let them take pictures of her in the nude and then she was too good to be kissed. It was amusing. She must have thought I was some hick who didn't know a right turn from a left turn.

"Jerry, Jerry—"

I was after her, really after her now. I had the dress down over her shoulders, almost to her waist, and she was crying hard. I didn't pay any attention to her tears. I had heard prostitutes cry because the fee wasn't large enough. Tears were for good girls and she wasn't a good girl. She was a woman, raw woman, and I was going to have her.

"Don't—"

I wished there were a light—I wanted to see her in the flesh. But I settled for the touch of my hands and I knew what I found. The picture hadn't lied.

"No, Jerry!"

But this time when I kissed her she kissed me back, just as I had been sure that she would. Her lips were hot and wet and they were wide apart. Our tongues met, retreated, met again.

"I don't want you to, Jerry."

"Why not?"

"Because I never have."

"Don't lie."

"I'm not lying. Jerry—"

She begged and pleaded but she might as well have been crying into the emptiness of the night. I cared nothing for what she felt, for what she said. The one thing I wanted was there and I was going to take it.

She had told the truth.

There had never been anyone else before.

Later, driving back to town, I kept the Plymouth at thirty, trying to kill some of the sounds of the exhaust.

"I'm sorry," I said once.

"Are you?"

"I wouldn't have done what I did if I had known."

"But I told you."

"I know, but I didn't believe you."

It was the second time in my life that I had been first and it wasn't a pleasant thought. With Mary there was love, but with this girl there wasn't anything but sex. It wasn't right. It was so wrong it was almost enough to make me ill.

"Care for a drink?"

"No."

"It wouldn't do any harm."

"It wouldn't do any good."

We entered Sayville and I turned in the direction of the hotel.

"When can I see you again?"

"You can't."

"Why not?"

"It's simple. I always told myself that when this happened it would be forever and for keeps. I always said that when a man took me I would marry him and raise his children."

I began to sweat.

"Maybe you did," she said.

"Did what?"

"Start something."

"Hell, don't worry about it."

"Why shouldn't I worry about it? I've got a right to worry about it. What worry do you have? None. You had your moment and that's all that matters to you."

I wanted to take it back, all of it, and I couldn't. She was a nice girl and I had misjudged her. I thought of all the other men who must have done the same thing. It wasn't fair.

"Jerry?"

"Yes?"

"Are you in love with me?"

I had done enough to her; I couldn't lie, too.

"I don't think so," I said.

"You mean you don't know?"

"I just don't think so."

She looked straight ahead.

"I wish you were. It would make everything so easy."

"Would it?"

"I'll feel this shame as long as I live but if you loved me it wouldn't be shame. It would be beautiful. It was wonderful and good but there could be so much more to it than that."

Love her, I thought; she's a good girl—love her. Fall in love with her. Forget the other one, the one at The Dell, and just remember that moment with her. She'll be good to you and good for you. She's something like Mary, a lot like Mary, and with Mary it was always right.

But I couldn't.

"I'm sorry," I said again.

She was crying when I left her at the hotel. I tried to find something to say to her. There wasn't anything. Anything I might have said should have been said before.

"Good night, Norma."

She walked toward the entrance without speaking.

I didn't get back to The Dell until after four.

I was drunk, stinking drunk.

This time I had something to get drunk about.

PART THREE

10

It wasn't a very big funeral, just Mrs. Sprague, Linda, myself and a couple of boys who had known Frank in school. The minister stressed the pity of a man dying so young but he pointed out that only the good go early. He said there would be another world for Frank, another place, and that in this world he would find himself.

"Amen."

I had driven Mrs. Sprague and Linda in from The Dell and I drove them out to the cemetery, behind the hearse. It was hot, standing in the sun by the side of the grave, but the services were short and soon it was all over.

"My boy," Mrs. Sprague said as we rode toward home. "My boy is dead."

"And my husband," Linda put in.

"Yes, dear." Mrs. Sprague reached for her hand. "My son and your husband. Gone. We'll never see him again, never hear his laughter, never see his smile. We must be brave."

They were both wearing black and Linda had a big pin on the front of her dress. She had shown too much cleavage and Mrs. Sprague had objected to that. The pin belonged to Mrs. Sprague and it looked like something her grandmother had given her.

"Well, back to work," I said.

Mrs. Sprague sighed. "I'll be glad to get back to work. These past few days have almost been the death of me. Now that it's over I think I see things more clearly." She leaned forward and glanced at me. "You've been kind, Jerry. I don't know what I would have done without you."

"You're welcome."

"I'll make it right with you."

"No hurry."

Linda was sitting between us and I could feel her thigh against me. I thought it was deliberate because there was plenty of room. Every once in a while she moved her leg and I was more aware of her than ever.

"It doesn't seem possible," Linda said.

Mrs. Sprague grabbed at that the way a dog would grab for a bone.

"No, it doesn't, and I ask myself why it had to happen. He was so young, so full of life. Why, just the other day—the day I gave him that hundred dollars—he said he was going to get a job and make something of himself. Mostly, I feel it's my fault, that it's in payment for my own sins."

"You don't sin, Mother," Linda said. "If there's anybody who doesn't sin it's you."

"But I do. Sundays I used to go to the mission and join in prayer, but since I've been so busy I've let it slide. A person shouldn't do things like that. You let money rule you and you ruin yourself—or somebody you love."

I drove as fast as I could. It had been "Mother" this and "Mother" that on the way out and I had had enough of it. Linda had even managed some tears. It had been enough to make me sick.

"This car," Mrs. Sprague said. "What's the matter with it?"

"The muffler."

"Get it fixed the next time you go into town."

"Okay."

"If Frank was alive he could fix it. Frank knew cars. He knew as much as anybody about cars."

"Indeed he did," Linda agreed.

It was late when we got back to The Dell and there was plenty to do. I had left the dinner dishes in the sink and these had to be washed and dried. Linda, who had changed into her pink uniform, helped me. Again she got soaking wet down the front.

"How do you do it?"

"Do what?"

"Get so wet?"

"Oh, that. I just get my belly too close to the sink."

"It's so small you think you'd miss."

"It isn't that small."

The old lady went down to look at the sump pump and I started the potatoes.

"You could help with the carrots," I told Linda. "That's your job."

"Well, thanks."

I peeled both the carrots and the potatoes and then I took the broom out front to sweep. I didn't sweep. I got the magazine from behind the counter and looked at her again. She had been just as good as she looked and that was something. I was still staring at the picture when the man from the oil company came in.

"Mrs. Sprague?"

"She's down cellar fooling with the sump pump."

"Can I go down there and see her?"

"I don't care."

When I returned to the kitchen Mrs. Sprague was just coming up the cellar steps, the oil man following her. He was puffing when he got to the top.

"Those are steep," he said.

"They sure are," she agreed.

"A woman your age shouldn't be going up and down them. You might fall."

She wiped her hands on her apron.

"Did you come here to talk about my age?"

He shook his head. "Well, hardly. The company says it will go fifty thousand on your property and not a cent more. That's quite a bit more than the original offer."

She wiped her hands again.

"I'm not interested."

"Why not?"

"What would I do if I sold out? Curl up and die?"

"Retire. On that kind of money you could live the rest of your life."

Mrs. Sprague nodded toward her daughter-in-law. "What about Linda? This way she has a job and we all make a fair living."

The oil company man looked Linda over real closely. "They'd give her a job," he said. "She'd make a very beautiful waitress."

The old lady walked over to the stove, opened the oven and tested the ham with a fork.

"I'm not interested," she told him. "Work is the only thing I know and without it I'd be dead. Can you imagine me cooped up in a room for the rest of my life? I can't. What you people should do is find another spot."

"There isn't another spot as good."

"That's not my fault."

He picked up his briefcase. "I'll talk to the company again," he said. "They may go up a little more but I don't know. If you had some buildings that we could use, it would be another story. As it is, they have to be all torn down."

"What's wrong with my buildings?"

"They're old."

"They suit me."

"I'm sure they do but what we would put up would be something modern."

"Not here," she said. "Not while I'm alive."

The fellow finally left and she kept on complaining about the oil company bothering her all the time. She wasn't going to sell and that was all there was to it. Why didn't they leave her alone?

"When I'm dead they can have it," she said.

A couple of the men were drunk but other than that we had a full house for supper. Mrs. Sprague used side dishes for the creamed cabbage and that added to my work. It was almost eight before I got the dishes done.

"I'm the one who gets it in the neck," Linda said after the old lady had gone upstairs. "I have to wait on all the tables, clear them off and then I have to help you dry the dishes."

"I'll do it myself."

"Don't be that way."

"You made your nest," I said. "Sleep in it."

She playfully snapped at me with a towel and it caught me across the backside.

"I haven't found my nest yet and you know it."

We finished drying the dishes, hung up the towels and I turned off the lights, all except a twenty-five watt that burned near the entrance to the dining room. She was close to me and for a second I thought of grabbing her, of putting my lips over her mouth and getting a little bit of what she had. But I didn't. She was playing this to the hilt and I could do the same thing.

Outside it was hot, sticky, and as we walked toward the cabins she opened the top buttons of her uniform.

"Boy, I wish there was a place to swim!"

"There is. Down the road."

"Far?"

"Too far to walk."

"The car runs, doesn't it?"

"Sure. And the key is in it. Go ahead and have yourself a time."

We paused in front of her cabin.

"Don't you want to go?"

I wanted to go and I didn't. If I ever got her alone in the woods I knew what would happen—the same thing that had happened the night before. And I didn't want it that way for us. I didn't want to fight her or hurt her. She had walked into my life and if anything was love, this was it. Oh, I wanted her physically but I wanted her in another special, different way. I wanted her mine, all mine, every inch of her soul.

"I don't have a suit," I said.

"You've got shorts, though?"

"Yeah, I've got shorts. What do you think I wear?"

She laughed and said she didn't know.

"I don't have a suit either. All I've got is underwear but it's dark and if you're a good boy it won't matter."

"Please yourself. Don't wear anything."

"Fresh!"

She wasn't offended, however; she was pleased. I could tell she was pleased. She leaned toward me and told me to smell her hair. I did.

"Grease," she said. "You get it every time you're around a kitchen. That's what I hate about a restaurant."

"I don't smell anything."

"Your smeller must be out of whack."

I sniffed again.

"Just some perfume."

"That stuff! Frank gave it to me last Christmas. He always gave me perfume at Christmas. You'd think I never wanted anything else."

She was closer to me than before and I had a terrible urge to overpower her.

"Don't," she said.

"Don't what?"

"Don't do what you're thinking about doing."

I didn't.

"I'll wait for you," I said.

"In the car?"

"In the car."

I didn't have to wait very long. She came out in about five minutes and got in beside me. She had put on some more of the perfume and the odor was strong. She was wearing shorts and a halter.

I wasn't sure exactly where the swimming hole was, but the spot wasn't hard to find. There was a small sandy beach, big enough for several dozen people, and the water toward the end of it was deep.

"Hope you're not embarrassed," she said.

"Why should I be?"

I got out of my pants, shirt, shoes and socks. While I was doing this she took off her shorts and halter.

"I feel naked, Jerry."

The moon was out but it wasn't up high and I couldn't see very much of her. All I could see was the whiteness of her skin and the darkness of the things she was wearing.

"Now that I'm here," she said, "I don't feel like swimming. I just feel like staying here on the sand and feeling the night air all around me."

I felt like doing something else.

"You came here to swim," I said, "and you're going to swim."

I caught her before she could get away from me. She threw one arm around my neck and squealed as one of my hands went where it shouldn't have gone.

"Jerry!"

She made a big splash as I threw her in and then I went in after her. I found her under the water but she got away from me. When I came up she was treading water and breathing heavily.

"That wasn't in the deal, Jerry."

"Wasn't it? Well, if you don't know your own mind somebody has to show you."

"But what you did!"

"That was an accident."

"I'll bet it was."

The stream was narrow and we swam over to the other side. She was a good swimmer and her strokes cut the water smooth and sharp. But there wasn't anything but a steep bank over there and it was impossible to get up on it. We sat there in the water, about a foot deep, and relaxed.

"There's something after one of my toes," she said. "It gives me the darndest sensation."

"Probably a minnow."

"Do they do that?"

"Or a turtle."

"Don't say that!"

Playfully, I reached down and grabbed one of her feet.

"Take off a toe," I said.

"Oh, cut it out."

Most of her body was in the water, but I could see the upper part of her. Her body was white in the shadows and the black bra slashed across it.

"You're a funny one," she said, splashing the water with her feet.

"Why?"

"Coming down here with me."

"Who wouldn't?"

Her feet remained still.

"You mean who wouldn't try?"

"Try what?"

"You know."

The mud on the bottom of the stream was cold on my skin but there was sweat on my face.

"I'm human," I said. "I get the urge once in a while."

"If I know you, it's more than once in a while. It's all the time."

"Well, every other hour."

She laughed and her laughter was soft and deep.

"You're honest, anyway. Frank wasn't. Frank would see a girl and he would say he wasn't interested, but the next thing I knew he was in bed with her."

"With all the work he had to do at home?"

She took a deep breath and let it out in a rush. I couldn't imagine Frank or anybody else trading this for what was on the other side of the fence. What did you get on the other side of the fence? I knew what you got. You got booze and a cheap room and a woman who didn't care. Or you got somebody far above you, like Norma. Either way, it was bad.

"He didn't have much at home," she said.

"Oh?"

"Some of the things he wanted me to do I wouldn't do." She hesitated. "He wasn't normal. He wasn't the way you are or the way most men are. He was—different."

"Holy hell."

"You don't know what life was with him. Nobody knows. I didn't have anybody I could talk to."

"You can talk to me."

"I think I can. Yes, Jerry, I think that. A girl could cry on your shoulder and feel better for having done it. Men of your type are few and far between."

"Don't flatter me. I might take it to mean something else."

"No, you won't."

"Why?"

"Because you know how it is with me."

I wasn't far away from her and it was easy to put out my arm and reach her. She didn't pull away. She just sat there in the water with my arm over her shoulder.

"How is it with you?" I wanted to know.

"I told you before but if you didn't get it all I'll tell you again. What have I got except this? What have I got except her? Nothing, that's what. Nothing."

"You could have me," I said.

She moved slightly and my arm fell down into the water.

"And what are you? A dishwasher? A potato peeler? I don't mean to hurt you," she hastened to add. "It's just that it's the truth."

"That isn't all I can do. Most of my work has been on construction, running a dozer or a shovel. Sometimes I make four bucks an hour—sometimes a little more, sometimes a little less. With overtime I knock out two hundred a week, give or take a few bucks. That may not be big money but it isn't hay. I was married before and we lived on it. We lived on it fine. We had an apartment, decent clothes, and before the accident we had a car. We even managed to save a little. The same thing could be true again."

"What are you asking me?"

She let me put my arm around her again, and this time I felt the softness of her flesh.

"You know what I'm asking you."

"We hardly know each other."

"Does that matter?"

She thought for a moment.

"No, I guess it doesn't. In fact, if it weren't for other things I might say yes."

I knew what the other things were. There were fifty thousand of them. She was the only relative Mrs. Sprague had and if the old lady died she would get the place. It wasn't hard to guess what she would do with it if she ever got it.

"I see," I said.

"It wouldn't be possible for me to marry you right away, anyhow."

"Why not?"

She reached up and pushed my hand away.

"He just died," she said. "Doesn't that mean anything to you?"

"You didn't love him."

"She thinks I did. What would she say if I took on another husband? She would kick me out so fast I wouldn't know whether I had my suitcase packed or not."

"And you'd lose fifty thousand bucks?"

"I might."

"Is that so important?"

My hand found its way back to where it had been before and she didn't stop me.

"Fifty thousand is a lot of money, Jerry. It has to be important."

"But—"

"No, you look at it my way. See things as I see them for a minute. My family is a bunch of slobs and I have tried to be better than them. I want the things from life that any girl wants. Sure, I want a home and babies. But there has to be security, too."

"I'd work for you."

"I'm sure you would."

"I'd go back with Sparks tomorrow and when this job is finished there will be other ones. I belong to the union and they place us. There wouldn't be anything to worry about. We could get a car and a trailer and life wouldn't be so awful."

"We'd get a car and a trailer? On what?"

She had me there. On either a car or a trailer you had to have one-third down and if I had thirty bucks to my name I was lucky. I wished then that I had kept up my insurance after Mary's death, that I hadn't cashed the government bonds I'd purchased on salary allotment, but some of the money had gone for bills and the rest of it had gone for whiskey and women. I had tried to forget the shock of the accident, that terrible surprised scream just before the crash; but I hadn't forgotten any of it. It was still with me, still there, even as I sat there in the water with Linda. It would always be there. I had to accept that.

"We wouldn't need a car right away," I said.

"How would you get back and forth to work?"

"Ride with somebody else."

"I see."

"And we could pick up a furnished apartment. Later on a trailer would be nice—some of them are out of this world—but it wouldn't be necessary at the start."

The silence closed in around us and I could hear some frogs along the bank. Further down the stream there was a splash, like a beaver giving a signal. I remembered living with my aunt and trying to trap beaver in the spring. My traps had been too small, and I had cried when the beavers sprung them and got away. Once, though, I had caught an otter—how the trap held him I don't know because an otter is stronger than a beaver—and I had gotten twenty dollars for the skin. I had thought then of becoming a professional trapper, of going to Canada or Alaska, but nothing had ever come of it. I had drifted into construction, working first as a laborer for a buck an hour. On one of the jobs an old man had showed me how to run a dozer and after that things had been better.

"It sounds comfy," she said.

"Does it?"

"But not for me, Jerry. The thing for you to do is find a nice girl and settle down."

My hand felt for her and found her and she didn't seem to object.

"You're a nice girl," I said.

"I'm a bitch."

"No, you aren't."

"You don't know me."

"I don't have to know you. I know what I want."

She sought my hand and took it away from her, but she left my arm around her shoulder.

"I know what you want," she said.

"Don't you?"

"I'm not sure."

"You were sure before."

"No, I wasn't sure then. It was one of those things, Jerry. You were there, the time was right and I was wild. I was thinking of Frank and that car and his drinking and I didn't honestly know what I was doing. It might have been the same if it had been somebody else."

I was hurt.

"You don't mean that."

"I don't know what I mean."

We sat there, my arm just over her shoulder, and when I moved toward her I felt a stone or a small stick jab me in the thigh.

"You're mixed up," I said.

"I know I am."

"You want me as much as I want you."

"Maybe."

"No maybes about it."

This time my hand went all the way to its destination and I felt her tremble and lean toward me. Her hand came up, and went over mine, her fingers digging in.

"You like, Jerry?"

Now I was really sweating.

"Is this all I mean to you?" she asked again.

"You mean more than that, far more than that. Why do you think I didn't go back on the road? I wanted to be around you, near you. I wanted to see you every minute that I could, every second."

"Do I remind you of your wife?"

"No, not exactly." I tried to be honest with her. "It would have been the same if she were alive. Once I saw you I would have wanted you. Not that my marriage wasn't good. Don't misunderstand me. It was. But you represent more, far more. You represent something that I've been looking for all of my life."

There was no doubt about it; I had it bad. I had it so bad that it was a great big ache inside of me. A numbness had gone down into my legs and the only thing I could think of was being with her, of having her again. And I was positive she wanted the same thing.

"Nobody uses the beach," I said.

"Jerry."

"We're alone and the night is ours."

"Sounds like part of a poem."

"It isn't part of a poem. It's what I feel, what I have felt all along."

"You've forgotten your wife and you may forget me, Jerry. I'm just one girl and there are millions. You're attractive. You talk well." She turned her head quickly and kissed me on the mouth, her lips wet and soft. "And you do things to a girl."

My hand became more desperate.

"What am I doing to you?"

"Can't you guess? Do I have to write you a letter?"

"No. Just kiss me again."

She did and this time it was longer, better.

"I love you," I said.

"How much?"

"All the way."

"What would you do for me?"

"Anything."

Run, I told myself; run, you crazy bastard, run. But I couldn't run. My hand was holding her and she was all through my blood. I remembered her lying on the bed, remembered the fury in the cabin, and I wanted all of this to be mine again. I wanted to hear her pant and moan, to cry out in pain, and I wanted the burning desire in me to roar out in a giant flame.

"Don't make me wait," I pleaded.

Her lips searched for my mouth, found it, pressed in, lingered, then slipped away.

"Am I stopping you?" she asked softly.

11

The old lady was feeling better the next day and she gave me the afternoon and evening off.

"Linda and I will take care of things," she said. "You've been wonderful these past few days."

"What about the car?"

"You can use that, too. And I'll give you some money to get the muffler fixed."

"Okay."

"And I'll bring your pay up to date. You might need it."

"Fine."

While she was upstairs getting the money Linda and I kissed by the sink. She was wearing the pink uniform and I ran my hands over her body.

"Don't do that, Jerry."

"Don't you like it?"

"I like it but you know what it does to me. You know what it did to me last night."

I spoke against her mouth.

"Last night was good."

"The best," she agreed.

"I wish you could go with me. We'd get a room in a hotel and really go to town."

She buried her face against my chest.

"Why do we have to hide?"

"Because you want to hide. I don't. If I had my way—"

The old lady came down the stairs and we broke apart.

"The muffler shouldn't be more than twenty dollars," she said.

"I wouldn't think so."

"And here's fifty for you."

"Thanks."

I was on my way out of the door when she called to me.

"I'll phone in an order for groceries and you pick them up, will you?"

"Sure enough."

The day was hot, hotter than the day before, and I broke the handle off the window on my side trying to get the glass down. I threw the handle on the back seat. The car was a mess if I had ever seen one.

Once I was away from The Dell I was able to think about the night before. It was late when we returned to her cabin and I had stayed with her the rest of the night. It had been a night to remember, one of passion and love—but there had been something else there, too. There had been fifty thousand dollars and we had talked about it, a lot—when we hadn't been doing something else.

"She can't live forever, Jerry."

"Who can't?"

"The old lady. The way she works she'll be lucky to last five years."

"And?"

"I can wait. I can wait that long." A moment of silence, lying there in my arms, her head under my chin. "But I don't want to wait. I'll go crazy here if I have to wait."

"If that's what you want, you haven't got much choice."

"Haven't I?"

"No."

"But there is a choice."

"What?"

Soft lips on my mouth, warm lips on my mouth, lips that were meant to be possessed.

"If you don't know I won't tell you."

Riding along in the car I knew. Those steps. She went up and down them half a dozen times a day, checking on that sump pump, and if she ever fell from the top it would mean the end of her. There was cement on the bottom and she would go almost straight down. She was sure to kill herself. It would be a cinch.

I tried to roll up the window and couldn't. I cursed and lit a cigarette. I was cold, cold, even in that hot afternoon. It was in my guts, twisting, turning, and the rest of the night came back, the things we had said, the things we had left unsaid.

"Someday she'll slip, Jerry."

"How do you know?"

"I know. That railing isn't very solid and if it was loose—"

More kisses, more love.

"Even the man from the oil company said she ought to be careful. Remember that?"

"Yes."

"I'm her only living relative."

"I know."

"I wouldn't keep the place five minutes. Not five minutes. I'd have that fifty thousand so fast they'd hardly have time to write out the check."

"Is money that necessary?"

"It is to me. To us."

"Us?"

"What we could do with it! Just think! Fifty thousand dollars—maybe more, as the man said—and we wouldn't have a worry in the world. There would just be us, the two of us, and we could do anything. Anything. Don't you see, Jerry?"

I saw. I saw the old lady plunging down those steps, saw her smacking her head on the cement, heard the bones in her neck breaking. And I saw other things. I saw the aftermath. It would be called an accident, pure and simple, and the cops would say it was tough, real tough. Reverend Stark would wring his hands and pray for her. She would be buried beside her son, buried as cheaply as possible. The oil company would pay fifty thousand, perhaps more, and that would be all there would be to it. The only thing left would be my conscience. And hers—if she had one.

Somebody started blowing a horn and I realized I had almost hit a car. I flung the cigarette outside and held the wheel with both hands. This wasn't right, even thinking about it. None of it was right. Money wasn't everything. Money was only about ninety-nine percent.

The first thing I had done when I reached Sayville was to have the muffler fixed. The charge was twelve dollars and I told the guy to make the bill out for twenty. He did and I gave him a buck for his trouble. I didn't feel like a crook. I thought I had it coming. She had promised me an extra ten and I hadn't seen anything of that. She was getting all she could for nothing.

"I won't get a dime for my work," Linda had said. "Just my room and board and a dress when I'm half naked."

Maybe she was right.

"Business would really boom if you ran around that way."

"The way the Sparks girl does?"

"She's all right."

"I figured you would know."

"How would I know?"

"Your kind would."

I picked up the groceries at Bertie's and he mentioned the ten percent again. I told him it was all right with me, that I would take everything I could get.

"Guess you can use it. She don't pay much."

"No, not much."

"Never did. Had a fellow out there once for twenty-five a week. He stole her blind. It was the only way he could live. Had a wife and a kid. What can you do on twenty-five a week?"

"Starve."

"And fast."

I took the groceries out to the car and piled them in back. I put the butter in front where I could get at it in case I stopped in some bar. I didn't want the butter to melt and if I stopped at a bar I could always get the bartender to put it on ice for me.

I stopped at a bar, all right.

I had three doubles of rye, real quick, and then I asked the bartender about the butter.

"Why not?" he said. "I've done crazier things."

The bar was small and friendly and the guy who sat next to me started unloading his problems.

"Insurance," he said. "You can't give it away in this stinking town."

"I always thought it was a pretty good racket."

"It is, but when you have a debit they drive you nuts. Come back next week, they say. Come back next week and I'll give you three weeks. The lying bastards. You go back the next week and they've had the doctor, or the old man got drunk, or some other damned thing happened."

He got to talking about fishing and he said it was good out along the creek north of town.

"Bass and perch."

He had been out there all morning, knocking around, but the afternoon was too hot to work or fish. Besides, he had something on the string and he was waiting for her.

"Young," he said. "Nineteen."

It wasn't long before the girl came in and she smiled at him. He lost interest in me right away. She was a short girl with bright red hair, cut short, and she had huge eyes.

"We can go up to the house," she said.

"What about your mother?"

"She's at a meeting."

"Will it give us time?"

The girl was frank. "If it's like the last we'll have time to spare."

The man laughed, sharing a special secret with the girl, and they departed.

I continued to drink and tried not to think of Linda or The Dell. But there was no getting around it—fifty thousand dollars was a lot of money. Even for a big shot it was a lot of money. And I was a little shot. Hell, I felt myself growing smaller every minute.

Mary ...

Why did you die? Why did it have to end? If you were alive it wouldn't be this way, nothing like this. I might have come to Sayville, I might have met her, but that would have been all. I would have felt a need for her, but I would have satisfied that need in your arms, with your body. I would have given myself to you the way I gave myself to her, and that would have been all. I would have lost myself in your love, and the need for her might never have grown to be the monster it is now.

"Another drink?"

"Keep them coming."

"This is on the house."

"Thanks."

Give me a baby, she had begged; give me a baby, Jerry, that looks like you.

No, like you.

It doesn't matter. Just give me a baby.

I had tried, tried, but nothing had happened. We had waited from month to month, hoping, praying, and always we had failed. We had bought books on the subject, read them together, but they all said the same thing. There were just a few hours during the month, just a few when it could happen.

"Another?"

"What?"

"You were falling asleep."

"Was I? Sorry."

"You can't do that in here. The boss comes in and finds you snoozing on the bar and it's my job."

"I'll stay awake."

"Sure?"

"Just try me."

I was getting drunk, drunk, but I didn't care. I had to do something. I had to forget that old lady and those steps and fifty thousand dollars. It wasn't easy.

"Where's the diner?"

"Two blocks down and one to your left."

"Thanks."

Go to see her. She's a good kid. Go to see Norma. Put everything on the line. So what if you don't love her now? You will later on. She'll make a good wife. She'll give you kids—she's built that way—and she'll keep you happy. Like Mary.

Mary ...

You were just a kid, Mary, just a kid, but you loved me and that made a difference. You were there, always there, and I never had to ask you. You knew. You were fine, Mary; solid and fine. Why did you have to die?

"Hey!"

"Sure, sure."

"You're going to sleep again."

"The hell."

"No more for you."

"Just one."

"No, no more."

"One for the road and then I'll get it under my feet."

"Your feet won't find the road."

"Let's find out."

Somebody down the bar laughed. It was a girl. What was so funny?

"All right. One."

It tasted like ginger ale but I didn't put up a holler. Right then I needed something mild.

Linda ...

Why can't it be the way it should be, the way it ought to be? What is the money?

"I might wander," she had said. "How do you know?"

"You won't wander. I'll keep you pregnant nine months out of the year."

"And the other three?"

"I'll be getting you that way."

Linda ...

I can make good money. Two hundred a week is better than a lot of folks do. You can have nice clothes and we can eat steak and we can have a bottle when we feel like it. We'll travel on my jobs and you won't get bored—I promise you that. We'll save some of our money and someday we'll have a home, a nice home. Maybe I can start in the contracting business, get my own dozer, and then we'll be all set. What do you want out of life? What do you want?

I knew.

Fifty thousand dollars.

"Gimme another."

"Where's your money?"

I fumbled in my pocket and found a bill.

"Here."

"Nothing less than a twenty?"

"Take it or leave it."

"I'll take it."

He made up for lost time on that drink. It was strong and it made me cough. The girl—why couldn't I see her plainly?—laughed again.

"Bitch," I said.

"Cut out that kind of talk, mister."

"Sorry."

Sorry for what? Sorry for everything. Sorry for myself. Sorry for Linda.

Forget the fifty thousand dollars, baby. Forget all about it and I'll make it up to you. I don't know how, but I will. We'll be nice to Mrs. Sprague, tell her how things are with us, and she'll be sure to understand. We can't go on this way. We simply can't. We can't go on stealing what we should have rightfully and even if we could there isn't any sense to it.

I'm getting drunk.

Drunk.

Drunk on booze and on you. One is as strong as the other. Or maybe you're stronger, stronger than the booze, stronger than I am. I think I recognize that. That's what scares me. All you have to do is whistle and I'll fall flat on my face. It isn't good. Not good at all. It should be the other way around. The man should be strong, the leader.

"Another."

"Cripes, where are you putting it?"

Drunk.

Stinking drunk.

Once, after Mary's death, I had been drunk for a week. I remembered little of it. All of the bars had seemed the same, all of the drinks the same. And the women—well, they were the same, too. Different color hair, different eyes, different shapes, but beyond that the same. Some had charged and some hadn't. One had been young, real young, and she had been looking for a father for her unborn child.

"I'll be a good wife to you, mister. I'll get a job and I'll work and I'll support the baby. All you have to do is give it a name."

"Sorry."

There was one house I went to, where I had sobered up. The girl was about my age, perhaps a year or so older, and her husband was on the road selling for a paint company. He got home every other week and while he was gone she had to have her fun. She locked all of the doors, pulled down the shades, turned on every light in the house and ran around naked. She had made me do the same thing, chasing her and eventually catching her in the bedroom and throwing her on the bed.

"You're a stranger and I can talk to you."

"Who wants to talk now?"

"I do. About me."

"Oh, well, go ahead."

"I'm afraid of men."

"Tell me more."

"I am. I always have been, even my husband. I do this to try and cure myself but I can't. It's there, inside of me, and it won't let go."

"Maybe you need another girl?"

"How did you guess?"

I had left there broke, ashamed of having known her, ashamed of what I had done.

Mary ...

I'm not forgetting you, Mary. You're there, always there, but you are in your grave and I'm alive. I have to go on living. I can't stop now. I don't want to stop. I want to find part of what we had and lost. I want to find the beauty in life, the goodness of it. Help me, Mary. Help me.

"On the house."

"Again?"

"You're not spending pennies."

"Dimes."

"But get your head up off the bar."

"Naturally."

Stop drinking. It only clouds the issue. You can't think straight when you're drinking. When you drink, everything, no matter what it is, is possible. You can see her dead, see that fifty thousand dollars, see—

Norma.

I'm a rat. I'm a stinker. I didn't mean to do that to you. Do you believe me? I didn't. I lost my head, went crazy over that picture. I believed— what was I to believe? You read about models—or girls who say they are models—and you get the wrong idea. Am I to blame for that? They pick up a girl in a house and she says she's a model, out of work, down on her luck. That's what they print in the papers, that's what you read, that's how you get to think. If I had realized—oh, I won't lie about it. If I had realized, it would have been the same. I wanted you the way a starving man wants food, the way a thirsty man wants water.

Marriage to you would be good, Norma, solid. I might not love you now—I don't know—but in time I would. Together we could make a home and be reasonably happy. The first thing we should do is have a child.

"Have another drink?"

"No."

"Don't tell me you're quitting?"

"I quit."

"Get your head up off the bar."

"Yeah, yeah."

"And pick up your change."

"If I can find it."

I found the bills and some silver and stuffed all of it in my pocket.

The girl laughed again as I staggered toward the door but I didn't bother looking at her. I couldn't look at her. I had all I could do to see where I was going.

I had trouble with the ignition key but after a while I got the Plymouth started. I turned on the headlights and pulled away from the curb with a jerk.

I'm not quite clear on how I got to the hotel but I made it. I walked inside, started past the desk and was stopped by the clerk.

"Where are you going?"

"Upstairs. Why?"

"You don't have a room here."

"But a friend does."

"Aren't you drunk?"

"Slightly."

"Who is your friend?"

"Norma Sparks."

"We don't allow—"

"Oh, hell."

When I got to her room I had to knock several times before she answered.

"Who is it?"

"Jerry."

There was a brief silence.

"Go away," she said.

"I have to see you."

"Why?"

"I just do."

There was another silence.

"I'm not dressed."

"Put something on. I won't run away."

"Well, all right."

She was wearing a robe when she opened the door. The robe was high on her throat and she had belted it around the middle.

"What a time of the night to show up."

"I guess it is."

I walked in and she closed the door. She leaned up against the door and stood there staring at me.

"You smell like a bottle of whiskey."

"I should."

"Where were you?"

"Just some bar."

Now that I was there with her I wasn't sure what I should say.

"Look," I began. "About the other night."

She looked down at the floor.

"Shall we forget it?"

"How can we?"

"I'm trying."

"I've tried, too, but I can't. I thought—well, I thought you might want to make the arrangement permanent."

Her eyes lifted to my face.

"Marriage?"

"Exactly."

She smiled for the first time since I had come into the room.

"You don't love me, Jerry."

"Who says I don't?"

"I do. You wouldn't have come here in this condition if you loved me and you wouldn't have done what you did if you loved me. No, you don't love me. You may think you do but you don't. I wouldn't want that kind of a marriage. With me, marriage has to be the answer to everything."

"Nothing is the answer to everything."

She shrugged. "I'm willing to wait."

I sat down on the bed and rubbed my face with my hands.

"You don't love me," I said. "I never thought of that."

She remained silent, standing there.

"Do you?" I asked.

She started to cry, softly and terribly.

"Now what did I say?"

"Nothing."

"I must have."

"Please, Jerry."

I got up and moved toward her.

"I didn't mean to hurt you. Honest, I didn't. It's the last thing in the world I would want to do."

She came into my arms and cried against my chest.

"Stop it, will you?"

"I can't help it."

"Just because a guy asks you to marry him is no reason to cry."

She moved her head from side to side.

"It is for me."

"Why?"

"You wouldn't understand." She pulled away from me. "You don't understand anything. You're big and strong and you think everybody else is the same way. Well, I'm not. I can stand just so much, take just so much, and that is all."

I didn't know what she was talking about but I knew one thing—she wasn't going to marry me. And I knew something else—she wasn't going to let me have her again.

"I'm sorry I bothered you," I said. "If I had been sober—"

"If you had been sober you wouldn't have come here."

"I might have."

"I doubt it."

I didn't try to kiss her or anything like that. I just left. What else was there to do?

On my way out to The Dell I had difficulty seeing the road.

Sometimes even a man has to cry.

12

The minister came out several times during the next week and he held long conversations with Mrs. Sprague. They talked out front when the place was empty, and a couple of times I thought they were arguing.

"He's stubborn," she told me once.

"About what?"

"Oh, things."

I was off the booze and I felt good. Even when I went to town for groceries and meat I didn't stop for a drink. I had lost the butter that one night and she has raised hell with me about it. The first couple of trips I had stopped at the diner for coffee but Norma had treated me like any other customer and I had stopped that, too. And there was something else I had given up on. I had given up on Linda—or I thought I had.

"What's the matter with you?" she asked me more than once.

"Nothing."

Then she would rub up against me.

"I don't keep my door locked," she would say.

Nights I lay on my bed and thought. I was in love with her. I was so crazy-wild in love with her that it frightened me. I wanted to go to her, to know her again, but the implications scared me.

I thought of quitting The Dell and I tried to get back with Sparks but he had hired another shovel operator, a man from Sayville, and there wasn't anything open. So I stayed on, washing the dishes, helping around the kitchen and seeing Linda every day. One night I borrowed the Plymouth and drove in to the movies but I didn't even watch the picture. On the way back I thought of hitting a bar but discarded the idea. I would save my money and when I had a small stake, I would move on. I would move on and forget her.

But I didn't move on and I didn't forget her. She was with me every day, working close to me, and when the old lady was out of the kitchen she didn't try to hide what she wanted to do with me.

"Kiss me, Jerry."

"No."

"You're afraid."

"Maybe I am."

"Don't be afraid. All I can give you is pleasure."

The minister came out on Saturday and Mrs. Sprague was down in the cellar when he got there.

"She shouldn't use those steps," he said. "One tiny slip and it's difficult to tell what might happen."

"Tell her that."

"I have but she won't listen. I even told her to get a new sump pump, one that she wouldn't have to watch. They only cost about fifty dollars."

When she came up he suggested sending a plumber out but she wouldn't hear of it.

"I've got better places for my money," she said. "Fifty dollars for going up and down those steps is pretty good pay."

After the minister left Linda asked the old lady for a couple of new uniforms.

"This one is too tight."

"Let out the seams."

"I don't know how."

"Oh, you don't know how!"

"Well, I don't. And, anyway, I ought to have two uniforms so one can be clean all the time."

"You can wash that one out before you go to bed and it'll be dry by morning."

"Gee, thanks."

That afternoon while the old lady was taking her afternoon nap I scrubbed the kitchen floor.

"Did you hear what she said about the uniforms?" Linda asked me.

"I heard."

"The old rip. All I get is my board and room and she can't afford a few lousy bucks."

"I thought she was paying you."

"Did you ever see her give me any money?"

"No."

"Well, I don't get a cent. I've got a home, she says, and I ought to be glad of that. Oh, sweet heaven, can you imagine? I'd be better off with a job where I worked for nothing and boarded myself."

I could see her point. It wasn't right and it wasn't fair. She should be paid the same as anyone else. The fact that she had been Frank's wife shouldn't enter into it.

"Talk to her," I said.

"I've tried that but it doesn't work. She listens but she doesn't do anything about it."

"Are you that broke?"

"You know what Frank left me."

"Nothing."

"And that's what I've got."

I finished the floor and we had some coffee at the kitchen table. There were still potatoes to peel but they could wait.

"I'll fix her," Linda vowed. "I'll wear shorts and halter in the dining room."

"She won't like that."

"What do I care if she doesn't? It's no worse than this uniform. In this uniform I show off half of what I've got."

"That's a lot of showing."

"Why? Don't you approve?"

"One hundred percent."

Linda drank some of her coffee.

"You get your money?" she asked.

"If I don't I don't work."

"She says she's going to cut you down to forty."

"Like hell."

But she did and she did it that night. She hoped I would understand. Frank's funeral had cost her a lot of dough and she had to cut corners wherever she could. I felt like telling her what she could do with her job but at the moment I was unable to do so. I needed some money to go somewhere else and this was the only way I had of getting it.

"I told you," Linda said when we were doing the dishes.

"So you did."

"How do you like it?"

"Not very much."

"The worst part of it is that she's got it all salted away. Plenty."

"How do you know?"

"Remember the day she went to town with you?"

"I remember."

"I went through some stuff in her room, snooping, and I found her bank book. She's got almost ten thousand put away."

"No kidding?"

"I'm not kidding. She's sitting on top of the world and she doesn't know it."

"With ten grand anybody would be."

"And this place."

"And this place."

Before she went upstairs Linda asked Mrs. Sprague about using the car to go in to the movies and, strangely enough, the old lady gave her consent.

"The only thing wrong is that I don't drive," Linda said.

"Jerry could drive you."

Linda looked at me.

"Would you?"

What was I to say?

"Okay."

She wore the black dress she had worn at Frank's funeral but she didn't have the pin on the front of it. The opening was deep, and I hated to admit it but she looked good in that dress. But she looked good in anything—or nothing.

"I don't care about the movies," she said as we drove down the road. "I just wanted to get out of there."

"Can't blame you." I couldn't.

"All I see is that cabin and the dining room and kitchen. It's enough to drive me nuts."

"You don't have to stay."

"You know why I stay. And I'm staying. I'm staying right here. I'm staying here to get what's coming to me."

I didn't know how she figured she had anything coming to her but a lot of people think that way. They sit around waiting for a mother or a father to die, or an uncle, or somebody, and after they get the money they blow it.

"Let's get a drink," she said.

"I'm not drinking."

"You can watch me."

I watched her every day, all the time. And at night, alone, I wanted to go to her. I wanted to go to her and tell her that I loved her and ask her to give up this insane business. I wanted to be in that bed with her, and I wanted to make love to her until I was blinded by it. But I had fought it down, just as I had fought down the urge to drink.

"Where do you want to go?"

"I don't care. Do you know of a place?"

"We can always find one."

I didn't take her to the bar where I had gone a couple of times with Norma. I stopped at the first neon sign I came to.

"Got your butter," the bartender said. "You still want it?"

"Take it home."

"Thanks."

Linda ordered scotch on the rocks and I had a plain ginger.

"You sure had it the night you were here before," the bartender told me. "You had a dandy."

"That's no word for it."

Linda asked me what he meant and I told her. I didn't tell her that I had gone to the hotel and asked Norma to marry me. She was a girl and I didn't think she would appreciate it.

"The old lady was sore about the butter."

I nodded. "You can say that again."

She had three drinks rather quickly, and I got tired of the ginger. I switched over to rye with a tall beer chaser.

"Might as well be plastered as the way I am," I said.

The rye burned going down and the beer was flat. When I ordered the next drink I had it with plain water.

"Why fight it?" she asked.

"Fight what?"

She reached out and touched my hand with the tips of her fingers.

"You and me, Jerry. You're fighting it."

"Now you're guessing."

"No, I'm not guessing. I've seen the way you watch me and I remember how you were that night along the creek. There are some things you don't get over so easily."

We were sitting close and our legs touched.

"Give me time," I said.

"Do you really want to?"

She moved her leg and pressed it against me. The saliva in my mouth became thick.

"Do I want to do what?"

She gave it to me straight.

"Forget me?"

I waved for another round and I gave it to her just is straight.

"You want one thing and I want another. The things we want just don't match."

"One thing we want is the same."

"Tell me."

"Money."

She was right there. I did want money—who doesn't? I wanted money for the good things in life, the better things that life had to offer. I was willing to work for it. She wasn't. There's a big difference.

"Yes, I want money."

"You can have it."

"When I get a decent job I'll have some."

"No, not that way. That's the dumb way."

"Name me another."

She did. "Her."

"The old lady?"

"The old lady. All she has to do is go down those steps, end over end, and we're sitting pretty."

I had another drink real fast. I had seen this coming, even thought about it myself, but now that it was there with me it came as a shock. I had actually thought of killing her.

"Fifty thousand," she said.

"Sixty."

"Oh, the bank book. You're counting ahead of me."

"I'm counting for you."

"Or yourself?"

"Nuts."

Her leg was still there, and once I reached down and touched it. It was a good leg, soft to the touch and strong enough to create desire.

"You do want me," she said. "Don't you?"

"Pretty bad." I had to admit it.

"I'm yours, Jerry. All yours."

"All?"

"Or I can be yours. It's up to you."

"But there's a price?"

"There's always a price, honey. Some things have one price and some things have another."

"Higher?"

"After it's over we may not want each other," she said. "You have to face that. But half of it would be yours. If you want me go along with it but if you don't you'll have more money than you know what to do with."

"The big split?"

"Call it what you will. We've both taken a lot from her, a lot. You saw how she was about those uniforms today. You saw how she cut you from fifty to forty when she knew you couldn't get back on the job. She's that kind, Jerry She's old and ugly and anything she gets she's got coming to her."

This was what I had been trying to run from. This was what had scared the hell out of me. But I was no longer scared. How do you explain these changes in a man? One day you're an average guy, nothing special, and the next day you're on the verge of being a killer. I didn't hate her; I couldn't say that. She hadn't been exactly fair with me but most people you work for aren't fair at one time or another. They give you a song and dance and after you're sucked in they play you the sad tune. They can't pay this, they can't pay that. You get so you wonder if they can pay anything at all.

"Knock it off," I told Linda. "This is a hell of a conversation."

"But to the point."

"That isn't it. You know what you're asking me to do?"

"I know and so do you. I'm asking you to put a bundle of money in our hands."

"Is that all you care about?"

Her leg moved against mine.

"No. I care about you."

"How much?"

"A good share of the world."

"If you did you wouldn't ask me to do what you're asking."

"Wouldn't I?"

"No. You'd go away with me and forget all this."

"Go away with you? To what?"

"To another job. There are lots of jobs and I can do well. We can get along. Things might not be easy at first but things would get better."

She laughed. "And you'd keep me pregnant nine months out of the year?"

"I'd try."

She put her hand on my leg.

"I think you could," she said. "I'd be as big as a house for the rest of my life."

"You could do worse. You could be in jail."

"How is that?"

"What we were talking about before—the old lady."

"There wouldn't be any risk."

"I don't see why not."

"Everybody knows she goes up and down those steps to check on that sump pump. The minister told her she shouldn't and so did the man from the oil company. A lot of people fall down steps all the time. It's just an accident. They say more accidents happen in the home than anywhere else."

I wished that I could feel the liquor but I didn't. There was too much inside of me, too much that even the liquor wouldn't still. The old lady was worth quite a load of jack and if we had it we wouldn't have any worries. We could go to Florida and lie around in the sun or buy a small business and settle down. It would be with us for a while, what we had done, but someday we would forget. You always forget. What is big to-day is nothing tomorrow. And I would have her. I would have her forever. She would be mine, all mine, and everything she had would belong to me.

"I don't know," I said.

"Well, I do. This is perfect, Jerry. Perfect. You wouldn't find anything more perfect in a hundred years."

Mary ...

Tell me what to do, Mary. Tell me what to do!

"I still like the other way better," I told her.

"Is there another way?"

"Sure. We can go away together. We can get married. I'll find work. I'm bound to find work. And if it's necessary, you could help out for a little while. It would be better than—that. We would wake up at night, knowing what we had done to her, and it would be hell."

"It's hell this way. And it would be the other way."

"Why?"

"Because I want things, things that you can't give me. Is that wrong? For the first time in my life I'm close to a lot of money and I don't intend to walk away from it. Love has nothing to do with it, Jerry. Love is just a part of it."

"A big part."

"I'm not saying it isn't, but—Jerry, how much money you have?"

I wasn't sure. "Forty or fifty dollars, maybe."

"And I have nothing. How far could we go on that? There would be room rent to pay and food to buy and you'd still have to locate a job. What if it took you a week? It might, or even longer. Where would we be?"

"She owes me a few dollars," I said stubbornly.

"Do you think you would get it if you quit her? You've seen how she is. When Frank died I was her daughter—for a few days. We had to stick to this together, she said. We had to remember Frank, how good he had been—all that bull—and face the future. How long did it last? Hell, she won't even buy me any uniforms and she doesn't pay me wages. You've got a home, she says. Can you tie that? I hop tables for those crumbs and all I've got is a home. Wash out the uniform, she says; wash it out at night and it'll be dry in the morning. What kind of a life is that, Jerry? You know what I'm talking about. I don't have to tell you. She sits with ten thousand dollars in the bank and I can't even have a uniform. If it saved her money she wouldn't care if I waited on tables in my bare skin."

She spoke the truth. The old lady had not been fair with her and she hadn't been fair with me either. Cutting me from fifty to forty a week had hurt and it had made me sore. I was still sore about it.

We had two more drinks and we didn't say very much. I guess both of us were thinking. I was thinking how it could be done, easy as nothing, and what things would be like afterward. I also thought about sixty thousand dollars; it was a lot of money.

"Let's forget her," I said finally.

"No."

"We'll forget her and get out of here."

"If you go you'll go alone."

"Is money that much to you?"

She looked up at me as though she wanted me to kiss her right there at the bar.

"You and money," she said. "I want both."

I knew that she wasn't very much different from me. I wanted her and I wanted the money, too. I wanted all of the things I had never had in life before, all of the things Mary and I had dreamed about. I wanted nice clothes and cash in my pocket, enough cash so that I didn't have to worry. And, even more, I wanted this girl. I had been out of my mind to have asked Norma to marry me. What kind of a marriage would that have been, anyway? I'd go back to running a shovel or pushing a dozer and in a year or less there would be three of us. With this girl, three seemed to be just right—three or half a dozen. The girls would be like her, soft and slightly pouting, and the boys would be like me, big and strong. What difference did it make where the money came from? The old lady was going to die someday, wasn't she?

"I need a drink," I said.

"We're already had a lot."

"Not enough."

She laughed at me. "You're scared, aren't you?"

"No, I'm not. I was before, but I'm not now. I just want to be sure that we could get away with it."

"All you need is a wire across the top step."

"I know. That and some luck."

"We won't need any luck."

"You always need luck."

The bar began to fill up suddenly and we stopped talking about the old lady. We just talked about where we would go and all that we would do after it was over.

"I've never been to Florida, Jerry."

"I have. When I was in the army."

"Is it nice?"

"All I saw was sand and scrawny-looking trees. We weren't near the big centers. Once a week they gave us a pass but there wasn't much where you could go. There was a town nearby, a small town, and all you could do was sit in the park—they called it a park—and watch the rats run across the street."

"Rats?"

"They lived in some trees that were hollow inside. I don't know what you call the trees but I've never seen bigger rats."

"I'm not interested in the rats," Linda said.

"Neither am I."

She turned on the stool and shoved her knees up against my leg.

"Maybe some other place would be better," she said. "With all of the pretty girls down there I might lose you."

"Not a chance."

"Kiss me and make me sure."

"Here?"

She leaned forward, her lips parted.

"Here. Right now."

I did.

Her lips were soft and warm and eager. They moved under my mouth, saying things that I didn't understand, and her little hands gripped my shoulders.

"I love you," she said.

"And I love you."

"Forever and forever?"

"Forever and forever."

"No matter what happens?"

"No matter what happens."

"Kiss me again."

"Don't you ever get enough?"

"Not enough of you."

We didn't stay long after that. I paid the bill, which was over ten dollars, and we walked outside. She hung on to my arm and before she got into the car she kissed me again.

"I'll never make you sorry," she said.

"I hope you don't."

"I'll be good to you for the rest of our lives."

"You're being good to me now."

She sat close to me as we drove toward The Dell and I had my right arm around her.

The road got rough but I didn't shift into second. I forced the car along in high, slipping the clutch when we came to a chug hole.

"I wish we were there," she said.

"Why?"

She squeezed my hand.

"You know why."

I parked the car in back of The Dell and didn't lose any time getting out of it. We walked toward her cabin and I hoped nobody saw us. I glanced upstairs over The Dell but everything was dark. The only light was in the cabin where the men shot craps and played cards.

Once inside the cabin she pulled down the shade and snapped on the light.

"We don't need a light," I said.

"I want a light."

Somehow, it reminded me of Mary. Mary had always wanted it dark, as though she were ashamed of what she was doing.

"You're all apart," I said.

She looked at herself in the mirror and smiled.

"Am I nice?"

"Would I be here if you weren't?"

"Am I as nice as that girl in the magazine?"

"What magazine?"

"The one you used to look at all the time."

I hadn't realized that she had seen me, but then, there were a lot of things I hadn't realized.

"Better," I said.

"I could pose for pictures, too."

"Yes, you could."

"But I wouldn't. I wouldn't let every man see me the way I am now."

"I should hope not."

She tossed her head and fluffed out her hair.

"Am I shameless?"

"No."

"Pretty?"

"Oh, baby!" I went to her and pulled her body into my arms.

This was one night when I wouldn't sleep alone. One night when I wouldn't have to think. Tomorrow was tomorrow, and today is today. To hell with all the rest of it.

13

I intended to do it the next day and get it over with as quickly as possible, but everything went wrong.

"The minister is coming out for me," Mrs. Sprague said after breakfast. "Because of Frank's death I've got some things to do in town. I doubt if I'll be back until around three."

"What about dinner?"

"There's stew fixed and you can serve that."

She went down the cellar to check on the sump pump but I hadn't had time to rig up the wire and nothing happened. She came up, puffing, saying that if she ever got a chance to get a secondhand pump she might consider it—if it were cheap enough.

"Twenty dollars," she said. "I wouldn't pay more than that."

"You won't get one for that kind of money."

"Then I'll keep what I've got."

She went upstairs to change and Linda and I worked on the dishes.

"The old bag," she said. "Just when we were set."

"Yeah."

"You got the wire?"

I nodded. "In my pocket."

"She would have to take off today and mess the whole thing up." Furiously, she dried a plate. "Waiting makes me nervous."

"Me, too."

"It isn't that anything can go wrong. It can't. It's just the idea of it."

Mrs. Sprague came down, dressed in black, and sat at the table drinking a cup of coffee.

"About that butter, Jerry," she said. "I don't know what you did with it but I got charged for it and I'm taking it out of your pay."

She was a bitch.

"Okay."

"You understand?"

"What if I didn't?"

She pushed the coffee cup aside. "Money doesn't grow on trees, Jerry. You have to learn that when you work for me."

I let the water out of the sink.

"I'm learning."

The minister arrived shortly after that and said he would like some coffee. He sat out front drinking it and she sat opposite him. I didn't know what they were talking about but I got the impression that they were arguing. Once she said something about not going to church and he said going to church wasn't the only sign of being a good person. She disagreed with him, I thought, and he didn't have any more to say about it.

They left shortly after ten and then we were alone. I checked on the stew and it smelled fine. The old lady really could put out a meal when she felt like it.

"Jerry?"

"Hello."

"What are we going to do?"

"What we were doing before. Wait."

She kicked at the garbage can and it made a racket.

"Dammit," she said. "Dammit to hell!"

"I don't feel any better about it than you do."

"And we were ready. For sixty thousand dollars we were ready."

"We're still ready."

There was plenty of time before dinner and there was nothing else to do. I poured a cup of coffee and then threw it out. It was strong enough to float an iron wedge.

"Don't you feel the heat, Jerry?"

I was wet with sweat.

"Sure, I feel the heat."

"What about a swim?"

"No. But you go ahead. Somebody has to stay here."

She came into my arms and I kissed her.

"You won't mind?"

"Not at all."

"But you'll miss me?"

"I wouldn't if we went down to your cabin."

"Oh, you!"

As soon as she was gone I took the broom and swept up out front. The wire was in my back pocket; every once in a while the end of it stuck into me.

When I finished sweeping I examined the top of the cellar stairs. There was nothing clever about my plan. All I had to do was fasten the wire to a couple of small nails on either side of the first step and away she would go. After it happened I would remove the wire and that would be that.

"Hello, out there!"

I closed the cellar door and walked to the front of the building to see who it was.

"Hi," Norma Sparks said.

"Oh, hi."

"I suppose my father is up on the job?"

"He must be."

I noticed a cab out front and it was waiting.

"If I stayed for lunch how would I get back to town?"

"Well, if the cab came out here once I guess it would come again."

She frowned.

"I'll tell him. I did want to see my father." She walked to the door but then stopped, swung around. "And you. I wanted to see you, too."

"Okay."

She walked outside and I watched her through the window. She was wearing a blue dress that hung to every curve and I decided she was better in real life than she was in that magazine picture.

The cab drove away and she came back into the restaurant.

"Hot, isn't it?"

"Yes, it is."

"Do you have any iced coffee?"

"I could make you some instant."

"That would be fine."

She followed me out to the kitchen and I scratched around until I found the jar of coffee. I put some of the coffee into a glass, ran water in on it and got a couple of ice cubes out of the refrigerator.

"Milk?"

"No. Black. Without sugar."

I put the glass in front of her.

"You wanted to see me?" I asked.

She tasted the coffee and said it was just right.

"About the night you were up to my room."

"Go on."

"I wasn't very polite to you."

"Well, I was pretty drunk."

"And when you came in the diner, I wasn't nice to you either of those times."

I didn't know what she was getting at but whatever it was she was breathing heavily, filling out that dress so that it was tight across her breasts.

"I'm thinking of going back to New York, Jerry."

"Are you?"

"I have to be honest with you, Jerry."

"All right."

"My father came to the hotel last night and he apologized for what he had said. He just asked me not to pose for nudes again."

"Somebody is going to get cheated."

I thought her face colored slightly.

"I told him I wouldn't. I have plenty of other work and—Jerry?"

"I'm listening."

"A lot depends on you."

"How much?"

"A lot." She put the glass down and she almost missed the table. "I have to be honest with you, Jerry. I have to be honest with myself. I just can't go away and leave anything undone."

"I'm glad your father saw the light."

"It isn't that, Jerry. It's us."

"Us?"

"You and me. You were—well, you know that you were the first one for me. I thought I would hate you for it, and I tried to hate you. But I can't. You made me live but you did more than that. You walked into my life and—and, Jerry, I'm glad that you did."

I could have used a drink. I knew what she was driving at now and I respected her courage for having come to me. It must have taken a lot of guts. But it was too late for that. I was on my way and there was no turning back. From now on there could be no change in my plans. I knew what I wanted and I was out to get it. I wanted the money and I wanted the girl and I was going to have both.

"I'm sorry," I said.

She came toward me.

"You don't have to be sorry. There's nothing to be sorry for. It was my fault as much as it was yours."

"But—"

"We can make it right, Jerry."

She was close to me, looking up at me, and what I saw in her eyes was more than mere emotion. It was love, the kind of love you dream about. The kind of love I had known with Mary. Something clean, something fresh, something decent.

"I'm sorry," I said for the second time.

I didn't have to tell her. She knew. The knowledge was in her eyes and I had to look away from the pain. I had put the pain there and before it was done there would be more pain. In that second I hated myself.

"You're a good girl," I said.

"Is that all you can say?"

I shrugged my shoulders.

"What else is there?"

"Jerry?"

"Yes?"

"Why can't it be for us?"

"You'll find somebody else."

"I didn't ask you that."

I could smell the stew and I knew that I should look at it.

"What would we have?" I asked her.

"I could work."

"And I don't have anything. How much do you think I make here? Peanuts."

She brightened.

"That's nothing to worry about. The man Daddy has on the shovel isn't any good and you could have your job back. We'd be together, the three of us, going from one job to another. It would be fun."

Fun? I didn't know. She was a wonderful girl, wonderful, but I was sure that I didn't love her. She deserved something better than what I could give her.

"It wouldn't work," I said.

"You thought it would the other night."

"That was the other night."

She started to cry softly and steadily.

"There's somebody else, isn't there, Jerry?"

"Don't torture yourself."

"But there is?"

"Yes."

"The girl out here?"

"Yes."

"But her husband just died."

"I know."

She sighed.

"You knew her before, didn't you?"

"How do you mean?"

"You know how I mean."

"Yes."

"And before me?"

"Yes."

"Oh, Jerry!"

There wasn't much to say after that and she went outside to wait for her father. While she was out there I got that copy of the magazine and looked at her again. Maybe I had made a poor choice but I had made it and I had to stick to it. If Linda and I didn't get along we could split the money and part. And maybe someday ...

We got through dinner all right and everybody said the stew was good. I had made fresh coffee but it was weak and I had some complaints about that.

"You'd think this was the Astor," Linda said. "And that guy with the traveling hands—he makes me sick."

"Slap his puss."

"I did before but all it does is make him more eager."

She helped me with the dishes and we were finished by two. She said she was going out to get some sun and did I want to come along?

"No. I want to look at those stairs again."

She was pleased.

"When will you do it?"

"I thought of tomorrow but today might be better. As soon as she gets back from town she'll want to look at that pump. If she hits it around three there won't be anybody around and that's the way we want it."

"Now you're talking."

"The quicker the better."

"'Boom' and it's over with."

"We hope."

She kissed me before she left and if it hadn't been for what I had to do I would have taken her down to the cabin for an hour of play.

"You can wait," she said.

"It'll be rough."

I didn't hear the cab come for Norma and I didn't see her go. I was putting that wire across the top step, drawing it straight and snug. The wire was thin, just enough to make her trip, and it was impossible to see it in the dim light. I closed the cellar door and felt satisfied.

I prowled through the restaurant, looking for a drink, even a beer, but I couldn't find anything. I finally tried some coffee but it wasn't any good and I threw it out.

Mary ...

I had to forget about her. What we had had was in the past, as dead as she was. Tomorrow I would be rolling in money and I would have a girl who could make up for everything that I had to do in order to get her.

Everything ...

Shortly after three I walked outside. Linda was stretched out on the grass, her halter untied so that the sun could get at all of her back.

"Where is she?"

"I don't know."

"Is it ready?"

"As ready as it will ever be."

She sat up, not caring what she displayed and I didn't mind seeing what she had.

"Looking at something?"

"Yep."

"I guess I'm not so bad."

"That's the understatement of the year."

I sat down beside her and we kissed.

"She ought to be getting back, Jerry."

"I hope so."

"This can't go on forever."

"Hardly."

"What if she's late?"

"Then we'll have to put it off until tomorrow."

"Oh, hell."

A few minutes later I heard a car coming up the road and I told her that she better put her halter on.

"Tired of what you see?"

"I'll never get tired of that."

She got into the halter and I tied it for her in the back. The car pulled in alongside of The Dell. It was the minister. The old lady got out and walked inside and the minister drove off.

"My feet are cold," Linda said.

"They'd better not be."

I left her on the grass and entered the kitchen. Mrs. Sprague was putting on her apron.

"How did it go at noon, Jerry?"

"All right."

"The stew suit them?"

"Fine."

She poured a cup of coffee, drank some of it and made a face.

"This is terrible."

"It couldn't be worse," I agreed.

"I'll have to show you how to make it sometime."

"Okay."

She got a couple of prime ribs out of the meat box and put them on the work table.

"Hot in town," she said.

Sweat was pouring down over my face. If she didn't go down the cellar fairly soon I would have to take up the wire and call it off for the day. This had to take place when there was just the three of us around. It would have looked better if somebody else was too but there was the problem of removing the wire.

"Oh, that sump pump," she said, starting for the cellar door. "I'd better see that the float isn't struck."

For a second what I was doing came over me. Sweat dripped into my eyes and I began to tremble.

"I'll look at it for you."

"You don't know the first thing about it."

"Well, it's time I learned."

"Learn how to make coffee first."

She pulled the door open and I wanted to shout at her, to tell her not to go down there. But I didn't. I stood there, my body cold and my belly on fire, and I saw her take the first step.

I heard her go.

She screamed as she went, screamed terribly, and the whole thing ended in a shriek.

"God," I said.

I couldn't move. She was down there at the bottom of the steps and I couldn't move. What if the fall hadn't killed her? What if the fall had only broken a hip? What would I do? Club her to death? Strangle her?

I walked to the steps, looked down, and saw her lying there on the cement floor. She lay still; she didn't move. I watched her, feeling miserable. Why had I done it? There must have been another way.

I found the wire and unhooked it from the nails. It was still in one piece and I rolled it up and put it in my back pocket.

I descended the steps, slowly, and knelt beside her.

I felt her wrist. There was no pulse. She was dead.

I climbed the stairs and walked through the kitchen. I was in a daze.

Outside, Linda was still lying on the grass.

"You can call the doctor," I said.

She sat up and I could see that I hadn't tied that halter very tight.

"Is it over, Jerry?"

"Yes."

I was wrong.

It had just begun.

14

The doctor told us what we had already known—she was dead.

"Broken neck," he said. "Maybe her back, too. I don't know. The neck was enough."

We were in the kitchen. I had given the doctor a cup of coffee and he had tried it but now he wasn't drinking it.

"We'll have to notify the coroner," he said. "And the police."

Linda and I had expected this and had talked about it. There was nothing to fear, however. Who could prove anything?

The doctor put in his calls and then the three of us sat and waited.

"She was a fine woman," he said.

"Wonderful," Linda agreed. "She was like a mother to me. After Frank died there was just the two of us."

I sat at the table, facing the doctor, and I could feel the end of the wire sticking into me. I put my hand back there, pushing the wire down, and it felt better.

"She had no business going up and down those steps," I said. "But she did it all the time. She didn't think anybody else around here knew enough to take care of that sump pump."

"There was nothing for her to trip on," the doctor decided. "She must have blacked out or something. No one can be sure exactly what happened."

"Except that she's dead."

"Except that."

The coroner arrived first. He was a small man with a flat, bald head and he owned a farm a few miles distant. He listened while the doctor described the old lady's injuries.

"An accident," he said. "Pure and simple."

"No doubt about it." He shook his head. "She sure did a good job on herself."

I looked at Linda. Everything was going all right. Everything was going fine. I smiled at her but she didn't smile in return.

The troopers were both big men, young and clean-shaven. We stayed in the kitchen while they went down into the cellar and when they came up they were in agreement with the doctor. It had been an accident. Again I smiled at Linda and then the smile slid away into nothing. There was a hardness about her face and her eyes that I didn't understand.

"You're wrong," she said suddenly.

One of the troopers looked at her.

"What are you talking about?"

"It wasn't any accident."

"Well, she didn't do it on purpose."

I saw it then, saw it as clearly as though it had been there all along. She didn't love me. She didn't give a damn about me. It was the money she was after, the whole business. She had never intended to split it with me, never intended to marry me. There was sixty thousand bucks or more, and she wanted every cent of it.

"Search him," she said.

Everybody looked at me.

"Search him," she repeated.

"For what?" the one trooper wanted to know.

I just sat there, my belly an empty shell. What a fool I had been. What a stinking, rotten, terrible fool I had been.

"For the wire," she said. "I'll bet he's got it in his pocket."

"What wire?"

"The one he used on the top step. The one he used to trip her. He said he was going to do it and he did it."

I tried to get away from the table, tried to get out of there, but they were too fast for me. Strong hands pinned my arms behind my back and equally strong fingers searched my pockets. They started at the front and worked around to the back. In the last pocket they found the wire.

"Interesting," the trooper said.

I remained silent while they looked at the top step.

They found the nails and the wire fit perfectly.

"I wouldn't have guessed it," the doctor said. "I wouldn't have guessed it in a thousand years."

"Nor me," the coroner added.

Numbly I stared at her but her eyes were averted. She was breathing rapidly.

"It was her idea," I heard myself saying. "It was her idea from the start. After Frank died she wanted the old lady's money and this was the only way she could get it."

"Prove it!" she flung at me, her eyes flashing. "You can't prove a thing you say." She turned to the trooper. "It was his plan, all of it. He was after me and the money. I told him not to. I begged him not to. She was such a wonderful person, really wonderful. She was like my own mother." Tears filled Linda's eyes. "And he did this to her. Oh, my God!"

She had sucked me in and I was in it deep. I was in so deep I would never get out of it.

"Want to say anything?" one of the troopers asked me

"Only that she's a bitch."

"Watch what you say."

"She's a bitch."

They put the cuffs on me and the one trooper guarded me while the other went down the cellar again. When he came up he was smiling.

"You can see the marks on her legs," he said. "Just above the ankles, where the wire caught her. One of her stockings has a run in it and it starts right there."

"I wonder how many murders are committed that people get away with?" the doctor asked.

"Not many," the trooper said. "They get away with it for a while, maybe, but sooner or later it catches up with them."

I knew I was done. Finished. She would get the money and I would get the chair. If I had only gotten rid of that wire. If only ...

"Mary," I said.

"What's that?" the trooper wanted to know.

"Nothing. Nothing at all."

A car turned in off the road and stopped. From where I was standing I couldn't see who it was but pretty soon the door opened and the minister came in. He was carrying a woman's pocketbook.

"Well," he said. "What is this?"

"Who are you?" one of the troopers inquired.

"A friend of Mrs. Sprague. She left this in my car and I thought she might want it."

He put the pocketbook on the kitchen table.

"Mrs. Sprague is dead," the trooper nearest me said. "This man killed her."

"Dead?"

"Very much so. He rigged a wire and she tripped going down the cellar steps."

"I am shocked."

"Well, it happened."

The minister walked over to Linda and took both of her hands.

"You must find strength," he told her. "Strength to go on without her."

"I'm trying to."

"She was a fine woman but in some ways she was odd. You are her only living relative and I thought, if anything should happen to her, that everything she had should go to you. But she blamed herself for Frank's death, for not going to church, and in spite of my advice she had me take her to town today to make out a new will. She left all that she had to the church."

I was laughing when they took me away.

It was the funniest thing I had heard in years.

You've probably read about the trial. It wasn't much of a trial and they found me guilty. I'm waiting now for them to come and get me, to take me to that little room from which you never come out alive.

Norma and her father helped me all they could. They spent every dime they had saved in my defense but there are some things that money can't buy. I didn't want them to do it but they insisted.

I saw Norma for the last time yesterday and I won't see her again. She tried not to cry but she did and when we kissed she told me that she still loved me.

"It should have been different, Jerry."

"But it isn't."

Linda didn't appear against me at the trial. She took an overdose of sleeping pills and the county had to bury her. I guess she couldn't stand losing all that money, couldn't face life the way both of us should have faced it before.

She has paid her price and now I will have to pay mine.

THE END

ORRIE HITT BIBLIOGRAPHY
(all paperbacks unless noted)

Love in the Arctic (Red Lantern hb, 1953)

I'll Call Every Monday (Red Lantern hb, 1953; Beacon, 1954)

She Got What She Wanted (Beacon, 1954)

Shabby Street (Beacon, 1954)

Cabin Fever (Uni-Book, 1954)

Leased w/Jack Woodford (Signature hb, 1954; revised by Hitt & retitled Trapped)

Trapped (Beacon, 1958)

Unfaithful Wives (Beacon, 1956)

The Sucker (Beacon, 1957)

Nudist Camp (Beacon, 1957)

Pushover (Beacon, 1957)

The Promoter (Beacon, 1957)

Ladies' Man (Beacon, 1957)

Dolls and Dues (Beacon, 1957)

Trailer Tramp (Beacon, 1957)

Teaser (Woodford hb, 1956; Beacon, 1957)

Devil in the Flesh (Valentine hb, 1957; Kozy, 1957, as Sins of Flesh)

Ellie's Shack (Beacon, 1958)

Suburban Wife (Beacon, 1958)

Summer Hotel (Beacon, 1958)

Wild Oats (Beacon, 1958)

Affairs of a Beauty Queen (Beacon, 1958)

Call South 3300: Ask for Molly! (Beacon, 1958)

Burlesque Girl (Beacon, 1958)

Girl's Dormitory (Beacon, 1958)

Woman Hunt (Beacon, 1958)

Hot Cargo (Beacon, 1958)

The Cheat (Beacon, 1958)

Rotten to the Core (Beacon, 1958)

Love Princess (Saber, 1958)

Hotel Women (Vantage hb, 1958)

Hotel Confidential (Vantage hb, 1958)

Sheba (Beacon, 1959)

The Widow (Beacon, 1959)

Add Flesh to the Fire (Beacon, 1959)

Private Club (Beacon, 1959)

Carnival Girl (Beacon, 1959)

The Peeper (Beacon, 1959; Softcover Library, 1973, as Twisted Passion)

Too Hot to Handle (Beacon, 1959)

Sin Doll (Beacon, 1959; Softcover Library UK, 1973, as The Excesses of Cherry)

Tawny (Beacon, 1959; Softcover Library, 1964, as Lovers by Night)

Ex-Virgin (Beacon, 1959; UK Softcover Library, 1969, as Made for Men)

Suburban Sin (Beacon, 1959)

Pleasure Ground (Bedside, 1959; Kozy, 1961)

Affair With Lucy (Midwood, 1959; Midwood, 1961, as Married Mistress)

Girl of the Streets (Midwood, 1959)

Summer Romance (Midwood, 1959)

As Bad as They Come
   (Midwood, 1959; Midwood,
   1962, as Mail Order Sex)
Hotel Woman (Valentine hb,
   1959; Kozy, 1960, as Hotel
   Hostess)
Wayward Girl (Beacon, 1960)
The Torrid Teens (Beacon, 1960)
From Door to Door (Beacon,
   1960)
Motel Girls (Beacon, 1960)
Tell Them Anything (Beacon,
   1960)
Call Me Bad (Beacon, 1960)
Untamed Lust (Beacon, 1960)
Never Cheat Alone (Beacon,
   1960)
The Lady is a Lush (Beacon,
   1960)
Sexurbia County (Beacon, 1960)
Tramp Wife (Chariot , 1960)
Hotel Girl (Chariot, 1960)
Lonely Flesh (Chariot, 1960;
   reprinted 1963 as Lola)
Suburban Interlude (Kozy, 1960)
The Cheaters (Midwood, 1960)
A Doctor and His Mistress
   (Midwood, 1960)
Two of a Kind (Midwood, 1960)
I Prowl by Night (Beacon, 1961)
Dirt Farm (Beacon, 1961; UK
   Softcover Library, 1968, as The
   Hired Man)
Summer of Sin (Beacon, 1961)
Four Women (Beacon, 1961)
The Love Season (Beacon, 1961)
Frigid Wife (Beacon, 1961)
Virgins No More (Beacon, 1961)
Party Doll (Chariot, 1961;
   reprinted 1963 as Strange
   Longing)
Man's Nurse (Chariot, 1961)

Hot Blood (Chariot, 1961)
Diploma Dolls (Kozy, 1961)
Dark Passions (Kozy, 1961)
Twisted Lovers (Kozy, 1961)
Suburban Trap (Kozy, 1961)
Carnival Honey (Kozy, 1961)
Wild Lovers (Kozy, 1961)
Easy Women! (Novel, 1961;
   reprinted 1963 as Inflamed
   Dames, 1964 as Love Seekers,
   1965 as Jenkins' Lovers)
Shocking Mistress! (Novel, 1961)
Peeping Tom (Wisdom House,
   1961)
Love Thief (Beacon, 1962)
Dial "M" for Man (Beacon,
   1962)
Torrid Cheat (Chariot, 1962)
Twin Beds (Chariot, 1962)
Naked Model (Chariot, 1962)
Libby Sin (Chariot, 1962)
Passion Street (Chariot, 1962)
Bad Wife (Chariot, 1962)
Passion Hostess (Chariot, 1962)
Bold Affair (Kozy, 1962)
Campus Tramp (Kozy, 1962)
The Naked Flesh (Kozy, 1962)
Violent Sinners (Kozy, 1962)
Love Slave (Kozy, 1962)
Frustrated Females! (Novel,
   1962; reprinted 1963 as I Need
   a Man!)
Warped Woman (Novel, 1962;
   reprinted 1963 as Taboo
   Thrills, 1964 as Wilma's
   Wants)
Abnormal Norma (Novel, 1962)
Bed Crazy (Novel, 1962;
   reprinted as Perverted Doctors)
Man-Hungry Female (Novel,
   1962; reprinted 1964 as More!
   More! More!)

Carnival Sin/Playpet (Vest-
Pocket, 1962)
Torrid Wench (Kozy, 1963)
Strip Alley (Kozy, 1963)
Nude Doll (Kozy, 1963)
Loose Women (Lancer Domino,
1963)
An American Sodom (Novel,
1963)
Male Lover (Gaslight, 1964)
Passion Pool (Lancer Domino,
1964)
The Color of Lust (Lancer
Domino, 1964)
The Passion Hunters (Lancer
Domino, 1964; Domino, 1966
as This Wild Desire)
Lust Prowl (Lancer Domino,
1964)
The Love Seekers (Novel, 1964)
The Tavern (Softcover Library,
1966)
Woman's Ward (Beacon, 1966)
While the City Sins (Ember
Library, 1967)
The Sex Pros (Beacon, 1968)
Panda Bear Passion (P.E.C.,
1968)
Nude Model (MacFadden, 1970)

As by Kay Addams

Queer Patterns (Beacon, 1959)
Lucy (Beacon, 1960)
Three Strange Women (Beacon,
1960)
Warped Desire (Beacon, 1960;
UK as Night of Desire, 1975)
The Strangest Sin (Beacon, 1961)
Autobiography of Kay Addams
(Novel, 1962)

My Secret Perversions (Novel,
1962; reprinted as Hidden
Hungers)
My Wild Nights With Nine
Nudists! (Novel, 1963;
reprinted as Nocturnal Nudists)
My Two Strangest Lovers
(Novel, 1963; reprinted 1964
as Beyond Love)
Cherry (Novel, 1963)

As by Joe Black (as told to Hitt)

Unnatural Urge (Midwood,
1962)

As by Roger Normandie
(co-authored with Joe Weiss)

Run for Cover (Key hb, 1957; as
Race With Lust, Kozy, 1959)
Web of Evil (Key hb, 1957)
The Lion's Den (Key hb, 1957;
as Tormented Passions, Kozy,
1959)

As by Charles Verne
(co-authored with Joe Weiss)

Mr. Hot Rod (Key hb, 1957)
The Wheel of Passion (Key hb,
1957)

As by Nicky Weaver

Love, Blood and Tears (Kozy,
1963)
Love or Kill Them All (Kozy,
1963)

www.ingramcontent.com/pod-product-compliance
Lightning Source LLC
Chambersburg PA
CBHW070925190726
48292CB00004B/1113